ASHES
ON THE
WIND

Books by John Fischer

FROM BETHANY HOUSE PUBLISHERS

Ashes on the Wind

Making Real What I Already Believe

Real Christians Don't Dance

Saint Ben

The Saints' and Angels' Song

True Believers Don't Ask Why

ASHES
ON THE
WIND

JOHN
FISCHER

BETHANY HOUSE PUBLISHERS
MINNEAPOLIS, MINNESOTA 55438

Ashes on the Wind
Copyright © 1998
John Fischer

Cover design by The Lookout Design Group

Published by Bethany House Publishers
A Ministry of Bethany Fellowship International
11300 Hampshire Avenue South
Minneapolis, Minnesota 55438

Printed in the United States of America by
Bethany Press International, Minneapolis, Minnesota 55438

Library of Congress Cataloging-in-Publication Data

Fischer, John, 1947–
    Ashes on the wind / by John Fischer.
        p.   cm.
    ISBN 1-55661-678-3 (pbk.)
    I. Title.
PS3556.I762A94   1998
813'.54—dc21

97-45419
CIP

If a snake bites before it is charmed,
there is no profit for the charmer.

Ecclesiastes 10:11

JOHN FISCHER, pioneering musician, songwriter, popular speaker, and award-winning *CCM* columnist, is also the author of many books, including *Saint Ben, The Saints' and Angels' Song, Real Christians Don't Dance, True Believers Don't Ask Why*, and others. A graduate of Wheaton College, John and his family now live in California.

To Doug

CONTENTS

O N E

Our Betty Lies Over the Ocean

The ashes hit the water in a manner unlike anything he had expected. He had purposely positioned himself where he could not see over the railing, never thinking there would be any sound associated with this rite. But these were not mere fireplace ashes. The pouring sound went on and on, and Jack Acres wondered how there could be that much left of her—she had become so frail.

She had always been frail anyway, even in her more healthy days, though health for Betty, as long as Jack had known her, had been a relative matter. Jack's concept of a healthy mother-in-law was when she used to have only three coughing spells a day, which she would always wave off as "something down the wrong pipe." That's why he had been surprised to hear the loud pouring sound. A silent dust cloud of ashes flying out over the water was more along the lines of what he had imagined. Besides, he remembered stories from others who had experienced cremation rites like this at sea, complete with jokes about brushing Uncle Something-or-other off their shoulders where he had settled on the wind.

Bobbi Acres was surprised that the ashes were thrown out so abruptly, but unlike Jack, she noticed nothing unexpected about the sound. She was already training her memory to a time when her mother's soul had more gravity. A committed marriage, an extended family . . . Sunday afternoons at Grandmother's farm after singing in the First Presbyterian Church choir . . . her mother's accomplishments as a medical research assistant . . . her mother as best friend to all her high school boyfriends (something that still stirred a playful jealousy in her). To Bobbi, the remnant that now remained of her mother gave little tribute to her true essence.

Bobbi already decided she was going to remember Betty in her childhood home on a farm in New York State rather than in some pastel condominium in Cocoa Beach, Florida, where she lived out her final years devoid of history and family roots. In Bobbi's mind, her mother would always be a woman of substance. The person she became at the end was a mere shadow of her former self, cast on the perfectly manicured lawn of a Florida golf course. She might have gained some security when she married Sam, but Bobbi was convinced her mother gave up far too much in the exchange. If only she and Bobbi's father, Ruddy Brewster, had stayed together. Then, instead of being in a boat off the coast of Florida, they would all most likely be in Shaughnessy, New York now, laying Betty to rest in the Brewster family plot across from the church. Or perhaps on the Martin farm where Betty had grown up, overlooking the rolling hills outside Parker Corners. Either would be preferable to being thrown to the wind, only to disappear within the vast, aimless blue water.

No one knew Betty's wishes until after her death. She had instructed Sam, but he had seen no need to convey that information to anyone else in the family. Never mind that Bobbi had already made a trip to the funeral home to pick out a coffin.

"What'd you go and do that for?" Sam said when he found out. "I'm not paying for any fancy box just to burn her up in. Makes no difference once it burns."

"Pop, you never told me she wanted to be cremated."

"Well, I'm telling you now. I don't want anybody gawking at her, and I don't want any funeral service either."

Samuel Dunn never talked about anything before it was absolutely necessary, and even then, a person often had to pry it out of him. He was now twice a widower, and that alone was enough to make him matter-of-fact about the whole experience—except that he was already like that anyway. There wasn't anything Sam went through, including the death of two wives, that didn't have him looking as though he'd already been through it so many times that nothing fazed him. Sam lived as if it were his dying duty to never let another living human soul know a thing about what he was truly thinking or feeling.

Jack always wondered what his mother-in-law had seen in Sam, besides someone to care for her, if you could call his abruptness "care." Perhaps that was enough for Betty. Give him credit; that much he did, right up to the end.

Sam had taken Jack to the marina in his car right after the service at the Palm Avenue Church. The memorial service Sam had never wanted, but got anyway at the insistence of the rest of the family, had made him antsy, so when it was over, Bobbi had suggested the two of them go on ahead. They had ridden most of the way in silence. This, too, was not unusual, since Sam only spoke when asked direct questions. When he'd answered one of Jack's questions with a comment about Betty being in the back, Jack had been tempted for a split second to turn around and see her sitting there. Of course, Sam had only meant that the ashes were in a box in the trunk.

Sam popped the trunk lid open as soon as they pulled into the marina parking lot and immediately went around and got out the box. They walked in silence to the boat, where the captain met them with a large bouquet of flowers from which he gave them each a handful.

"These are nice," Jack said, looking at them quizzically.

"They're for marking the spot in the water," Sam stated, looking for a place to sit. He found one near the engine housing, where he sat with the box on his lap looking like a schoolboy with his lunch. A green sport coat hung loose and unwelcomed on his shoulders. It covered the only thing anyone had ever seen him wearing: a pastel polo shirt, open at the collar. This one was a graying yellow from being washed too many times with dark colors, a detail he'd missed while caring for himself and his dying wife for the last six months. He had a drawer full of bright new shirts, but Sam was a creature of the familiar.

On the left side of his forehead, Sam bore the signs of recent brain surgery: a dent the size of a golf ball. The surgery had made him more reluctant to speak than he already was, though Bobbi thought he only used that as an excuse to stay even further removed from those around him. His sky-blue eyes under snow-white hair stared directly forward, and ever since his surgery they had a startled look, as if everything he saw contributed to a sort of chronic low-grade irritation.

The box on his lap was small, about the size and shape of a pastry box—something that would more likely accommodate half a dozen donuts than the remains of a loved one. He had already gotten rid of his flowers, setting them on top of the engine housing, where they trembled along with the idling motor. Flowers did not suit Sam, but something about the box did. Maybe it was the fact that he finally had Betty reduced to this. Not that he wanted her dead; he just wanted her under control. No one ever had any of the Brewster women under control unless they were in a box, and this was undoubtedly the smallest box any of them had ever been in. No one remembered any other cremations in either the Brewster or the Martin family history. This only served to underscore the sadness of Betty Brewster ending up in a pastry box on the lap of Sam Dunn on a smelly, chartered deep-sea fishing boat in a Cocoa Beach marina, awaiting her final demise on the water. It was not supposed to end this way.

Barbara Ann Brewster Acres was proud of her heritage, even though Betty had rejected it, and in some ways, Bobbi identified more with her two grandmothers than with her own mother. This echoed a practice not uncommon in upstate New York, where "old money" often skipped a generation in the family trust funds and endowments. Bobbi felt skipped over by both money and tradition. When her mother had divorced out of the Brewster family, that took care of the money, and when Betty married Sam and moved to Florida, that pretty much severed any traditional ties to either side of her family.

Bobbi loved both her grandmothers and bore strong traits in her character from each of them. From her paternal grandmother Brewster she inherited style, social acumen, and a spirit of philanthropy; from the Martin side she got her faith in God and a genuine, welcoming personality. In Grandma Martin's home there was always something warm in the oven, as well as something warm for the heart. And many a needy woman in the poorer sections of Shaughnessy knew the compassion of Grandmother Brewster as they were warmed by a blanket, a meal, and shelter that came through her kindness, right on through the Great Depression.

To Bobbi, the differences between these two families were a great benefit to her. But to her mother, they were only a source of conflict. Bobbi often doubted that her mother, after growing up in Parker Corners, ever fully adjusted to being a Brewster in Shaughnessy. Betty's social graces always seemed stiff and somewhat contrived, manifesting in a tendency to laugh too loudly and drink too much at cocktail parties. In the end, she adjusted just enough to lose the charm of the farm and yet never quite enough to embrace the Brewster style. And when she and Ruddy, short for Rudyard A. Brewster Jr., divorced shortly after Bobbi and her brother, Will, were out of the nest, Betty lost even what she had tried to adopt as a Brewster. It was a bitter divorce, and Betty dealt with it by leaving behind every single piece of silver or crystal or fine embroidery with a *B* on it. Bobbi still refused to believe that the attic fire on Bingham Street that destroyed all the Brewster heirlooms was an accident. Even the family films were burned up. God knew that if Betty hadn't torched it, she *wished* it torched enough times to be held responsible.

"*You* might not want to be a Brewster anymore," Bobbi once

told her mother, "but you seem to forget that I was born into this family."

So Bobbi had ended up with one grandmother's faith and another's fortitude, and a sense that her heritage had been stripped from her by her parents' divorce. Like many other difficult marriages in their generation, Bobbi's parents had thought they were doing best by the kids to fake a happy marriage until after their offspring were out of the nest, figuring that a divorce would be easier on their children if they already had their own marriages going. Bobbi knew that divorce at any time was costly. It wasn't money she had been cut from; it was history, tradition, and some tangible connection to the women who had made her who she was. What Betty had tried to discard, Bobbi was trying to find. Betty's funeral was no exception.

"He didn't show *you* the will, did he?" Bobbi had asked Jack while they were getting ready to attend the memorial service.

"Nope."

"So we're taking Sam's word for it that she wanted to be cremated?"

"Are you thinking it was his idea?" Jack asked as he leaned over his wife in the mirror and tied his tie. "I guess I wouldn't put it past him to save a few extra bucks and a lot of hassle." It was cramped quarters in the small second bathroom of Sam and Betty's two-bedroom condo.

"I don't know. It was probably her idea." Bobbi was a little annoyed at Jack's intrusion and purposely took up more of the mirror, relegating her husband to one last glance at his Windsor knot from the upper left corner of their reflection. "She burned up everything else—might as well burn up herself. But what about her jewelry? Where do you suppose that is?"

"I'm sure Sam has it."

Jack didn't mind his fragment of functioning mirror. It was a trade-off for the joy of watching his wife primp. One of the most underrated pleasures of married life, he always thought: watching beauty maximized before your very eyes.

"She wore Grandma Martin's wedding ring," Bobbi said, tossing her hair. "The diamond is probably not worth fifty cents, but it's the only thing Mom kept that belonged to her past. With my luck it got cremated too. Could you zip me up, please? And remind me to ask Sam about the ring."

The memorial service at the Palm Avenue Church had almost been one of those pitiful events full of prayers and readings that boil down to a feeble hope that maybe—just maybe—the resurrection of Christ actually happened. It was going to be one of those services where the minister says some of that resurrection verbiage just in case, while the bulk of it is a kind of passing on of the baton of life, the present runner having given out entirely on the race. Fortunately—or unfortunately, depending on one's perspective on these things—Bobbi had gotten wind of this ahead of time and made sure her mother's funeral service had more substance to it. The minister was one of those who thought it was unfortunate. One would think that, being the minister, he would have been in total control of these services, especially in retirement-centered Florida, where churches abound more in funerals than weddings. But then again, he had never dealt with a female Brewster before.

There were more nice things said about Betty Brewster Dunn in that hour-long service than were ever said of her in her entire lifetime. The Reverend William Oglethorpe had been able to manage only a brief session with Bobbi and her brother, Will, in advance of the service. At times the family wasn't sure the reverend was talking about the same woman they knew, but that's one of the casualties of dying in a place where few know you.

Sam and Betty had lived in Cocoa Beach, Florida, for almost ten years, but Sam was not the churchgoing, community-oriented type. Betty had developed a casual relationship with a few women at the church, more through a bridge club than anything that had to do directly with religion. It wasn't anything like her former marriage and life in Shaughnessy, New York, which was centered around church and community. But that's why Sam had wanted to move to Cocoa Beach in the first place: to get away from all of that. It was a sad commentary that a woman who had expended such effort trying to live a socially oriented life, in the end, had to have a minister presiding at her memorial service whose primary information about her came from a two-hour briefing with her adult children the day before.

That was one of the reasons Bobbi had wanted Jack to take part in the service along with Reverend Oglethorpe. He had a knowledge of Betty that the minister did not possess, and from what Bobbi and Jack could tell, a faith in God that also seemed to elude the aging reverend. Over her husband's protests, Bobbi had insisted that Jack rewrite the service. It turned out to be a task he had actually relished, replacing all those vague, flowery sections with Scripture like "faith is the substance of things hoped for," and "though outwardly we are wasting away, yet inwardly we are being renewed day by day. For our light and momentary troubles are achieving for us an eternal glory that far outweighs them all." The Reverend Oglethorpe was undoubtedly going to be glad to see these folks leave town.

The most poignant verse Jack picked for the memorial service turned out to be the one about Christ in the life of a believer being like a treasure in a jar of clay. It was hard, given the context, for everyone not to imagine Betty in an urn.

But Betty never saw the inside of an urn. No, Sam's treasure was in a box—a cardboard box—with a plastic bag and the dust of Betty inside, closed up with a wire twist. "I don't need a fancy urn," Sam had insisted. "I just need to get her out to sea. Doesn't matter how I get her there."

Jack didn't mind that sentiment, but Bobbi was having a harder time with it. She simply had not been ready to part with the material presence of her mother, even if it was only a handful of ashes now. Bobbi had watched her mother's true essence spill out of its spent vessel three days earlier. She had smelled the scent of death in the small condo where Betty had breathed her last. Bobbi knew her mother was safe and happy now, but she herself felt suddenly, strangely alone.

In this, she and Sam shared something in common. Though Bobbi firmly believed in a resurrection, she lived in the here and now. As far as Bobbi was concerned, her mother was in two places at once. She was in heaven—of that Bobbi was certain—but she was also in the cardboard box. What was left of Betty had material significance. Though Bobbi had gone along with the cremation, she was not happy about letting her mother disappear on the wind. She would have preferred to have the remains in a place where she could visit and remember.

As far as Sam was concerned, *all* of Betty was in the box. There wasn't anything else. He mocked all that Christian talk about resurrection. For him, a cruise on the ocean was the quickest and most efficient means of getting this whole thing over with and getting on with his life, whatever that would mean for him now.

"The service is over," he said to Jack as he scanned the parking lot for the arrival of the others. "No more holy talk."

"No more Scripture?" Jack said, half joking but half serious. He had been thinking about some kind of final word as they scattered the ashes at sea.

"Nope."

"Nothing about coming from dust or going back to dust?"

"Spare me." Sam clutched the box tighter, as if Jack were trying to wrestle it from him. "If you want to do something, you can sing some songs. Songs that everyone knows. Just as long as they're not religious."

Jack realized right then that Sam had probably been subjected to more religion in the last hour and a half than he had experienced in ten years.

"No problem, Pop. You've got it."

Sam had visibly endured the church service well enough. Though there were moments when something might have touched him, his eyes stayed dry. And yet there were other signs of weakness. Bobbi would later show Jack bruises on her hip bone where Sam had a vise grip on her in the receiving line. And then there was the time during the service when Sam's estranged youngest son came over and gave him a big hug from behind. That had made his eyes brighten. It happened during a camp song that Jack was teaching everybody. The song has a part where everyone reaches out and touches the people around them—a calculated risk at a Florida funeral attended mostly by elderly retired folks who were all strangers to them—but Bobbi had been clear about making sure they gave Betty what she would have liked regardless of anyone else, and Betty would have liked the reach-out-and-touch-someone camp song. It was what she had been trying to do with her life when she lived it, for in spite of whether she was happy or not, Betty always wanted everyone else to be.

The service had started with four hymns Jack picked out about the Resurrection and ended with a Catholic folksong that Bobbi's sister-in-law had taught him about rising up on eagle's wings. Bobbi's brother, Will, had surprised everyone by ushering his whole family up front to help sing it, while motioning vigorously with his arms to the rest of the immediate family until they were all up there singing too. Sam wasn't singing, but they got him out of the pew and up there with them. That was enough of a miracle.

The people loved it. A change of pace from the typical dirge was a welcomed experience. The brightness they emanated as they came through the receiving line afterward made it seem more like a wedding than a funeral.

Sam had never wanted a funeral in the first place, and Bobbi could smile afterward and know that, in a way, he had gotten his wish. This was nothing like a funeral.

"Will you do mine?" one spry Floridian had beamed at Jack as she shook his hand. Bobbi, Jack, Will, and his wife, Jackie, would later joke on the boat about going into business. "On Eagle's Wings Funeral Coordinators" was what Jackie wanted to call it.

"Where are they?" Sam kept saying impatiently from the boat. The trembling flowers over the engine compartment were dusting the panel with yellow pollen. Some of them had broken away from the bunch and were working their way to the edge. Jack wondered why the captain had left the motor running.

Whenever Jack and Bobbi visited Florida, Sam acted like he was always waiting for Bobbi. This time was no exception. Bobbi had her mother's gift of gab, and when she was around people, she was never conscious of time. Jack paced the boat, impatient as well. He couldn't think of anything to say to Sam at the moment and wished for the quick arrival of the remainder of the funeral party to come and save him from the awkwardness he was feeling.

"Sit down," said Sam. "You're making me nervous."

Jack obliged and sat on one of the white wooden chairs along the railing. The sun was about to dip behind one of the many condominium towers that line the more popular Florida beaches. The captain came and spoke a few words to Sam that Jack could not hear over the gurgling engine.

"What was that all about?" asked Jack with his expression.

"He wants to know how much longer," shouted Sam. "I told him we leave in fifteen minutes whether they're here or not." And Jack knew that he would.

Luckily, they arrived in exactly fourteen minutes. The entourage piled out of two cars. Will and Jackie along with their two young sons, Kyle and Kevin—they lived locally in Cocoa Beach— and then the out-of-town guests: Jeffrey, Kate, and Jeremy, adult children from Sam's previous marriage whom Betty had raised since their adolescence, Sam's brother Albert, and Bobbi. Jack and Bobbi had left their own two children home with their neighbor in Ipswich, Massachusetts—a decision Bobbi was now regretting. The absence of her children only added to her loneliness.

The fact that Albert Dunn and Samuel Dunn were from the same background and the same family defied reason. Albert was everything Sam was not. He was as positive as Sam was negative, as kind as Sam was gruff, as believing as Sam was unbelieving, as religious as Sam was pagan. It was almost as if they had sworn a pact during childhood to take the opposite side on everything. The one thing that betrayed their kinship was their orneriness. Uncle Albert was as ornery about doing good as Sam was ornery about being nasty.

"What have you got there?" said Albert as he pulled up a white chair next to his brother.

Sam made no reply.

"Betty's not there, you know." Albert leaned over and turned his ear, as if listening for something from the box.

"She's not anywhere else, either," Sam said. "And don't start in on me."

Uncle Albert winked at Jack and smelled the batch of flowers that he waved in front of his nose. He never gave up on Sam, though they were hardly ever together except for important family events such as this one. Uncle Albert had not made the expected geriatric migration south; his home would always be in upstate New York, where everyone knew him well. When Albert Dunn died, no one would have to brief the minister. And when Albert died, it would be hard to find a place to park in the church parking lot.

Albert had lost his own wife in a violent automobile accident, and though it had been sixteen years since her passing, he talked about her as if they were still married. In his mind they were. People at his church were always trying to fix him up with some spry young widow, but Albert would have nothing of it.

"So what are you going to do now, Sam?" Albert said.

"Travel" was the reply.

"Where?"

"Maybe I'll come up and see you."

Anybody who heard Sam's response over the roar of the engine was a little surprised. Sam had never indicated before any desire whatsoever to leave Florida, even for a trip, and it certainly was a shock to hear him talk about seeing his brother. The words exchanged between them over the last thirty years could fit on one sheet of paper.

"That would be splendid," said Albert, quite pleased with the news. He then threw in an idea of his own. "Or we could go back to the Keys."

Everyone in the family knew that stories of a dark, mysterious past in the Florida Keys haunted the brothers' childhood, and Sam's permanently startled eyes seemed to focus on some distant memory with the suggestion.

The boat pulled out of the marina as the sun slipped behind one of the resort towers on the beach. By the time they got out to the open sea, there would be a painted sky. Betty had always loved a sunset cruise, and Bobbi tried to comfort herself with the thought that her mother would find her resting place on such a perfect evening. Bobbi was trying as hard as she could to keep a positive attitude, but her mind was on the rolling hills of her childhood and her grandmother Martin's farm outside Parker Corners, where she wished they were placing Betty's remains. In such a place, she could remember her mother in her best years, return to visit with her own children, show them the farm where their grandmother had grown up, and teach them about their great-grandmother Martin.

Jack, unaware of her struggle, lovingly caught her eye, and she managed a smile back.

"What are you thinking?" Jack spoke into her ear, moving closer to her.

"Oh, I was just thinking about how Mom wanted her bed turned toward the door the last couple days of her life so she could welcome her guests. Imagine that. The sorry state she was in, and she was still trying to be a proper host."

They stared silently out at the brilliant water for a while until Bobbi spoke again. "Didn't Sam want you to play some songs?"

"Oh yes, I almost forgot."

Jack then got out his guitar and led everybody in "If I Had a Hammer," "Michael Row the Boat Ashore," and "This Land Is Your Land." Nothing religious, but it cheered everyone up. And then, just when Bobbi was about ready to make a move toward organizing the final ceremony of the ashes, Sam got up and took his box over to the railing, and before anyone could say anything, he undid the wire twist on the plastic bag and dumped Betty into the ocean. Unconsciously, Bobbi's hands flew out before her as the ashes poured out and then returned slowly to her lips as if they had been caught doing a silly thing. A look of vacant futility filled her eyes as she stared out at an empty sea.

Everyone quickly tossed their flowers onto the water, and as the boat turned back, the children spotted a school of dolphins diving in the very spot where the flowers were floating.

"She loved dolphins," Bobbi said softly to Jack, who was holding her at the railing. Her voice was immediately swallowed up by the roar of the boat's engine.

TWO

His Bonnie Lies Over the Sea

From all appearances, Sam Dunn was an agnostic. This is not to be confused with an atheist—someone who puts effort into the state of disbelief. An atheist is someone committed to maintaining a view of the world without God. Sam's unbelief wasn't that purposeful. He simply refused to believe anything he could not verify with his five senses. If there was a God, there would be no way for Sam to know about it short of a personal appearance by God himself. There was no fifth dimension to Sam Dunn. With one exception.

Sam kept orchids. It was more convenient to associate the orchids with Betty, and she may have been the one who got him started, but much to everyone's surprise, Sam kept the plants going for no apparent reason. He kept them going when she could no longer tend to them, which could have been explained as an attempt to cheer her up, but would not explain why he kept them going after she died. He even added to the collection.

Flowers and Sam made an odd couple, as they did on the boat. But orchids are not just any flower, and Sam knew that.

Some orchids are terrestrial; that is, they grow in the ground like most plants. Terrestrial orchids are found most often in cool, damp woods and swamps. But orchids most likely to thrive in the warm, tropical climate of Florida grow high up in the branches of trees. They do not need soil. Their roots gather in a loose mass along tree branches, and some of them even hang free. These roots are covered with a corklike substance that enables the plant to gather water and nutrients directly from the air.

Growing these kinds of orchids in captivity requires a special treatment because of this. They need water, but the water has to be able to run off, since there is no soil to hold it. For this reason Sam built an orchid greenhouse for Betty, off their porch. It had two tiers of wire-mesh shelves along three screened walls. These shelves were lined with non-blooming orchid plants. In the center of the small, roughly six-by-ten-foot area was a table, also covered with wire mesh, where the pots that were blooming at the time were placed to display their glory. Orchid blooms on live plants can last up to six weeks.

Bobbi always thought of Sam's plants on the tiered shelves as an audience cheering for their flowering companions, gaining inspiration for their own coming performance when they would get their chance on the blooming table. The floor of this growing area was covered with crushed white rock to absorb the large runoff from watering the orchids every other day. The plants were still in pots, even though there was no soil in them, only bare roots.

"Isn't it strange that such a beautiful flower would be found fifty feet up in the air where no one can see it?" Bobbi had said during one of the Acres' annual visits to Florida.

"Someone sees," said Sam, and the statement had bloomed like an orchid in thin air.

Bobbie dared not question him on it. She didn't want to ruin it. She preferred to hold on to this memory as proof of something good deep inside of Sam. She knew that if she insinuated in any way that the "someone" Sam referred to might possibly be God, he would undoubtedly deny it.

⌒

"I don't like it," said Bobbi the weekend after she and Jack returned to their home in New England following the funeral. "I've tried to reach Sam four times in the last two days, and all I get is his stupid machine."

"He doesn't know how to use it," Jack said. "He's probably so frustrated with it that he isn't picking up the phone at all. How many times does it ring before the machine kicks in?"

"Only once."

"That's why. He never gets to the phone in time."

"Great," she said sarcastically. "That means he's not getting any of my messages. I'm going to call Will and see if he's heard anything."

It was a Sunday afternoon in March, one of the first warm days of spring. The temperature had reached an unseasonable sixty-eight degrees earlier that day, but it was dropping fast again as the sun grew large over the golden marshes.

Jack and Bobbi's house sat alone in a field on the outskirts of the small borough of Ipswich. In its early days, it would have been a farmhouse, but now that these small towns north of Boston were all bedroom communities, it took on more of a town-and-country appeal. The nearby towns of Boxford, Rowley, and Essex are small and charming—not much different than they have been for three hundred years. In between these towns are two-lane rural roads with homes clustered in twos and threes or sometimes standing alone, as theirs did. Jack and Bobbi loved the area for its close proximity to Boston and yet the absence of housing tracts for miles in any direction.

The house was a pleasant blend of old and new. The front part of it was built in 1798 and had a huge fireplace with a built-in brick oven for baking bread. In the rear of the house was a new section with a two-car garage and a large family room over it that boasted an open-beam ceiling with two skylights and lots of large windows.

It was really like having two houses in one. The older section with its low ceilings, small, cramped rooms, and narrow windows was cozy and quaint, while the newer section was wide open and spacious. If you got tired of one, you could always move yourself to the other. Jack's home office as a second generation newspaperman was in a large upstairs hallway that connected the two. It had windows facing west over flat marshlands bordered in the distance by the hardwood trees lining Route 1. He had arranged his work schedule so that at least half of his working hours could be spent at this desk as opposed to his newspaper office in Salem. It worked well with Bobbi's schedule, which often took her on the road as a fund-raising consultant.

"No answer at Will and Jackie's," Bobbi called from the family room as Jack sat at his desk. He left the bills he was going over and joined her on the couch.

"You know what?" he said, remembering something. "I programmed his answering machine for checking messages from another phone in case we needed to do that while we were there. I think I remember the code. You want to see if we can find out anything?"

"What's the code?" she said, already dialing the number.

"Hit star nineteen anytime during the recorded message."

Jack watched as she listened. It took a long time; there must have been a lot of messages.

"These messages go back to when we were there," Bobbi said, then held up her hand to stop any reply Jack might make. Her face showed a growing concern.

"What is it?"

"Ssshhh!" she said, slightly annoyed.

A minute later, apparently done with the messages and holding the cordless phone out in front of her where she could see the dial, she asked, "What do I do now?"

"Hit one and it will erase the messages."

"I don't want to erase them."

"Then just hang up. . . . What? What is it?"

She clicked the phone off and set it down, puzzled.

"Do we still have the number of that cremation service?" she questioned.

Jack was growing angry. Bobbi's mind was on a direct link to her actions, and she always expected Jack to be able to read her thoughts without her having to bother with an explanation.

"Get me the number," she said, poised to dial again.

As Jack went to his desk to find the folder where he had put all the information from the funeral, he heard her say, "Cocoa Beach, the Neptune Society, please."

Jack found the card in his folder about the same time Bobbi got the number from information. *Neptune Society of Cocoa Beach,* the card read. *Private Charters for Sea Scattering. Simplicity. Dignity. Low Cost. Prices Quoted by Phone.* He put the folder away and picked up the phone at his desk right when the party answered in a cheery voice.

"Neptune Society, may I help you?"

"Yes, may I please speak with Mr. Gibbons?" Bobbi asked.

"This is Earnest Gibbons."

"Mr. Gibbons, this is Bobbi Acres."

"Oh yes, Mrs. Acres." Earnest's voice dropped noticeably in tone. "What can I do for you today?"

"I have not been able to reach my stepfather since we were there for the service two weeks ago, and I just noticed on his answering machine that there were a number of messages from you. I was wondering if there was something wrong."

There was a long pause.

"Mr. Gibbons?"

"You mean . . . you don't know . . . a-about the mix-up?"

"What mix-up?" asked Bobbi. "No. I don't know about any mix-up."

He cleared his throat nervously. "Well, it seems that we somehow mislabeled the remains."

"You did what?"

"Well, we got your mother confused with another woman with a similar name."

"You mean that was *not* my mother we scattered in the bay?"

"Ah . . . no. That was Mrs. Dean, wife of J.W. Dean, a traveling evangelist and faith healer who was in town at the time."

"And where is my mother?"

"Well, Mrs. Acres, I'm afraid your mother's remains are with Mr. Dean. We have been trying to locate him ever since we made this unfortunate discovery. He's on the road constantly. As far as we know, the man doesn't have an address."

"I can't believe this. Does my stepfather know this?"

"Yes. After we could not reach Mr. Dunn by phone, we went out and told him personally."

"Mr. Gibbons, this is something that I would have preferred to have not even heard about."

"Believe me, Mrs. Acres. If we could have avoided it, we would have not told anyone, but Mr. Dunn called us about your mother's jewelry. That's when we discovered the mistake. Her jewelry is also with Mr. Dean."

Bobbi was silent.

"How could this possibly happen?" Jack filled in.

"Oh, hello, Mr. Acres. Believe me, in thirty-five years in this business, it's never happened before. Betty Dunn, Bonnie Dean . . . The names are similar—"

"That's no excuse for such incompetence when dealing with something as important as a person's remains, Mr. Gibbons," Bobbi cut in. "Does my brother Will know about this?"

"I don't know. We assumed Mr. Dunn would inform you all."

"You've assumed a great deal already."

"Mrs. Acres, you don't know how sorry we are about this. Rest assured we are doing everything we can to locate your mother's remains."

Bobbi left a number with Mr. Gibbons, then tried Will again unsuccessfully. After the initial shock wore off, Jack allowed a chuckle to slip out to test Bobbi's emotions. He had been quietly amused on the other end of the line, listening to this incredible news unfold. Jack Acres was never one to hold much reverence for the body of the deceased anyway.

"No wonder so much of her went into the ocean," he said

when he thought about it some more. "Bonnie Dean must have been overweight."

"Jack, cut it out. Have some respect for the dead."

"I have enough respect for the dead. I just don't have much respect for phony preachers."

"Who says the guy's phony?" Bobbi asked. "You're jumping to conclusions."

"You're right. It's just that for every real one of these guys there seem to be ten impostors."

"Right now I really don't care," said Bobbi. "I just want to find him."

"That's not gonna be easy. What can we do? Check the yellow pages for traveling evangelists? He could be anywhere by now."

"We've got to do something, Jack. My mother's riding around in this guy's trunk when she's supposed to be at sea. And he's got Grandma's ring too."

"I wonder what it does to a faith healer's career to have his wife die on him. Probably doesn't help much."

"Will you please stop making light of this?"

"That's not a joke. If he has to stop traveling, he might be easier to find."

"What are we going to do?" Bobbi kept pressing.

"What is there to do? You want to go down there and look for him yourself?"

"Yes, I do!"

"Bobbi, neither one of us has time for that kind of thing."

"She's my mother, Jack."

"Bobbi, your mother's in heaven. This is just a box of ashes we're talking about."

Bobbi sighed impatiently. "It's not like we haven't talked about this before. Of course Mom's in heaven. I know that. But come down from your spiritual cloud for a moment, Jack, and see things from my perspective. What's left of her is important too. It belongs somewhere significant. I think of Mom and how it seems she's never had a place to be. Shaughnessy is as close as she came to roots. Or the Martin farm where she grew up. . . . It *is* important where you end up, Jack, if not for you, please believe it for me. Women are of the earth. That's why you can't pull us up by our roots without consequences. Where are you going to bury *me*, Jack, when *I* die?"

"Probably wherever we are at the time."

"See? That's what I mean. It doesn't matter to you—and that's all right, you don't have to understand. Just try and appreciate that it matters to me. Here I thought we had Mom delivered to the sea. I never liked the idea anyway, but at least the dolphins came." She paused a minute. "You know, I don't think that guy at the Neptune Society is telling us the whole truth."

"Why do you say that?"

"In the first place, everyone has to have an address or they're an illegal person. Don't you have to fill out an address on a death certificate? And this evangelist or faith healer—whoever he is—has got a ministry. He must have a place to receive funds. Whatever those guys do, they always get money from people. Where do the people send their money?"

"Unless he's an old-fashioned itinerant," Jack said, "and collects his money in each place before he moves on."

"Nobody does that anymore. Not with TV and radio and toll-free numbers and credit card pledges."

"I don't know. There's some pretty backward areas in this country."

"I'm going to call the Neptune Society back and have another little chat with Mr. Gibbons."

"And while you do that, I'll go try and find the manual to our answering machine."

"What for?"

"I think there's a way you can call in and turn the machine off since I know the code. Maybe we can raise Sam with a few more rings."

"Good idea."

So that was when Bobbi found out that J.W. Dean had put down a bogus address on the death certificate, as well as the phone number, next of kin, even place of birth. None of them checked out. Nor was Mr. Gibbons clear on why J.W. and Bonnie Dean were in Cocoa Beach, either, except he assumed Mr. Dean was holding services somewhere in the area. That was also when Bobbi found out that J.W. Dean was not only a faith healer—he handled snakes too.

"He does what?" Jack asked her.

"He handles snakes," Bobbi repeated, and the expression on her face when she said it made her look as if she had to hold one to say it.

THREE

J.W. Dean and the Last Crusade

Unlike Betty Dunn, Bonnie Dean wasn't wearing any jewelry when she died for the same reason she never wore any when she was living. She didn't wear any makeup either. Her appearance standards were drawn directly from the King James Version of the Holy Bible. Bonnie represented the perfect preacher's wife, at least in the circles J.W. Dean traveled, which, for the most part, were in and around the poor, rural areas of Florida and Georgia. She was quiet, chaste, and unadorned, and suitable for places like Lacoochee, Venus, Benbow, and Lulu, Florida, where her husband held crusades. As a traveling preacher, J.W. was safe with this bland profile for his wife, though it was becoming harder and harder for him to conceal his attraction for flashier women—an attraction that was cleverly justified in his own thinking.

In truth, J.W. only *preached* the virtues of the monochromatic female. The women in his mind were far more colorful. Though he would publicly read from the New Testament about "the out-ward adorning of plaiting the hair, and of wearing of gold, or of putting on of apparel" with a condemnatory tone, his imagination would often take long trips to these descriptions of what a woman was *not* to put worth in. Those were the very things Reverend J.W. Dean admired. He would have preferred to be around for the put-ting on of more exciting apparel than the limp, colorless, chin-hug-ging, ankle-length dresses that Bonnie wore. This was only one of the reasons why the death of Bonnie Dean was not too great a set-back for the reverend.

John Wesley Dean had his sights set on loftier things than the predictable traveling revival show that had become his stock-in-trade for almost ten years. (John Wesley went to his initials while attending a Pentecostal college and preparing for the ministry. The college did not take kindly to the anticharismatic doctrines of John Wesley, so John had taken up J.W. as his first name and it stuck. Anywhere else, the laborious four-syllable first name would have given people difficulty, but in the parts of the South that he trav-eled, J.W. rolled off the tongue in an easy three syllables, "Jay Dub-ya.") He had taken to the road after failing three times at the local pastorate. Though he would never admit it, the real reason he took up traveling crusades had come down to a choice between im-pressing a new audience every week with the same material, or stay-ing in one place and having to deepen his message and his rela-tionships over the long haul. When it came down to it, *deep* was not a word that described much about J.W. Dean, except perhaps the blue of his eyes that sparkled grandly underneath his silver hair. J.W. was convinced his good looks, his charisma, and his ability to move an audience were too important to waste on one small con-gregation. J.W. Dean would not plow the same field over and over again. J.W. Dean would cultivate the world.

It had been these strong urgings that had rendered Bonnie less and less desirable in light of J.W.'s future, for J.W. knew he was destined for greatness, and he was convinced that greatness was to come to him in the form of television. As sure as he was destined for the world, J.W. Dean was destined for a satellite network. He had known it ever since he appeared as a guest on the *PTL Club* back in 1984 and found himself hypnotized by the glory of the lights and cameras. "Lights, camera, ministry!" That had become J.W.'s new secret calling, a calling from which Bonnie had always been conspicuously absent. Whenever J.W. imagined himself on camera, it was never with Bonnie by his side. She was good for the road show—for praying fervently and playing the organ and singing passionately and handling snakes—but she presented serious problems on camera. Her drab, lifeless personality was simply unadornable. You could dress her up, but you could never put her on TV. This had become painfully obvious to J.W. in the videos of their appearance on the PTL show. Next to Tammy Faye Bakker, Bonnie's drawn face and pale, sunken skin made her look more like an escapee from a concentration camp than a television personality. And then there was the memo J.W. happened on quite by accident, from the makeup artist to the show's producer: *About the evangelist's wife . . . sorry, we did the best we could.*

J.W. knew that for television, he needed someone who was anything but quiet, afraid of no one, and adorned like the Taj Mahal. He needed someone who would rewrite the King James Bible for the Christian community and the tabloids. Someone who would spend most of the day plaiting her hair. Someone who would flaunt her gold and her jewelry and purposely qualify herself, every year, for the worst-dressed-women list in the *National Enquirer* by wearing the most outrageous of apparel. J.W. saw all this as a good thing—a necessary thing, in fact. It was a way of gaining attention for God. The New Testament was obviously not written with television in mind. A powerful television ministry required that the minister take out certain spiritual exemptions that did not apply to the majority of Christians. Effective, widespread television evangelism allowed for a reasonable bending of the rules. To the end of reaching more people for Christ, almost any means would be justified.

J.W. had actually taken to likening his problem with Bonnie to Abraham's problem with Isaac. God asked Abraham to sacrifice the very son of the promise, leaving him no choice but to obey God and trust that He knew what He was doing. J.W. knew divorce and certainly murder were out of the question, so if Bonnie was an obstacle to his television career, then that was God's business. It was precisely this kind of thinking that enabled J.W. to reconcile his wife's death as a sign of God's blessing on his vision. It signaled the end of his stint as a low-budget traveling revival show and the beginning of what he planned to turn into nothing short of a wealthy Christian television empire. If Jim Bakker could do it, J.W. Dean could do it better. And since Jim Bakker had fallen, there was a huge vacuum for someone like J.W. to fill. He had been waiting patiently in the wings for this moment; now, he believed, his time had come.

The autopsy report said Bonnie died of an untreated snakebite. It was an eastern coral snake that she had handled the night of her unfortunate passing, which was easily confused with the similar black-, yellow-, and red-striped nonpoisonous snakes Bonnie and J.W. were accustomed to handling in their "daring" demonstration of faith. It had behaved just like the other snakes, too, gripping its jaw onto her pale white flesh as she casually held it up, dangling, in front of the astonished crowd. She never noticed the different configuration of colored bands on this particular snake. She never knew, as it fixed its blunt black snout on her wrist, that deadly venom was slowly and methodically entering her veins. Never knew, even as she had difficulty breathing that night, that anything serious was amiss. And never suspected, as sleep quickly overcame her, that she would never wake up in this world again.

J.W. smiled as he eased his green Ford Torino onto Interstate 95 heading south. He had six more months of crusades booked and that should be enough time to find him a new bride for the cameras. The smile on his face right then came from the thought that a bride suitable for television would also be a bride suitable for bedding down. He was going to relish this new assignment, after an appropriate period of mourning, of course. But the way women came on to him, even when Bonnie was alive, made him certain that period would be relatively brief. People would understand. No one expects him to be lonely.

J.W. caught his face in the rearview mirror and allowed himself just a little admiration. He was a youthful fifty. He'd kept nearly all his hair, and he wore it thick and loose, though always in place. It wasn't a coincidence that he often reminded people of Kenny Rogers. He could have won a look-alike contest.

He suddenly remembered something and popped open the glove compartment of his car, revealing a small plastic bag of dark gold jewelry. God truly had His hand on him, he thought. He had even provided J.W. with a solid gold bracelet and a fine antique diamond wedding ring for his new, yet-to-be bride. Assuming some mix-up at the morgue, he had endured only a twinge of guilt about keeping it—a twinge that was easily eradicated by a confident sense of God's calling on his life. It was someone else's mistake, not his, and whenever the twinge came back, he would remember the real guilt-clincher: God never makes mistakes. The jewelry in the box was his now—just one more sign of his manifest destiny.

Right about then, J.W. caught something other than himself in his rearview mirror. It was the flashing blue light of a Florida patrol car that had been on his tail while he surveyed the ring and bracelet one more time. J.W. Dean swallowed hard, passed a car he had been even with on the Interstate, and pulled over to the right lane. He then let out a big sigh of relief as the patrol car raced on by, lights flashing.

⌒

Bobbi kept trying to reach her brother, but Jack was the one to finally get him at Sam's house, of all places. He had figured out how to discharge the answering machine, and in the process of checking the rings, someone actually picked up the phone.

"Hello."

"Will?"

"Jack! Is that you?"

"Yes, but what are you doing over there?"

"Looking for Sam."

"So are we. You mean he's not there?"

"Nope. And you won't believe this—"

"Wait a minute. Let me get Bobbi."

"Bobbi!" Jack called, covering the receiver. "Pick up the phone—I've got Will on the line!"

Jack could hear Will expelling his breath in short bursts, then the static of the cordless broke in as Bobbi clicked on.

"Hi, Will. Where have you been? We've been trying to reach you."

"I'm over at Pop's place right now, and you won't believe this—he's gone."

"Gone where?"

"He bought a new pickup and left town yesterday."

"You're kidding," Bobbi said. "Did he tell you where he was going?"

"He didn't tell us anything. I came over here because I couldn't get him to answer the phone."

"How do you know he's gone?"

"George, next door, told me. He said Sam drove up Friday with—get this—a new blue Chevy pickup and said he was going on a long trip. Didn't know when he'd be back. He asked George to take care of the orchids. He left yesterday. Can you believe that? He didn't even tell us. Did he tell you anything?" Will asked.

"No. We haven't talked to him since the funeral. Why, that little rascal! He always wanted a truck, but Mom wouldn't have it. He sure didn't waste much time."

"There's more to the story, sis. I'm not sure I want to tell you this part."

"Why? What is it?"

"Well, I think he may have flipped out. George told me he said he was going to look for Mom."

"He hasn't flipped out," Bobbi said flatly, after a brief pause. "He really has gone to look for Mom."

"Oh, great," Will sighed. "That makes me the only sane one left in this family. Jack, are you still there?"

"I'm still here, and we're all sane. You must not have heard about the ashes."

"What ashes?"

"I'll tell him," Bobbi cut in, pausing for a second before proceeding. "Will, that wasn't Mom we poured into the bay. It was someone else. The Neptune Society got the ashes mixed up."

"You're kidding."

"No, I'm not kidding. We've been on the phone with Mr. Gibbons all afternoon."

"I told you that guy was a bonehead," Will said. "But I still don't get it. Where are Mom's ashes?"

"They're with some itinerant preacher who could be anywhere by now," Jack said.

". . . with Pop on his trail," Bobbi finished. "That's where he's gone, I bet. He's gone after J.W. Dean."

"Wait a minute. What did you say his name was?"

"J.W. Dean."

"Does this guy handle snakes?"

"Yep."

"I bet that's the same guy who's been in the news here—that is, if you call the *Rockledge Ledger* the news. His wife is supposed to have died from handling one of their snakes, but he got out of town before anyone at the church could find out about it. Some local reporter picked up on the story a couple days ago when he was collecting information for the obituaries, and they're making a big deal of it in the paper. The church is up in arms."

"Sounds like our man," said Bobbi. "And to think, we dumped his wife in the ocean."

"And he's got Mom!"

"And Sam is out there somewhere trying to find him," Jack added.

"What'll we do?" Bobbi asked.

"What can we do?" countered Will. "Wait to hear from him, I guess."

"Oh, that's good," Bobbi said sarcastically. "When do either of you remember ever hearing from Sam about anything? I would have missed Mom's death if I hadn't called." Then she added to the knowing silence, "This guy also has Mom's wedding ring and the bracelet Sam gave her for their tenth anniversary."

"For a preacher, he sure didn't grieve very long, did he?" Will commented.

"Maybe he thought he could get out of town without anyone finding out his wife handled one too many snakes," Jack said.

"He almost did, if it weren't for that newspaper report," said Will. "You know, with all the negative press preachers are getting these days, I bet this story is going to get a lot bigger than the *Rockledge Ledger.*"

It was Bobbi's turn. "Will, you said something about a church in the article. Do you remember which one?"

"No, but it was one of those with a long, funny name, you know, the kind that looks like a mobile home with a steeple on top and one of those yellow portable signs blinking out front."

"With yellow lights and wheels under it," Jack added. "I know exactly what you mean."

"Why don't you check it out, Will," said Bobbi. "That church might know something about J.W.'s next crusade."

"Okay. I'll call you if I find out anything," he promised. "Can you believe this?"

"It's just like Mom to not settle down just yet," Bobbi said, and they all agreed that pretty much summed up all this new, somewhat overwhelming information they had received.

A little later, when Jack and Bobbi were snuggled in bed, Bobbi had one more thing to say.

"Sam has just gone up a notch in my book."

"How's that?"

"He went after her." She paused for a minute and went on. "You know, this means we may get Mom's ashes back. I might have a second chance. If I do, I'm not giving in so easily. I'm not letting anybody throw her in the ocean. I did that once. Never again."

Jack knew this was virtually impossible, seeing that Bobbi was in Massachusetts and Sam, in Florida, would obviously be the first to recover the ashes, if in fact they were recoverable. And when and if Sam did, he would most likely do whatever he felt like doing with them and not tell anybody. Not to mention her unrealistic expectation of Sam giving them over that easily after being the one to find them. Bobbi was into some very wishful thinking, Jack thought, but he did not want to bring that up, not when they were in bed and ready to go to sleep.

"Jack? Are you asleep?"

"Huh?"

"Cut it out. You're not asleep. Not that fast."

"Almost, though."

"I just have one question. Would you go out after me—after my ashes?"

Jack thought about saying yes, but it wouldn't have been the honest answer.

"What am I saying? Of course you would," she said, giving him a big squeeze. Bobbi knew the real answer to that question, but she chose to think otherwise of her husband. It was the way she often encouraged people, and sometimes it had an effect on him.

This time it did, for as he drifted off to sleep, he dreamed about driving around Florida in a pickup, trying to find the ashened remains of someone he loved. He just couldn't remember who.

FOUR

The Road to Okeechobee

By Monday morning, it was clear that Will's research was unnecessary. By Monday morning, a good percentage of the population of the United States knew not only what church J.W. Dean's last crusade was held in, but where the next one would be. All the pertinent information was as handy as the front page of *USA Today*. You couldn't miss it. It was the featured cover story, complete with a chilling picture of a sweaty-faced pale woman, dazed and dangling a small color-banded snake that had a jaw-hold on her wrist. The other hand was raised in praise as her glassy eyes rolled upward.

Death of Evangelist's Wife Raises Venomous Questions

By Brad Lane
USA TODAY

Snake handling has seen a steady following in America, especially in the South among certain denominations and cults who take literally the words of the apostle Mark that disciples of Christ "shall take up serpents, and if they drink any deadly thing, it shall not hurt them." A recent NBC special has brought snake handling to the forefront of a nation's religious consciousness that is already severely taxed by the dubious prof-iteering of brazen televangelists. But now a new story is threatening to add yet another bizarre twist to religion in America.

Authorities in Cocoa Beach, Florida, are investigating the mysterious death of Bonnie Dean, wife of traveling evangelist, faith healer, and snake handler, J.W. Dean. Mrs. Dean died two weeks ago after handling snakes during a revival service in Rockledge, Florida, a small rural town about fifteen miles inland from Cocoa Beach. The cause of death, as reported on her death certificate, was an untreated snake bite.

According to Sheriff Buck Buford of the Cocoa Beach Police Department, there may be more to the story. "We're concerned that we cannot locate the Reverend J.W. Dean, that he left town abruptly following the death of his wife, and that he had the body cremated, obviously ruling out any possibility of further autopsy."

Is the sheriff implying foul play? "The Deans have been performing this snake-handling business for nine years," says Buford. "Why should something suddenly go wrong this time? In my opinion there's nothing supernatural in this. It's more like a circus act. And if a death like this happened in a circus, you can be sure an investigation would ensue." No formal investigation is planned at the moment, though Sheriff Buford does not rule it out as a possibility pending further findings.

Earnest Gibbons of the Neptune Society, the service in Cocoa Beach that performed the cremation, doesn't see anything unusual in the events surrounding the death of Bonnie Dean. "There was nothing out of order. The coroner conducted his investigation, the death certificates were completed, everything was done by the book. We handled this matter as discreetly as possible, at Mr. Dean's request, so as not to jeopardize the faith of the local congregation. Wherever possible, we respect the wishes and the confidentiality of our clients."

Sheriff Buford disagrees. "The death certificate is completely bogus. Nothing checks out. We have no reliable information on Mr. Dean. The only thing we know is that he has another crusade in two weeks. Needless to say, we have a few questions to ask the reverend."

Will the court bring a charge of negligence on the part of J.W. Dean? "It's unlikely," says District Attorney Warren Anderson. "The courts have usually steered clear of religious matters involving fringe elements such as this one." But with a death involved, all that could change. Sheriff Buford has received a court order to question Mr. Dean, which he intends to do as soon as he can locate the evangelist.

Meanwhile, the Reverend J.W. Dean is scheduled for revival services in East Naples next week. It sounds as if he may have a few interesting guests waiting for him when he arrives. Until then, the verdict on his wife's death remains in question. The coroner's office is standing by the results of its investigation naming an untreated snakebite as cause of death. Sheriff Buford is quick to point out that Reverend Dean neglected to get her treatment. "There should have been ample time to get the patient to the hospital for an antidote, once he realized she was ill," says Buford.

"To take her into the hospital would have been the same as denouncing his faith," insists Billy Bobb Battson, pastor of the Holy Ghost Gospel Temple, host of the Dean crusade. "He had to give her the chance to recover on her own. This is the way we handle these things. The Lord took her. That's it—plain and simple." These two conflicting points of view show the complexity of this incident should this, or any story like it, ever enter the courtroom.

Sheriff Buford, who comes from two generations of traveling evangelists, seems bent on getting to the bottom of this one. But until then, it remains a matter of opinion as to whether the death of Mrs. J.W. Dean was due to lack of faith or lack of care. It may always be.

Jack saw the article Monday afternoon in Beverly, waiting in a salon for a haircut, and called Bobbi right away. Will saw it when one of his desk clerks showed him the paper after she picked it up on her coffee break. Sam Dunn saw it over blueberry pancakes at the Central Cafe in Indiantown, Florida, eight miles east of Lake

Okeechobee. J.W. Dean didn't see it right away. He was staying at his cousin's mobile home in Port Mayaca, a mere six miles down the road from where Sam sat.

Sam had no idea he was that close to J.W. All he knew was that the part-time secretary at the Holy Ghost Gospel Temple in Rockledge thought she overheard J.W. mention something about Lake Okeechobee as a place he might vacation until his next crusade. Sam was planning on making the rounds to all the motels and campsites in the most popular towns around the lake, looking for the 1972 green Ford Torino with a faded, peeling vinyl top she had described. But that was before he picked up Monday's *USA Today*.

Now he could hardly believe his luck. Right there on the front page of the most popular newspaper in America was the crucial information he had not been able to find yet: the site of J.W. Dean's next crusade. His excitement over this new discovery probably explained why he failed to notice the green Torino pulling into the parking lot of the Central Cafe as he walked out of the restaurant that morning. His mind had quickly switched from Torinos to religious revivals in East Naples.

J.W. Dean poured imitation maple syrup over his stack of famous buttermilk pancakes with satisfaction and noticed that the customer who had just vacated the booth next to him left his copy of *USA Today*, so J.W. helped himself. The front section was missing, but J.W. didn't mind. He never cared much for world and national news anyway. He liked reading about the celebrities in the "Life" section and strike-it-rich tips in "Money." The thought did cross his mind that he would need to catch up on major news items once he got his TV program going, but then again, he would also have an expert research-analysis team combing all the major papers and giving him a distilled update each day before his show. No need to bore himself with world news now.

A shiny blue pickup pulled out of the parking lot and headed west as J.W. made the first cut into his fluffy stack of favorite hot cakes with his fork.

Through his home office window, Jack watched as nighttime hesitated in the sky over the golden marshes of Ipswich, signaling the promise of longer days to come, then shut out the horizon altogether. Bobbi was still out, working late, and Jack had already fed Alex and Brook so they could get to their homework and he could finish up his own work at the computer.

"Hi, Mom!" Jack could hear the children say after the car finally rolled into the gravel driveway and the kitchen door slammed. He knew Bobbi would be talking to each of them in their rooms and catching up on the events of the day, so he stayed at his computer. He was making final corrections to an article that needed to be e-mailed that evening.

"So this is it," Bobbi said minutes later as she came up to his desk, already absorbed in the snake article in *USA Today*.

"Hi," Jack said as he stood up to kiss her, having to squeeze his head between her face and the newspaper to do so. She gave his lips little cooperation and went on with her reading.

"I can't believe this," she said. "Earnest Gibbons is even in here."

"Yeah, don't you love that? 'Nothing out of order,' so he says, and 'everything by the book.' Right. Switching ashes? Whose book is he talking about?"

Suddenly something startled Bobbi and she looked up from the paper. "Jack! What was that? It sounded just like a mouse in the room!"

Jack laughed. "It *was* a mouse. It came from my computer. That was just my alarm going off."

"Thank goodness. It sounded so real. I liked the screaming monkey sound better."

While Bobbi finished reading the article, Jack sent off a couple of faxes that the alarm had reminded him about. Then Bobbi got an idea.

"Jack, I have to go to Naples on business soon anyway. If I go next week, I can be there during J.W.'s crusade and I know that's our best chance of finding Sam. Why don't you come with me?"

What Jack wanted to tell her was that one crazy person running around Florida trying to find someone's ashes was enough. But instead he said, "We can't afford another trip to Florida, and we've used up all our freebies."

"Well, my trip will be paid for by the company. We can afford one ticket. Come with me. The timing is perfect." She hesitated. "I can't believe the mess Mom's gotten herself into!"

"I know," Jack agreed. "I was just thinking, if she only had half this excitement when she was alive."

"She had boring husbands."

"So? You have me."

Bobbi looked at Jack holding his arms out and a hundred things filled her mind to say right then, but she decided to have mercy on him and kiss him instead.

"Well, that was certainly better than the first one," said Jack.

"Come with me to Florida," she said in the little-girl voice that she knew would melt his heart. It did, but not enough.

"I can't do that, babe. I have too much work here. Besides, what do you really expect to accomplish there?"

"I'm mostly concerned about Sam. He still gets terrible headaches—even after his operation. He could black out on the road somewhere, and no one would know where he was."

"And that could happen a mile away from his house on the way to the golf course too," added Jack. "I have a feeling what you really want is to beat him to the ashes."

"I am going to do everything in my power to bring Mom back to New York and lay her to rest where she belongs. You're right about that."

"Good luck getting her away from Sam," Jack retorted, realizing he was doing it too—equating Betty's ashes with Betty.

"Oh, I know. He's set in his ways. I just think if I were down there, I might be able to influence him. He does listen to me sometimes. At least I can try. So you'll come with me? Paid hotel room . . . No kids . . ."

She knew how to get him. Bobbi knew anything free was one of Jack's biggest weaknesses. "I'll look into it, but don't count on it."

She stepped up, wrapped her arms around his waist, and rested her head on his chest. "I'm going anyway. It would just be nice to have you there with me."

They stood there holding each other for a few minutes and then the mouse squealed again.

"Will you shut that thing off? What is that, a snooze alarm?"

"Sorry, I'll take care of it."

Jack reached for his mouse in order to dump the alarm signal, and Bobbi sat down on top of his desk and started going through a pile of mail. They often had conversations in odd places in this house. Rarely in a spot where one would sit down for such a thing. There was something about Bobbi that always resisted using things for their intended purpose. That seemed too average to her—like giving in to the status quo—and if there was anything that Bobbi didn't want to be, it was average. So they put the television in Alex's room and watched it sitting on his bunk bed or the floor because she hated TVs in family rooms, and they had chairs in the formal room that looked nice but didn't sit nice, and they spent long conversations in hallways and bathrooms and sitting on desks and kitchen counters, and Jack went along with all of this because all of this went along with Bobbi, and the one thing he knew about Bobbi, above all else, was that he loved her. As long as he kept his mind on that, they could have a meaningful conversation anywhere.

So Jack sat in his chair and they exchanged questions and answers about the day. Jack answered Bobbi's questions with a string of forgettable news items, most of which she was now sitting on. He preferred her to the things she was covering up on his desk anyway, and told her so.

"I should hope so," she said, crossing her legs with a swish. Jack leaned back in his chair and clasped his hands behind his head. Bobbi saw this as an opportune moment for one of her favorite things while she and her husband talked. She laid her stockinged feet in his lap and looked longingly at him. Jack smiled and started rubbing her feet.

"Are you at all surprised that Sam went after the ashes?" he said after Bobbi returned a few moans of appreciation. "That he would care that much?"

"Yes," she replied.

"I am too."

"I would have expected him to make some comment about all ashes being the same and how we should just forget about it," said Bobbi.

"Exactly. What do you think all this means?"

"I have no idea."

"Maybe he just wanted an excuse to take a trip."

"Maybe," she said. "Did Will call?"

"Yes. He saw the article too. He said he'd find out what church J.W.'s crusade was going to be at and let us know. He was talking about maybe driving out to Naples if he hadn't heard from Sam by then. You know, we're all assuming that Sam picked up a copy of *USA Today.* What if he didn't?"

"He did. He's never missed a day as long as I've known him," Bobbi stated. "Don't stop—that feels so good. . . . Even when he was in the hospital for surgery, he had it delivered to his room."

"You're right. I forgot about that." Jack continued to knead her feet and stared out the window at the headlights blinking through the tree trunks along Route 1. "That always surprises me about him. He can seem so dim-witted sometimes, and then other times he's as articulate as a journalist."

Bobbi let Jack massage her feet a little longer. "Thanks," she said finally. "I'm tired now. Will you put me to bed . . . and read to me?" It was that little-girl voice again.

"Sure," he said, looking around for the mouse to his computer, "as soon as I put this thing to sleep."

That wasn't soon enough for Bobbi. She knew that the things he would find on his computer screen even while shutting it down would keep him occupied for another half hour if she let him, so she scooted over on his desk until she was sitting right in front of the screen. "Now," she said with a playful grin.

He tried to reach around her, but she moved again to block him. Holding him off with one hand, she reached back with the other, felt for the mouse, and then sat on it, sending the little mouse sound squeaking repeatedly.

"Now look what you've done," Jack said.

Bobbi got a wild look in her eye. "I think your mouse is a little too excited to go to sleep right now."

"I don't blame him," he said, and with one swift move he swept her up off his desk, eliciting a scream of delight, and carried her down the stairs, barely under control.

"You haven't done *this* in a long time," she whispered in his ear.

His labored breathing confirmed her observation and betrayed his waning fitness, but her bright eyes gave him strength. He had forgotten what happened to his wife whenever he got her up off the ground . . . even if only for a few minutes.

She, on the other hand, never forgot.

FIVE

The Big Tent

"Get a load of this, you guys," Alex said, reading from the *Boston Globe* the next morning in the kitchen. " 'It has been reported today that sperm are terrible swimmers and need to surf on powerful muscle contractions in the female uterus to get to their destination. According to Doctor Tartabul of the R.B. Richter Institute, this could account for more than half of reported infertility cases.' "

Bobbi elbowed Jack, who was making coffee. "There you go," she said. "Good thing *I'm* in shape!"

"Good thing my guys are good surfers," said Jack, smiling broadly at Brook, who had a look of disgust on her face. Then he started singing and swaying with his own music, "Let's go surfin' now, everybody's learning how, come on a safari with me. . . ."

"Mom," Brook protested, "why can't we have a normal family? You guys are grossing me out!"

Bobbi sat down next to her daughter and poured herself some cereal. "There's nothing gross about sex," she said. "It's all very beautiful and it was created that way by God."

"Mom, microscopic tadpoles surfing around on muscle tissue is not what I call a beautiful thing," said Brook.

"Those 'microscopic tadpoles' are responsible for making you, and there isn't anything more beautiful than you."

"You only say that because you're my mother. Trevor doesn't think so. He never even notices me."

"Trevor is blind," said Jack, joining them at the table.

"Brook," Alex continued, unwilling to drop the subject, "did you know that you already have all the eggs you will ever produce? You were born with them. We learned that in Human Reproduction yesterday."

"Alex!" Brook cried, rolling her eyes. "Mom, please tell him to stop."

"Actually," Jack interjected, "Alex started us off this morning with an important report about male reproductive swimming deficiencies. I'm personally shaken by the news."

Brook was already rinsing her dishes and slamming them loudly in the dishwasher. "I'm going to go dry my hair. I've had enough of all of you this morning."

Alex was still at the counter with the paper spread out in front of him. "Hey, Alex," Jack said, "anything in there about J.W. Dean?"

"Who's J.W. Dean?"

"He's the one who has Gramma's ashes."

"Oh yeah, the snake guy. Why would he be in the paper?"

"The sheriff of Cocoa Beach wants to investigate his wife's death. It was the cover story in *USA Today* yesterday."

"Awesome!" Alex was impressed.

"Did we offend her?" Jack asked Bobbi after Brook was well out of the room.

"Of course. It's kind of hard *not* to at thirteen. Especially our daughter. It's not like she's opinionated or anything."

"Well, just checking. Are you done with the front section?" he said to Alex, simultaneously grabbing it from him. "Thanks." Jack scanned the first few pages, then found something on page three. "Here it is! A paragraph in the 'National News' sidebar. I can't believe the coverage this thing is getting! Now they even know the church in East Naples where J.W.'s next crusade is."

"Will keeps having his research done for him by the newspaper," Bobbi commented. "What church is it?"

"The First Apostolic Church of the Holy Ghost with Signs Following in East Naples. Boy, that's a mouthful. I wonder if J.W. ever does revivals in plain old Baptist churches."

"I doubt it," said Bobbi. "You've got to be a church with a long name to have a snake handler come. Can you imagine our church hosting J.W. Dean?"

"The pews would empty out in a second!"

"You know, with all this publicity, Jack, I wonder if J.W. Dean's going to show up at all."

Jack thought for a minute. "To not show up would be an admission of guilt."

"And then everybody would be after him, and Gramma's ashes would be in the middle of the news!" Alex's eyes were growing wider by the minute. "We could join the chase!"

"Hold it, McGyver," Bobbi said. "You guys are both jumping to conclusions. You're assuming J.W. Dean has something to hide. What if it was just a failed demonstration of faith? Maybe it was simply God's time for poor Bonnie."

"You mean to say you actually believe this snake-handling stuff—that God works through this kind of thing?"

"I'm more inclined to believe this than a boring pastor quoting platitudes every Sunday. If faith isn't exciting, I don't want to be a part of it. I want to be where God is happening. If J.W. has a line to God's power, then more power to him."

"You scare me when you talk like this—like you're ready to roll in the aisles or something."

"Jack, I'm always ready for God to touch my life."

"Well, of course . . . but you can't be naïve either. There are a lot of phony preachers out there—the Bible warns us about them all over the place. I was even thinking the other day that if J.W. did have something to do with his wife's death—and I'm not saying he did—it's just that if he could have arranged this somehow . . . well, it would make the perfect murder. Think of it. His wife dies at the hand of snakes they both handle all the time. How can they pin anything on him?"

"Come on, Jack, you've been watching too much TV."

～

J.W. Dean was watching a lot of TV at his cousin's house that week, but because he never strayed from the local Christian station, he missed the stories about himself that were everywhere else on the news. Christian television had no interest in a story that would further erode the credibility of preachers. J.W. never knew he was suddenly famous until he was standing in line at a convenience store near his cousin's trailer park in Port Mayaca and realized he had been staring at himself on the cover of the *National Enquirer*. It took a few moments for it to register in his mind—he was so accustomed to staring at himself in a mirror—only this time the image did not move when he moved. He bought himself a copy, and when the story referred to the *USA Today* article, he went out and found that one too. That's when he started watching network news, where he was popping up everywhere. Jay Leno had a joke about him in his opening monologue, and *Saturday Night Live* even brought back the Church Lady, who comically pulled a rubber snake out of her purse and fell over backward at her desk, stockinged feet up.

J.W.'s first reaction had been one of fear, especially when the *National Enquirer* headlined the church secretary of one of his former crusades—a certain Mallory Blaine—as claiming to have had an affair with him. Problem was, the voluptuous beauty on the cover of the tabloid was nowhere in J.W.'s memory. Seeing her there made him wish she had been. He comforted himself with the knowledge that fame comes with a certain price, and false accusations were part of what was to be expected. He soon became pretty smug about his instant fame that was already worthy of a scandal charge.

No, things couldn't go much better than this for J.W. Dean. A week's worth of free publicity for his television debut was in essence what had taken place here. J.W. Dean had suddenly joined the likes of Jim Bakker and Jimmy Swaggart as an illustrious group of ministers who had found their way to the racks of supermarkets and the talk shows of the nation. "The J.W. Dean Show" was suddenly not just a dream, it was a commodity that would be readily marketable. Almost overnight "J.W. Dean" had become a household name. All he needed to do now was make himself out to be the victim of everything and the perpetrator of nothing and he had a ready audience. J.W. understood publicity enough to know that it did not matter what kind of publicity you got. Publicity was publicity, and J.W. already had more of it in one week than anyone could afford to buy. J.W. was now "somebody" and he couldn't wait to get to East Naples and find out how big of a "somebody" he really was.

On Saturday, the day before meetings were scheduled to begin, J.W. drove up to the little country church on the edge of an open field of palmetto scrub and trash timber stands, east of the city of Naples on Florida's western Gulf Coast. Partially cleared once for cattle land and left to perish in the hot sun, this scarred land is typical of the areas of Florida that lie just inland from lucrative coasts lined with pink condominiums, aqua green swimming pools, and iron-gated estates. No more than a few blocks east of Highway 41, the thickly padded St. Augustine grass of manicured lawns disappears and modest mobile homes take over—aluminum boxes sitting on unpadded gray dirt.

J.W. immediately noticed that the meeting tent was larger than the one he requested in his letter of contract with the church. In fact, it was twice the size of any tent he had ever used in his crusades. The second thing he noticed was an *Action News* van parked next to the tent and a person getting out of it with a portable video camera. The third thing, which he failed to notice, was the un-marked police car parked next to the van with the official emblem of the Sheriff of Cocoa Beach on the side.

J.W. first went to the church offices and found the pastor, May-nard Filmore, who was an old college buddy from his denomina-tional school in West Virginia. Maynard slapped J.W. on the back and ushered him into his office. He was a big man, a foot taller than J.W., and as warmhearted and trusting a person as his stature.

"J.W., J.W., J.W., my old buddy, how ya doin'? So sorry to hear about Bonnie—she was such a blessed asset to your ministry. How will you ever replace her?"

"I don't know that I can," said J.W., eying the nice mahogany desk in Maynard's office. "Just got to keep going."

"I was a little worried when you didn't show up last night like you said you might, but then again, I knew that I would have heard from you if there was some problem. Did you see the tent?"

"Big tent. Why?"

"I ordered a bigger one, praise the Lord. I had to, J.W. Calls comin' in from all over the country. We had to put in a separate line in the office and hire someone just to answer it. It hasn't stopped ringing since last week. There's gonna be a harvest here, Dean boy—a harvest of many souls."

J.W. smiled when he heard Maynard call him "Dean boy." It brought back old memories of college days, pranks on campus, and real spiritual vision. It was as if all his youthful fervor came wrapped in the sound of that nickname, and he was suddenly reminded of the prophetic words that were said over him by his classmates, the calling he had responded to, and the resolute commitment he had made to the ministry as a young man. All of this came to him in an instant—in the purity of its first light—and forced him to concede a certain dimness that had dulled it. He looked into Maynard's firm, kind eyes and saw a strong light burning.

"J.W.," Maynard said in a more serious tone, "the sheriff of Cocoa Beach is waiting to question you. Half the calls we've gotten are from the news media. How are you going to deal with this?"

"The sheriff has something against preachers. He's trying to discredit my ministry and make me responsible for Bonnie's death. God will turn it around. You just watch."

"What *did* happen, J.W.?"

J.W. got up out of his chair and peered through the blinds of the office window to the large tent outside. The cameraman was zeroing in on a reporter with a microphone in front of the tent. J.W. spoke quietly, respectfully. "She was feverish when she went to bed, but I never expected anything other than the flu. I woke up next to a corpse. It was her time, Maynard." He turned to focus on his old friend and noticed how dignified Maynard's newly gray hair appeared against his shiny black African skin. "Her time."

"God will reach many people through this," said Maynard. "I know that's no consolation for losing her, but God knows what He's doing."

"Amen," pronounced J.W., looking outside again. "Look at that tent. You think we can fill it?"

"The glory of God is gonna fill this place, Dean boy. I know it!"

Maynard came over to the window, put his big hand on J.W.'s shoulder, and started to pray. J.W. went down on his knees, and Maynard rested his other oversized hand on J.W.'s head and prayed for the power of God to rest upon him. J.W. was shaking. After a number of minutes of fervent prayer, J.W. got up and they embraced and headed toward the door.

"Oh, J.W.," Maynard said, turning to look back at him with his hand on the knob, "this Mallory Blaine thing . . . tell me it isn't true."

"It's not," said J.W. "She's just someone trying to get attention."

"You will have to address it somehow," said Maynard. "It's unfortunate, but people believe what they read in those trashy papers."

"I've already taken care of it," said J.W. "I contacted the pastor there. She wasn't even the secretary when I visited. She filled the post for only four months last year. I have his statement in a news release for the papers here. It will put the whole thing to rest."

Maynard was visibly relieved. "Well, then," he smiled, "let's go meet the press."

SIX

The Keys to Florida

Sam took a roundabout route getting to East Naples. Now that he had a clear destination in mind and some time to kill before getting there, he decided to go southeast to Fort Lauderdale and Miami and then take the famous Alligator Alley across the Florida Everglades.

Sam had two vices from which he had taken a three-year hiatus due to his wife's illness. One was smoking cigarettes and the other was betting at the dog races. It was smoking that had ultimately choked out Betty's life, and Sam had stopped on her behalf as soon as the punishing emphysema set in. Now that she was gone and with no lingering incentive to care for himself, he had returned to his Marlboros with a vengeance, as if he had lost ground to make up. Greyhound racing was the other vice, and his three-year absence from the racetrack had no moral implications either. It was simply the constant demands of caring for his dying wife that kept him away.

It is not uncommon for an older person like Sam, whose life has been on hold for an ailing partner, to suddenly act as if he had his own life back when his partner finally passes on. Only for Sam, it was more like getting his own death back. Sam's new "lease on life" was really a "lease on death"—a destructive return to the vices that living with Betty had kept at bay. Betty was the last good thing in Sam's life—the last reason for him to care about living at all—and in this lay the irony of Betty's missing ashes. Even in her death, she provided him with one flickering spark in his otherwise hollow existence. Betty's ashes became a temporary salvation for Sam: They left him with one more thing to do. With Betty safely put away, Sam would be without the burden of a reason to live. But with Betty's ashes still at large, reason remained.

Sam had always been on the verge of self-annihilation. He had even been hell-bent in the pursuit of it when he met Betty, having lost his first wife five years earlier to a quick and painful cancer. So intent was he on reaching his goal that he never would have noticed Betty had she not wagered her way into his life.

They had known of each other through social ties, for both of their families were of the inner circle—the elite that dominated the society pages of the *Shaughnessy Press*. But it was at a wedding that their relationship began. It was not hard for them to find each other, even when they were not looking. They were both lurking around the circumference of the same circle: he, in pursuit of his own dark shadows, and she, thrown out from the center by an ugly divorce. When their eyes first met they had been sitting within speaking distance, staring inward at the milling crowd, so close, yet so unaware of the other's presence that they startled each other.

"Oh! Hi, Sam," Betty had said. "How are you doing?"

"Miserable" was his reply.

"This must be the black sheep corner," she had commented.

"No, it's the smoking corner."

"How long has it been since Helen died?"

"Five years."

"That's too long."

"You're right it's too long. One day was too long."

"Sam, I mean five years is too long to be *alone*."

"I like being alone."

"Really? You look gloriously happy." Her raised eyebrow had underscored her sarcasm.

"You don't know me. This is as happy as I get."

"I bet I could change that."

"I wouldn't have thought you were the betting kind," Sam had said. He then added as a joke: "Tell you what, if I win at the races tomorrow, I'll marry you."

"You're on," Betty had said, straight-faced, and she meant it. They even shook hands on it and the next day Sam hit the biggest win of his betting career. Three weeks later they were married, against the vehement protests of everyone who knew them, especially their children.

"Mom, are you crazy?" Bobbi had questioned. "This man is awful. He's mean. He's a grouch. Have you ever seen a smile on his face?"

"As a matter of fact, he smiled when he asked me to marry him."

"Yeah, because he won at the races! Mom, I'm just afraid you're the one who's going to lose here."

"I'll be the judge of that," Betty had said. "The way I see it, I've already lost. I had my Prince Charming, but your dear father rode off on his white horse, never to be seen again. Frankly, I just want someone to take care of me."

"Mom, I don't get this. You're willing to live with a miserable man just because you'll get taken care of? *I'll* take care of you if that's what you want."

"Oh, will you, now. You'll be with me when I get up in the morning and when I go to bed at night? You'll sit next to me and watch the days go by? You'll make sure my health insurance is paid up? You'll be with me when I'm sick? You'll bury me in the ground when I die?"

Bobbi had been unable to answer that barrage of questions with anything other than a prolonged silence.

"Bobbi, sweetheart . . . he's a good man. I've known him from afar for a long time. Sam's crusty on the outside, but he's got a soft center somewhere in there and I aim to find it. And you know what?"

"What?" said Bobbi, suddenly calmed by her mother's certainty.

"He's a man of his word. I'll admit he doesn't have many of them, but the ones he manages to use, he means. He made good on his promise to me, didn't he?"

"But, Mom, do you love him?"

Now it had been Betty's turn to be silent. Finally she spoke. "Love means different things at different times in your life. If you mean, do I respect him? Yes. Do I think he'll take care of me? Yes. Does he make me feel safe? Yes. Do I think about him night and day and has he swept me off my feet? Well . . . to be truthful, that already happened and look where it got me. No, I just want someone to stay. Someone I can count on. Someone who'll be with me to the end and bury me when I'm gone. Sam has promised to do these things, and I know he will keep his word. You can call that anything you like, but right now, from where I am in my life, that feels a lot like love to me."

That's when Bobbi had kissed her mother on the cheek and quietly vowed she would never again say a derogatory thing about Sam in her hearing.

Sam drove through the miles of sugar-cane fields and intersecting canals that feed into them south of Lake Okeechobee. One afternoon thunderstorm cleared only to have another one follow on its heels, leaving small lakes on either side of the two-lane highway. He could have gotten to the interstate quicker going due east, but he chose the back way. Soon the yellow ocher cane fields gave way to the sawgrass of the Everglades. Overgrown memories tugged at Sam's heart.

As a child he had been captured by southern Florida. Images of smugglers, pirates, crocodile hunters, bootleggers, and fishermen had dominated his unchecked imagination, mostly through stories told him by his grandfather. Vacationing in Florida was a tradition that went back through three generations of Dunns. As the story goes, Sam's grandfather fell so in love with the mysteries of life south of Miami that he simply refused to return to New York State one summer . . . and turned his back on everything—his position, his wealth, his wife and family—for a vagabond fisherman's life along the Florida Keys.

Sam was thirty before he found out the truth about his grandfather, though he had known him for twenty years by another name. This only added to the mystery and intrigue of the stories and the legendary lore Sam carried with him. Grandfather Dunn's abandonment had left such a black mark on the family that the grandchildren were kept from the truth, at least the women thought so. Sam grew up thinking his grandfather had been killed in World War I and would still believe that, were it not for his Uncle Charles. Charlie Dunn refused to have his father totally estranged from himself, and his own children from their grandfather. He was the only one in the family who didn't go along with the cover-up. On yearly family vacations to the Miami shores, Charlie would take young Sam and Albert along with his own children on overnight fishing trips in and around the Florida Keys. Known only to Charlie, the owner and operator of their boat every year was none other than the children's grandfather and his own father, Chadwick Dunn. Sam knew him then as "Crocky," short for tall tales of crocodile adventures that mesmerized them all as his salty voice crept out over the still water and echoed off the dark mangroves of Florida Bay.

As Sam drove through the Everglades, the cryptic names of the Keys they traversed in Crocky's sloop revisited his mind from a long-forgotten childhood: Snipe, Saddlebunch, Marquesas, Big Coppitt, Lower Matecumbe. The varying hues of aqua, turquoise, and indigo were suddenly vivid in his memory—hues that could change in an instant by a sponge field on the floor of a coral reef or merely the passing of a cloud overhead. He remembered the feel of his first snook on the line and the day Crocky reeled in a hundred-pound tarpon. Sam wondered what it would be like to go back and hear the sound of wings from the big birds again—the cormorants, white herons, and pelicans, their great wings slapping the water as they struggled for altitude or buzzed the bay like jets in formation before careening up to a thrashing halt high in the moss-covered cypress trees overhead.

As he approached the Hollywood Dog Track north of Miami, Sam Dunn surprised himself. Instead of turning in, as was his original plan, he turned onto Interstate 95 and headed for points south. He had enough time to kill before J.W.'s crusade. Something was stirring. He had known for some time that all the islands of the Keys, which in his youth were only accessible by boat or the old Flagler Railway, were now accessible by the Overseas Highway, a continuation of U.S. 1, but he had never availed himself of the opportunity to drive it. The knowledge that the islands of his memories were literally minutes away won over his desire to win some money watching greyhounds chase a mechanical rabbit. So Sam blew by Miami, Florida City, Key Largo, and didn't stop until he put up for the night in a little motel on Islamorada, one pearl on an emerald chain of coral islands that stretch a hundred and twenty miles out from the mainland of Florida.

SEVEN

The Arrest

There was a picture in the hallway opposite Jack Acre's desk in Ipswich that perfectly captured the essence of Barbara Ann Acres. Jack purchased it as a surprise for her one Christmas and had it framed. It was an original World War II recruiting poster that had the face and shoulders of a pretty woman in uniform superimposed over a life-sized Western Union telegram. Looming behind the ominous yellow parchment that in wartime was most often the bearer of bad news, one could see a treacherous, white-capped ocean disappearing into billowing clouds of black smoke.

The woman's face was soft and direct, her posture firm but not rigid. Her eyes were wide open and focused straight ahead, set under dark, lined eyebrows and a shadow cast by a white-and-blue uniform hat proclaiming in yellow letters: U.S. NAVY. Her sharp, delicate nose was the focal point of a feminine orb that featured full orange-red lips set determinedly under lightly rouged cheeks.

Two silver anchors graced each navy blue lapel, one slightly higher than the other.

The blowup of the telegram behind her was large enough to read, though partially covered up by her image. The message was addressed to a MISS NANCY HOLMES, and just above her name were the letters and numbers of what appeared to be its French origin: LD241 INTL SANS ORIGINE 174. On either side of her short, curly brown hair, one could make out the following words and fragments of words otherwise hidden by her face: IN HOSP—WOUND—EVERYTH—N'T WORRY—O.K. LOVE, DAN. Under the picture, in large red letters, was the caption: THAT WAS THE DAY I JOINED THE WAVES.

Had she been born thirty years earlier, Bobbi would have been the woman in that picture. Bobbi Acres, not content to stay at home while her wounded husband lay in a French hospital. Bobbi Acres, signing up for the Navy, requesting France, with every intention of swaying the entire U.S. military establishment to get herself assigned to LD241 INTL SANS ORIGINE 174, wherever that was. Bobbi Acres, doing everything possible to aid the cause, and if she couldn't get to *that* hospital, she'd get to *some* hospital. Same difference. Anyone who knew Bobbi and had passed that picture in the Acre hallway and taken enough time to figure out the story behind it had said the same thing: "Yep . . . Bobbi would do that."

Some might romanticize the blind love that would put a woman like that in uniform, as if her whole purpose in life was to get to her wounded husband. But Bobbi would not have been in it for her husband; she would have been in it for the war. Bobbi would've been thinking, *My husband's wounded; I've got to help the cause.* There would be no question about it; if he couldn't fight, she must. Many women in wartime helped the cause by working in factories in the States. That would not have been good enough for Bobbi. She would have had to get in uniform and get over there and fill in for him. And had she been over there in her dress blues, she would have had more drive than a regiment of male soldiers in her position. For Bobbi, it would have been all stars and stripes and blazes of glory and good triumphing over evil and coming home to a parade.

But there was still more. The truth of the matter was, Bobbi would have been a little put out at her husband in this situation for finding himself in a hospital when there was a war going on. Bobbi's philosophy of life left little room for being laid up for any reason.

She had never done well in hospitals. Once, when Jack was an outpatient for a hernia operation, Bobbi had managed to get herself in the door to see him, but she went to the wrong floor and walked in on the confirmation of all her fears. In the bed where she expected to find Jack, she saw a shriveled seventy-eight-year-old man hooked up to half a dozen tubes with his toothless mouth open and gurgling. Convinced it was what the operation had done to her husband, she stormed out of the room and demanded to see a doctor.

"Oh, thank goodness it's you," she had said when they finally got her straightened out and on the right floor.

"Why do you look so white?" Jack had questioned when he saw her. "You look like you've just seen a ghost."

"I just thought I saw the ghost of you, that's all."

"Are you sure you're okay?" Jack asked.

"No! I'm *not* okay! Can we go now?"

She never got over her disdain for hospitals, even through two reasonably good birth experiences. During each of those hospital stays, Jack had made note of the helpless look that came over her face the minute they put her in a wheelchair—a look that never left her until they wheeled her out. Her expression was so noticeable because it was so rare—an expression of not being in a position to control the situation. The one other time that look had crossed Bobbi's face was a time known only to Jack and God.

⌐

Bobbi was in perfect control of the situation (or so she thought) when she drove out to East Naples in a rental car, bent on finding her mother's ashes in the possession of Mr. J.W. Dean.

She fully expected to bump into Sam somewhere in the crowd, but nothing went as she'd hoped.

"Well, I got right to J.W.," she told Jack over the phone later that night from her hotel room in Naples.

"Great. And what did you find out?"

"Nothing. He knocked me out before I could ask him anything."

"He what?"

"He knocked me out."

"That's what I thought you said. What are you talking about?"

"It was so crowded, Jack. People were spilling out the back of the tent. Reporters were all over J.W. Dean like vultures. No one could get within fifty feet of him. So I figured my only chance was to go down front for prayer at the end of the service."

"Oh no." Jack sighed, seeing what was coming. "Was he handling snakes?"

"Nope. No snakes this time."

"Well, what did he say? What happened?"

"I waited in line while people were falling over right and left. Some of them he'd merely breathe on and they'd go down. When he got to me, he asked me what I wanted prayer for and I told him I wanted my mother's ashes back, and before I could explain, he had his hands on my head and was muttering something about Mom's eternal soul. That's the last thing I remember."

"I don't believe this. My wife got slain in the Spirit."

"Don't knock it, Jack. You know I've been wanting to experience more of God lately."

"You mean to say you're giving this experience credibility?"

"And why not?"

"Because this guy could be a crook, that's why! He slept with a church secretary, and the sheriff of Cocoa Beach thinks he's a murderer! Are you sure you didn't get bitten by a snake? Are you feeling okay?"

"Jack, I can't remember when I've felt better. And you don't know whether any of those stories about J.W. Dean are true anyway. They're tabloid stories. I mean, consider the source, Jack. The same folks brought us actual photos of the Loch Ness monster. Besides, whatever I received didn't have anything to do with J.W. if it was from the Lord. When I came to, I had the most wonderful sense of peace. I'm not even stressed out about work anymore."

Now Jack knew that meant something important, so he decided to refrain from any further comments right then about Bobbi's supposed spiritual encounter.

"So you never got to talk to him?" he asked.

"No. He was gone by the time I came to, and a counselor finished praying with me."

"What was that like?"

"It was wonderful. I got a sweet old lady . . . very genuine."

"And what about Sam? Did you find Sam there?"

"No sign of him," she said. "The crusade lasts for a week. Maybe he's coming later."

"Are you going to stay? See if he's there tomorrow night?"

"I can't. I have appointments in Boston the day after tomorrow."

"Is there a late flight you can catch?" Jack suggested.

"No. I've already checked into that."

"You can't afford to hang around there simply on a hunch that Sam will show up."

"No, I can't. I talked to Will, though. He said he might be able to get down later in the week."

"How frustrating to be right there and come away emptyhanded," Jack said.

"Not exactly. I got something from the Lord."

"Hey, maybe Sam will get slain in the Spirit too."

"Jack, don't joke about this."

"No, I meant that. Sam's going to have to get knocked in the head to get anything about God through that thick skull of his."

Bobbi knew that Jack was probably right about that. What Bobbi didn't know was that Sam *was* there that night. He came in late, after the meeting started, and left early, before it was done. Well, he didn't actually leave. He was escorted out, which is to say, he was actually thrown out. This all happened while Bobbi was oblivious to what was going on.

Sam had recognized her standing in line in the front of the tent and saw her fall over backward when she was touched by J.W. Unacquainted as he was with this kind of behavior, he made no small stir trying to come to her aid, so much so that he was subsequently removed from the premises by two muscular ushers—"holy bouncers," they called themselves—trained to keep an eye out for rabble-rousers, the demented, and the deranged. They were convinced that Sam qualified for all three. They even tried to exorcise a demon out of him, but he was more belligerent than any demon they'd ever encountered. They made it clear that he wasn't to be seen at these meetings anymore without a significant change in heart and escorted him to his truck to make certain of his departure. Sam circled back through the parking lot a couple times in hopes of locating Bobbi, but to no avail.

Maynard Filmore was in his office the next day when his part-time secretary came in and announced that there was a Mr. Dunn from Cocoa Beach who wished to see him. Maynard immediately thought of J.W. when he heard Cocoa Beach mentioned.

"Is he a reporter?" Maynard asked.

"He's awfully old for a reporter."

"Did he say what he wanted?"

"No, he just asked to see you."

"Send him on in," said Maynard.

When Sam entered the office, Maynard rose to meet him with a big grin and a warm handshake. Sam didn't even lift his hand.

"I want to know where you're keeping my daughter-in-law," Sam stiffly stated to a surprised Maynard.

"I beg your pardon."

"My daughter-in-law," Sam said, looking around the room. "I know you're keeping her here somewhere."

"There's no one here but the staff members who work here,

Mr. Dunn." Maynard looked confused. "This is a church, not a prison."

"She fell over last night like the others. Where do you take them after they fall over?"

Maynard broke into a big smile. "We don't take them anywhere," he said with a chuckle. "We have counselors who talk with them and pray over any of their needs."

"And after that?"

"After that they go home like everybody else. What is your daughter's name?" asked Maynard, reaching for a stack of cards on his desk.

"Bobbi Acres," said Sam. "And she's my daughter-*in-law*."

"Hmmm," he said, flipping through the cards. "We have a Barbara Ann Acres here from out of town. Could that be her?"

"Ipswich, Massachusetts," Sam said.

Maynard noted that his odd visitor was right about that, but he didn't feel comfortable saying anything about the hotel in Naples Bobbi had listed as her temporary contact. Too many crazy people in this world getting information for all the wrong reasons.

"Mr. Dunn, what exactly is it that I can help you with? Have you lost track of Mrs. Acres?"

"No," Sam replied. "But you could help me get in touch with J.W. Dean."

"J.W. Dean?" Now Maynard really was suspicious. "Mr. Dunn, it seems the whole world wants to see J.W. Dean right now, and because of that, he's not seeing anyone except the congregation he preaches to here every night."

"Do you know where he's staying?"

"I'm sorry, I'm not free to give out that information. We're just hosting this revival, sir; we're not a clearinghouse for Mr. Dean's affairs." Maynard flinched at his choice of words, but Sam didn't seem to notice.

"I have something that belongs to him." Sam rose abruptly. "Would you please see that he gets this?" He laid a white envelope on Maynard's desk and left the room before the pastor could even stand up to say good-bye.

Maynard slumped in his chair and stared at the envelope. It was on motel stationery from the Vagabond Inn in Naples, and it was open. He couldn't resist. The man's odd visit had captured his curiosity. He opened the letter to find the following scrawled unevenly on an uphill line. *I have your wife's ashes.* It was signed Samuel Dunn, and the phone number of the motel was circled. Maynard shook his head in amazement. The Vagabond Inn was where J.W. Dean was staying.

⌁

That night Sam was not only on time for the meeting, he was early enough to get a good seat. One of the ushers who had escorted him out the night before noticed him and consulted with his fellow "bouncer." After some discussion, they decided to keep a close watch on Sam but let him stay. He was on time, he was wearing a coat, and he was clean-shaven—three improvements from the night before that might indicate God was working in the man's life. Besides, their purpose was to keep the peace, not to keep anyone from meeting the Lord. They prayed that this might be the night for the gray-haired ornery man in the green coat to do just that.

But Sam was not interested in meeting the Lord. He was only interested in meeting J.W. Dean, and he had taken the clue from Bobbi and decided that he would go forward that night, if only to deliver another note directly to him—a kind of part two of the note he left with Maynard that afternoon. This note told J.W. that the ashes he thought were his wife's were in fact the ashes of Betty Dunn, and J.W. had them by the mortuary's mistake, along with Betty's jewelry. Sam knew this because he had in his possession the remains of Mrs. Dean. All he wanted was a simple exchange: Bonnie for Betty and Betty's jewelry—an exchange he proposed for the next day at noon at the coffee shop of the Vagabond Inn.

Sam was taking a chance in declaring that he had the remains of J.W.'s wife in his possession when those remains were, in fact, resting in the company of dolphins somewhere in the cold Atlantic. But he figured it wasn't that big of a chance, since he had created

Bonnie's mock remains out of barbecue ashes from outside his motel in Islamorada and the fine white sand of his favorite lagoon in the Florida Keys. It was a most incredible match, Sam thought, all tied up in a plastic bag with a twist-tie and resting comfortably in a bakery box from the same bakery on Highway 1 where he and his cousins would meet Corky for donuts before taking to the sea. The unique concoction had the same look, same consistency, same weight as the ashes he dumped off the boat near Cocoa Beach. Sam was convinced that it would take an expert to tell otherwise.

To his surprise, Sam found certain elements of the revival meeting interesting to him, even entertaining. The singing group at the beginning had a down-home country style that reminded him a little of the Carter Family that often sang with Johnny Cash, and Maynard Filmore, up in front of a crowd instead of in his office, turned out to be a rather entertaining comic. As the black pastor of a predominantly rural white congregation, he threw an odd twist on the norm for the South, but of course, Florida can hardly be considered part of the South, being, as it is, the vacation-retirement spot for so many northerners. True, Florida has its own history rich with Spanish conquistadors and Native Americans, but this history has been drowned by waves and waves of northern transplants, down either for vacation or to spend the waning years of their lives enjoying, or still grasping for, the American dream.

Maynard had no qualms about making light of his own minority status. He constantly chided the people for their lack of soul. He taught them how to "clap black" and how to speak up from the audience when they agreed with the preacher. "Give the man some feedback," he said to a chorus of newly liberated white "amens."

"It's lonely up here," he went on. "Preachers *need* your support. J.W. Dean needs your support. Lord knows he's not getting it from anyone else right now. I want you to know, I'm standing by this man. I went to school with this brother and I know his heart. His heart is solidly in the hands of the Almighty, Praise Jesus!"

"Amen!" went a chorus of more seasoned shouts from members of the guest choir for that evening, the Faith Center Gospel Tabernacle Choir from Fort Myers, an African-American gospel group that raised the flaps on J.W.'s revival tent right before the Reverend Dean got up to speak.

When J.W. Dean appeared on the stage, he prefaced his talk with a plug for the final meeting on Saturday night when he would be handling deadly coral snakes. "The ultimate sacrament" he called it, "so alive it can kill you." He went on to confess, in tears, how important this sacrament was to him, even though it had taken the life of his beloved Bonnie. In spite of how much he missed her, it had been her time to go. How her face had glowed when she realized that she was getting sick! He had offered to take her to a doctor, but she had refused, wanting only for God to do what He wanted with her. "Just like the blessed Virgin Mary," J.W. said, and then he quoted the mother of Jesus in her words to the visiting angel, " 'Be it unto me according to thy word.' These were the final words of my dear Bonnie. Whatever you do," he concluded with a final appeal, "don't miss Saturday night! It will be a life and death matter!

"As much as I miss Bonnie," he went on, a statement Sam thought was slightly dubious from the way he was eying a number of nodding beehive hairdos in the first few rows, "I know where she is. I cain't go to her, but she's safe, and she's happy. No, I cain't go to her now, but I will go to her someday. Hallelujah! Now, I know many of you think I'm talkin' 'bout heaven, but I ain't. I ain't just talkin' 'bout heaven, I'm talkin' 'bout a MANSION!"

Yes, Lord. (Pastor Filmore's loosening of the crowd had them ready for that one.)

"I'm talkin' 'bout rooms and rooms and rooms till you cain't come to the end of the hallway!"

Glory!

"I'm talkin' 'bout leavin' this place for a F-I-N-E-R place with streets of gold and diamond-studded doors and big fat rubies for doorknobs!"

Amen!

He was playing off their energy now, jumping up and down and shaking his shoulders. Then he walked down off the stage onto the sawdust floor and right up to a nodding hairdo and said, "I'm talkin' UPTOWN, honey!" and everyone squealed and clapped with delight. That's all it took. The congregation was enthralled with him.

"The Bible says, 'I go to prepare a place for you.' Now, what kind of place is that? Jesus said: In my Father's house are many . . . condominiums?"

No. And they all laughed.

". . . mobile homes?"

No! And they laughed even more at that one. Sam surmised that most of these people probably lived in mobile homes.

"In my Father's house are many . . . cottages?"

No!

". . . bungalows?"

No!

". . . shacks?"

No!

"How about: In my Father's house are many dwellings? Is that good enough? Certainly any kind of dwelling would be okay as long as it was in heaven, right?"

No!

"What's it say?"

Mansions.

"What was that?"

Mansions!

"I didn't hear you."

MANSIONS!

"Oh! That's what I thought you said." J.W. took out a handkerchief and dabbed his forehead with it while the audience applauded itself with glee, and then he walked back up to the platform. Now he could lean into the microphone and say, "And Bonnie's in her mansion right now. Hallelujah." His voice was soft and deep like velvet. "And I know how she's got it decorated too. It's simply done because she was a simple woman. A good woman."

Here Sam thought he might have detected a degree of sincerity.

"You know, we're all lookin' for a place to call home, but I gotta tell you somethin': We're not gonna find it here. No, sir. No, ma'am. No home here. This here's temporary. Just like this tent."

Preach it!

That one came from the choir. J.W. turned around and smiled. "That's right, honey. This here tent ain't permanent."

Yes, sir.

"This was nothin' but an empty field a few days ago."

Yes, sir.

"And a few days from now, it will go back to being nothin' but an empty field again."

Right.

"Except for a TH-O-U-SAND holy feet stompin' on it all week!"

That sent the choir into ecstasy, jumping and stomping and whooping and hollering. Sam, along with many in the largely white crowd, looked a bit uncomfortable. J.W. waited for the choir to quiet down and the dust to settle before going on. He took a sip from a glass of water on the podium and dabbed his mouth with a hanky. Then he picked up a large blue leather Bible and started reading.

" 'In my Father's house are many mansions,' said Jesus, 'if it were not so, I would have told you.' You can trust Jesus, my friend. He wouldn't tell us somethin' that weren't true. 'I go to prepare a place for you. And if I go and prepare a place for you, I will come again, and receive you unto myself.' And here comes the good part: 'That where I am, there ye may be also.' " And then he repeated it. " 'That . . . where . . . I . . . am . . . there . . . ye . . . may . . . be . . . also. . . .' " He paused to let the impact of each word settle in.

The tent was quiet now except for a few coughs and the rustle of makeshift fans in the choir, where the lights were bright and hot. "Think about that for a minute. Where do you suppose He is? Heaven? Here on earth? How about a new heaven and a new earth? Or how about this: How about the fact that it don't matter where He is? That's right, you heard me right. It don't matter where He is. . . ." Here he paused a long time for the drama.

"Because wherever He is, you and I will be WITH HIM."

Glory!

"We're gonna be wherever HE is, precious friends. We're gonna be *with Him*. Never gonna be alone. Gonna be *with some-body*."

Hallelujah!

"Gonna be *with somebody!*"

The tent resounded, everyone voicing their praise. J.W.'s crescendo had swept them up into a frenzy.

"Carlotta," he said, turning to the pretty gray-haired, olive-skinned woman who was still at the organ, "play me the intro to 'Mansion Over the Hilltop,' " and J.W. launched into a verse and refrain from the well-known gospel song in a voice that reminded Sam of buzzing June bugs on a hot summer night. Then J.W. motioned to the gospel choir, and they mercifully drowned him out.

J.W. then went from talking about mansions to talking about how to get one. "You've got to believe. 'Believe in God, believe also in me,' Jesus said, and that's all it takes." And for all his emphasis on snakes and healing and emotional hype, J.W. delivered a gospel message plainly and simply that night. J.W. had the largest crowd of his life in that tent, and the importance of the moment pulled out of him all that was good and right and sincere about his calling. J.W. gave them the gospel, and when he asked them forward, it wasn't just for healing or for gettin' the Spirit; it was for getting right with God—to admit your sin and receive Jesus Christ as your savior.

"Right now, tonight, I can reserve you a mansion in heaven," he said as Carlotta continued playing on the organ. "Come down here right now and meet Jesus. We're takin' mansion reservations . . . tonight . . . right here . . . right now. . . . Glory!"

So strong was the call that it made Sam hesitate in going forward. Something about these people was a little too sincere for him. This was not what he was expecting. He had counted on J.W. being a phony, and for the most part, J.W. had delivered on that expectation. But the people threw him. He hadn't figured on their faith being so real. Whatever it was that made so many go forward that night was mighty strong stuff, and Sam was surprised at how hard he had to work to convince himself that it was not working on him—that if he went forward, it was not for this.

Due to his delay, he was one of the last people in line, and by that time, the nature of the meeting had altered somewhat. Many of the early arrivals at the altar were converts who were prayed over and sent off with counselors. That part of the service had a more solemn tone. Toward the end of the invitation time, however, the emotion seemed to pick up, along with the music, and people got caught up in the intensity. By the time Sam finally got his moment with J.W., the platform was strewn with bodies. Some were out cold; others were shaking on the ground as if they were lying on a slab of ice. The two ushers who had spotted him earlier caught each other's eye and praised the Lord.

There were two women in front of Sam. The way J.W. Dean grabbed the head of the first one made him think of her as a busted fire hydrant that J.W. was trying to turn off. She could barely stand under the pressure of his grip.

"You've got a mansion," he shouted, "and some doctors are telling you it's time to go see it, but God's tellin' me different. Can I get a witness?"

Amen!

"God's tellin' me it ain't *time* for you to go see your mansion yet!"

Yes, Lord!

Meanwhile, the woman under J.W.'s control could only shake and sob. She was severely overweight, and J.W. was having trouble keeping her steady. He motioned to a couple of attendants who came over and each took an arm. Then he exchanged a few words quietly with her.

"Hallelujah! Do you believe?" J.W.'s head snapped back with a twist.

"I believe!" shouted the woman.

Raising his voice and addressing the congregation, J.W. cried again, "Do you believe-ah!"

We believe!

J.W. then pressed harder on the woman's head until her face turned red, and he cried, "Demon of heaviness, come out!" And as he threw his arms away from her like a swimmer doing a backstroke, the woman's legs went limp, and she crumbled to the floor like a sack of potatoes. It took three men to drag her away.

Sam's forehead started to perspire. He wasn't sure what it was that went out of the woman, but he was convinced he was not going to let anything get away from him.

The next woman was handled differently. She whispered something to J.W., and he prayed quietly with her. The country music group started playing a hymn. When he was through praying, J.W. held up both hands in front of her and the woman's hands mirrored his, though not touching. For a brief moment, they were caught in a poetry—a symmetry of mime. And then without even touching her, she fell back softly into the waiting arms of the two assistants, lost in a dream state. On her face was a look of sheer bliss.

Sam had to step over her to get to J.W. The music was getting louder. J.W. took one look at Sam and immediately put his hands on Sam's head, feeling for the dent and praying fervently, his lips moving rapidly to no intelligible language. Sam seethed inside. He could not stand being touched. His reaction was quick and, without thinking, he locked his arms in front of him and raised them swiftly up and out, knocking J.W.'s arms away from his face and startling him out of his prayer trance. Sam's face was red with anger.

J.W. was relentless. "God sees a stubborn will before me!" he said, his voice trembling over the music. "Pray, my people. Pray for the wayward soul!"

Sam could hear a loud, murmuring babble come up from the crowd. J.W. was rocking back and forth, praying even more fervently with his eyes closed.

"You have my wife's ashes and her jewelry by mistake," Sam announced outright. "I would like them back."

J.W. kept on praying without any acknowledgment. Sam wasn't

sure he had heard him, so he leaned in closer and repeated the same thing.

Suddenly J.W.'s eyes opened and a look of horror came over his face as he stared into Sam's eyes. He raised both hands in front of Sam as he had done to the woman, and Sam stood there rigid. Then he cried, "In the name of Ja-HEE-zus, come out!" and he struck Sam so hard on the forehead with the palms of both hands that his head snapped back with the blow, but Sam stood firm.

"How about a trade?" he said, undaunted, and J.W. whacked him in the head again, but Sam stood like a boxer in a ring, absorbing blows without going down.

For the first time, J.W. Dean began to look worried. His eyes darted to and fro uncontrollably and suddenly alighted on something that filled them with more fear than a hundred Sams put together. Sam didn't see that look, however, because he was reaching into the pocket of his coat right then and pulling out an envelope and handing it to J.W. J.W. took the envelope—but in a daze, because what he had seen was two uniformed police officers forcing their way through the crowd and coming straight for him. The music played even louder, threatening to drown out the words that followed, and for those who didn't hear, it was a good thing.

"J.W. Dean?" said one of the officers, approaching.

J.W. made no reply. His head turned toward heaven and he closed his eyes.

"J.W. Dean, you are under arrest for the murder of your wife, Bonnie Dean." The other officer walked around J.W., drew his hands behind his back, and handcuffed them while the preacher kept his head toward heaven. Then J.W. opened his eyes and a change came over his face. It was as if he saw something or someone that no one else could see—something that gave him comfort and relaxed the anxiety on his face. Some would later say he saw an angel. Maynard would say that it reminded him of what Stephen must have looked like when he was being stoned. Sam was nonplused by the whole experience and primarily glad to be relieved from the assaults against his head that had already given him a migrain.

"You have the right to remain silent," the officer began methodically while the music played on. "You have the right to an
attorney."

I need no other argument, I need no other plea . . . went the
hymn lyrics sung by the choir.

"Keep in mind that anything you say can and will be used
against you in a court of law."

It is enough that Jesus died and that He died for me.

EIGHT

Murder by Rattlesnake

In 1991, Glenn Summerford was sentenced to ninety-nine years in prison on a manslaughter charge for attempting to murder his wife, Darlene, with a rattlesnake. Summerford, a serpent-handling preacher, had thrust Darlene's hand into a box of rattlers because of his own conviction that she had been unfaithful to him. The trial took place in the Sand Mountain region of northern Alabama.

Sheriff Buford had this story firmly implanted in his mind when he came upon the news of the death by snakebite and the hasty cremation of Bonnie Dean. Buck Buford was himself the son of an itinerant preacher who had left his wife, children, and ministry when Buck was six years old to run off with a choir member of a host church. He grew to hate traveling preachers and distrust religion in general, so when the J.W. Dean case fell in his lap, he had a vested interest in bringing the scoundrel to justice.

J.W.'s case was especially loaded because it had all the marks of an apparent homicide, similar to the Summerford case. Sheriff Buford's interest in it had grown as he found more pieces of the puzzle. The early cremation, the total secrecy of the funeral, the bogus addresses on the death certificate, all added up to something very suspicious. A thorough questioning of certain members of the Rockledge congregation for possible motives had turned up some questionable female liaisons on J.W.'s part, with far more attractive women than the homely Bonnie. And then the *National Enquirer* article about Mallory Blaine hit the newsstands, and Buford felt he almost had him. Enough, at least, to follow J.W. to East Naples so he wouldn't lose him, but not enough to bring him in. Buford was hoping that his mere presence would ruffle J.W. enough to reveal another clue about the strange passing of his wife.

He still needed hard evidence, and Sheriff Buford couldn't believe his luck when that very evidence arrived on the fax machine set up in his hotel room in Naples. It supplied all he needed to arrest J.W. Apparently, someone had come forward from the Rockledge congregation who was knowledgeable about snakes. He had observed that the snake attached to Bonnie's wrist on the night in which she died was indeed a poisonous coral snake. But what made him come forward was the fact that he had also observed J.W. and Bonnie both handling nonpoisonous scarlet king snakes on all the other nights. The two snakes are so similar in size, color, and behavior that, from a distance, and caught up in a religious frenzy, most people would not notice the difference. But Nathan Samuelson, a university professor writing a thesis on snake handlers for the University of Florida, had noticed. He also observed another piece of damaging evidence: On the night Bonnie died, J.W. himself did not handle any snakes.

Sheriff Buford now had a case, and it was even better than he had hoped for. Not only did he have motive for murder and a witness to the murder "weapon," he had proof of a hoax—one more way to reveal to the world the great religious lie that he spent so much of his life hating. These were not poisonous snakes J.W. was handling after all. They were harmless king snakes. This was not about miracles; it was about the manipulation of people and the murder of a wife. And if they put Summerford away for ninety-nine years for attempted manslaughter—and his wife hadn't even died— then J.W. could get the chair. Not to mention the attention the sheriff was already getting now that this whole story had been bumped up to a national level. He would be on the evening news. He could inform the world of crooks like J.W. Dean that prey on the sensibilities of weak-willed emotional cripples. This was justice. This was definitely Sheriff Buford's big day.

Sam woke up the next morning impressed by the fact that it surely wasn't his day. His head still ached from the pounding he took from J.W. Dean the night before. His head always ached, but this was worse than usual. He thought of the people who claimed to have been healed by J.W.'s touch. He could have used a little healing instead of the beating he got.

Sam rubbed his eyes, then checked his watch. Six A.M. He glanced around, realizing the light coming through the crack in the curtains was not the sun but the fluorescent tube outside his room, flickering for want of mercury vapor. The room smelled like the bottom of an ashtray, which was always a good rationale, he thought, for lighting up a new cigarette. Create some fresh smoke to get rid of the old.

He got up, took a couple aspirin, and recalled the arrest. He wasn't sure what to think about the event. It certainly meant he knew where J.W. Dean would be now, but it would definitely complicate getting Bonnie's ashes back. His mind had gone through all the possibilities many times. J.W. could have left them someplace where he stores things. He could have dumped them or buried them anywhere. But for some reason, Sam had a feeling that J.W. had the ashes with him.

Sam got back into bed and stacked the pillows so he could sit up. One smoke and then he'd get ready and go to breakfast. Room 127 of the Vagabond Inn was a typical motel room with everything bolted down—the pictures to the wall across from him, the lamp and TV to the end table and dresser, and the bedstead to the wall behind his back. The air conditioner had been on and off all night, waking him a number of times with its dramatic entry. The room was done in 1962 decor and it hadn't been redecorated since. Everything was one shade or another of orange.

Sam checked the Gideon Bible next to him on the end table to see if it was bolted down. It was not. He opened the front flap and immediately saw *Help in Time of NEED* on the facing page. Scanning the titles he saw *Comfort in Time of SORROW, Guidance in Time of DECISION,* and *Peace in Time of TURMOIL,* but the one that caught his eye was *Protection in Time of DANGER.* To the right of that heading there was a name, a number, and then another number. Assuming the last number was the page number, he looked up page 655 and found Psalm 91. Sam had just had his first course in Bible interpretation: how to follow the cover page in a Gideon Bible.

Sam started reading. *He that dwelleth in the secret place of the most High shall abide under the shadow of the Almighty.* No wonder he didn't believe in God, he thought. Who could understand this? Out of curiosity he finished everything that was in the 91 section. He especially noticed number 13, *Thou shalt tread upon the lion and adder* . . . Sam knew what an adder was. It was a poisonous snake. He wondered if this snake stuff was everywhere in the Bible.

Sam replaced the Bible on the table and as soon as it got there, it had that glued-down look. There was one other thing that intrigued him about his first encounter with Scripture. Number 15 of 91 had said, "He shall call upon me, and I will deliver him: I will be with him in trouble; I will deliver him, and honour him." This made Sam even more convinced that God didn't make any sense. How could God honor someone dumb enough to get himself into so much trouble? That had always bothered him about Christians; they seemed to be whining all the time. And they used God for getting out of jams that they were responsible for getting themselves into. Sam always thought that if you got yourself into a mess, it was your responsibility to get yourself out.

Sam showered and dressed and walked outside his door. The

air conditioner was louder outside than it was inside. Something was loose and rattling on the cover, and it reminded him of a '35 Buick he used to drive when he was a kid. It had a fender that rattled just like it.

The sun was not up yet, but a red glow was visible just behind the blinking neon "Vagabond Inn." Sam walked across the parking lot and found a table by the window in the coffee shop. The only other people there, besides a transient, were two police officers. Sam had noticed the police cars in the parking lot when he walked over. He also noticed the lack of business in the place. It was early, but not that early. Maybe the "snowbirds" were already heading north, back to their permanent homes. It was a welcomed departure for locals like Sam who deplored the constant flow of tourists during the winter months.

Sam ordered, got up and bought a *USA Today* out of a machine by the front door, and returned to his seat. He scanned the first three pages for something about J.W. He wasn't expecting it to appear that soon, but you never knew with satellite news—ball scores from the night before made it. There was nothing, but Sam knew it wouldn't be long. If they covered Bonnie's death, they would surely pick up on J.W.'s arrest.

No sooner had his pancakes arrived than a police car drove up alongside the coffee shop and the two officers inside settled quickly with the waitress and went out to meet it. Sam watched with interest as they conversed with the driver. There were two officers in the car, as well, and a passenger in the backseat. The car then followed one of the officers on foot to a sedan, where he opened the trunk, took out a small bag, inspected its contents, and handed it to the driver. The police car then backed up and pulled away as the officer who had taken the bag out of the trunk got into his own squad car and followed. The other policeman went inside one of the motel rooms.

Sam had been watching all of this with mild curiosity until the first squad car pulled away and he got a good look at the sedan from which the officer had removed the bag. He burned his tongue with coffee as he pulled it away from his lips. It was a lime green Ford

Torino! Sam couldn't believe his eyes. He could even see pieces of the weather-beaten vinyl roof sticking up, silhouetted against the pink wall of the motel that looked ruby red in the light of dawn. J.W. Dean must have been staying right there in the Vagabond Inn! By the time the second squad car pulled by, Sam had become more observant, and he caught the familiar Cocoa Beach Police emblem on the side. Sam quickly searched the fresh images in his mind for the officers and the passenger in the first car and was convinced that the passenger had to be none other than J.W. Dean himself. It all made perfect sense. J.W. had probably spent the night in a Naples jail and they were now taking him to Cocoa Beach. This stop at the motel was to pick up the bag from the trunk of his car. Probably some personal items.

Sam got up from his table and left three-quarters of a pancake stack and enough money to cover the bill. He started across the parking lot, remembering the other policeman who had gone into one of the motel rooms. He wasn't sure exactly which one, but he knew it was close enough to probably see the car through the window. He would have to be careful and casual. Walking toward the Torino, he noticed something dangling off the door handles, and as he got closer, he recognized it as the yellow tape that police use to seal off areas they don't want people to cross. It was wrapped around the handles of all four doors. He figured that gave him reason enough to be a curious bystander, so he took a few moments to scan the inside of the car. One glance in the backseat made his heart jump in his throat. There, sitting on the seat right next to the door, was a small square box, exactly like the box that the ashes of J.W.'s wife had been in!

Shaken, Sam walked to his room and sat on the bed. He tried to collect his thoughts, but he couldn't think sitting down, so he got up, lit a cigarette, and started to pace. The bed took up most of the room, so he walked back and forth around it, stopping each time by the window to look out at J.W.'s car and the police car that was only three stalls down.

What ironic luck that he was this close to Betty's ashes . . . and yet what obstacles to surmount in order to get them! It would be such a quick, easy take. Open the door and remove the box. That simple. Then he thought of his phony ashes. He could switch the contents and put the box back, and no one would ever know. But with every easy plan came the harder questions: Was the door locked? Was the tape hindering its opening in any way? Was the policeman looking?

Sam decided to wait for a while and hope that the officer might leave. But would the police leave the car unattended? What do they do with a car that might contain evidence in a homicide case? Tow it to the police station, probably. Impound it, most likely. Maybe that was why one officer stayed there. His sole job might be to protect the integrity of the car as evidence.

It was this line of thinking that made Sam's mouth go dry. Any attempt at entering this car put him squarely in the middle of a murder investigation.

But then he would think of how close he was to the ashes and how simple it would be to have this whole ordeal over with. He wondered about going to the police and explaining the whole mess. The mortuary had already admitted their mistake. There shouldn't be any problem with the police confirming the mistake and turning over the ashes to Sam, but a murder investigation complicated everything. They would need to pore over all the evidence. They would do tests. It could take months, years . . . and he might never get Betty back. This was the one thing that would make him take a risk. He wanted those ashes and he wanted to dispose of them where there would no longer be any chance of disturbing them.

Sam decided he would take a little trip to the ice and vending machines and stroll casually by the car. Check out the tape on the doors. See if he could tell whether the car was locked. As he shut the door to his room, he noticed the quiet. The air conditioner was off but still gasping. No one was stirring. He glanced at the windows of the rooms close to the car, one of which housed the policeman, and all the curtains were closed. Approaching the car slowly, he noticed that the yellow tape was not hindering the opening of the door in any way. It hung loosely on the handles only as a deterrent. He walked up to the side of the car and his heart started pounding. He looked through the window and saw the box. Betty! Sam's eye darted nervously, and he noticed a huge hole in the door panel where the lock should be, realizing then they couldn't lock the car if they wanted to.

Suddenly Sam knew the time was right. Walking around any more would only draw attention. He would never again have a chance like this. He would take the box to his room and then decide the next step. Who cared anyway? Just a bunch of ashes, important to no one as much as they were to him.

He tried the door and it opened easily. He lifted out the box, closed the door, and started back to his room, forcing his legs to walk when they wanted to run . . . wanted to fly. "It's okay," he said, giving the box a little squeeze. "I've got you now."

"Hold it right there, old buddy!" said a voice from behind him, and Sam turned around to face a police officer with a drawn gun. "Put the box down and your hands up!"

NINE

Hurricane Bobbi

Around noon the same day, Jack Acres drove up the gravel drive of his home in Ipswich after a morning conducting interviews at his newspaper office in Salem. Bobbi's car in the garage immediately surprised him, since she was supposed to be in Boston. He also noticed something else about the garage at the same time he saw the car. He could see it from the street: the familiar face of a female naval officer leaning against the wall next to the car. It was the World War II poster he had framed and given to Bobbi for Christmas, the one that should be on the wall opposite his desk, only it had been removed from its frame and was staring helplessly out at the world, naked and in exile, on top of a stack of boxes. Jack blinked and got out of the car. Closer inspection revealed a dog-eared corner and two bad scratches around the nose area.

"Hi, Jack, I'm up here," Bobbi called cheerily from the family room as the kitchen door slammed behind him. Jack immediately went up and found his wife pacing the room holding a framed picture while her eyes darted from object to object, wall to wall. She was wearing black leotards and a black high-necked turtleneck under one of his blue denim work shirts that scalloped at her knees. Her red hair was scrambled and she wore no makeup. Jack usually loved to see her like this, in contrast to the highly refined look she maintained for her business, but it was not for him that she was dressed this way.

"How nice to find you home," he said unconvincingly as he tried to kiss a moving target and almost tripped over the ottoman that wasn't where it was supposed to be. Then he noticed that a number of items in the room were not where they were supposed to be.

"Oh no," he said as he watched her eyes scanning, never once looking at him. If she looked in his direction, it was not at him that she was looking, but at the wall behind him or at the half of the room in which he was standing. He felt like an object somewhere in her depth of field. "You've got that I-don't-like-the-way-this-room-looks-anymore look in your eyes. Please . . . say it isn't so." But he knew it was too late. Bobbi was, by all indications, deeply enmeshed in the one thing about her he had come to dread the most in nineteen years of marriage: a bona fide Barbara Ann Brewster Acres rearranging mood.

"They canceled my meeting in Boston this morning, so I decided to stay home today," she said, holding up the picture at arm's length in front of her. "What would you think about this picture over the fireplace?"

Jack flopped down into the ill-placed armchair in the center of the room and assessed the damage. He knew Bobbi well enough to know that she wasn't telling him the whole story. It wasn't just because the meeting was canceled that she was doing this; it was also her frustration over knowing she could have stayed in Florida if she had known. She was probably worried about Sam and about the real whereabouts of her mother's remains. These moods were usually driven by some great sense of impatience over something she could do nothing about. The end result was meted out on what she could actually *do* something about. In this case it was the nature and shape of the house.

While he understood, at least in part, where she was coming from, Jack also resented her ability to take on a project of this magnitude with no apparent regard for his plans for the afternoon. He knew where this was going. She would tell him that she didn't need his help, while at the same time she would engage in an activity that dominated his work space. There would be no escaping this, apart from turning around and going back out the door. It made him wonder what would happen if, some morning when she was all set up for a few hours of business calls, he sauntered in with a bunch of power tools and casually announced he would be drilling and hammering and would she like to join him.

"Don't sit down; we have work to do," Bobbi said, still pacing.

"*You* have work to do," said Jack. "I have work to do at my desk."

"Fine," she said matter-of-factly. "Just help me find a place for this one picture."

Right, thought Jack. *This one picture.* He knew from experience that this rearranging cyclone—"Hurricane Bobbi," as he liked to call it—could strike anywhere, anytime, with merely a picture or a vase in question, and suddenly the end table had to be moved to accommodate the picture, then the couch to the end table, then the piano to the couch, and then the validity of the room itself was questioned when it didn't fit the piano, as if Jack could remodel the shape of the whole room in a couple hours, or better yet, buy them a new house that suited the piano. It had happened on occasions that the entire contents of a room had been shifted two or three ways until all the pieces finally came to rest in their original locations, with only a picture residing in a new spot on the wall, three hours and many sore muscles later.

By now Bobbi was growing more and more impatient with Jack, who in her mind was sitting there enjoying his peaceful reverie when she was obviously busy and needed some help. "Could you come over here and hold this for me, please?" She was trying to be polite.

Jack gave out an exaggerated sigh as he got out of the chair and held the picture up while Bobbi stepped back.

"I kind of like that. Here, let me hold it and see what you think."

Jack let out another sigh as he handed her the picture and they changed places.

"Jack, be careful. You might hyperventilate with all that sighing. It's perfectly fine if you don't want to join me in this project; it just would be more fun if you did. Now, tell me what you think of the picture. Hurry up, it's getting hard to hold."

"I like it," he said reluctantly, and then he couldn't believe what he said next, except that it was true. "But it would look better if the couch was over there too."

"Exactly what I was thinking!" said Bobbi, looking directly at him for the first time and smiling hopefully. "Let's try it!"

"You know, when we get to heaven, I bet you're going to want to rearrange the galaxies," Jack said as they struggled with the couch. "God must be preparing you for something big. I just hope He doesn't ask me to do the heavy lifting."

"I hate to tell you, Jack, but by that time, I won't need your help. Right now, though, you're pretty good slave labor."

Sometimes Bobbi needed more than Jack's help. Alex and Brook were occasionally swept into Hurricane Bobbi too. Once, they all four moved the piano twice in one afternoon, which may not seem like much except that the piano was a nine-foot grand that had to be put on its side and strapped to a special set of moving rails and relieved of its legs—an hour-long process—just to get it ready to slide to a new location and another hour to set it up. The children were known to vanish in an instant at the slightest indication that their mother might want to consider making even a minor adjustment in a room. They, like Jack, could spot that look in her eye in a second.

"There," Bobbi said, "now that side of the room looks great. What are we going to do over here?"

Jack still hadn't made up his mind whether or not he was in on this project. He surmised Bobbi was about two hours into her Barbara Ann Brewster Acres rearranging mood and about that far away from being out of it.

"Bobbi, aside from the fact that you always look dynamite in my shirts, I'm not sure I can do this. I had other plans for my afternoon. You weren't supposed to be here, you know."

"I told you that's no problem. I can do this myself."

Fine, he thought, *and how am I supposed to get work done at my desk with you over here going for a centerfold in* Architectural Digest *and asking my opinion every three minutes?* But Jack said nothing. Instead, he looked over at his desk and saw the empty wall opposite it and remembered the picture in the garage.

"You took the picture down. What happened to it anyway? It's all ruined now."

Bobbi looked at Jack and now *she* sighed. "Jack, it was ruined when you framed it. We've been through this before."

"I guess I thought that since you left it up for so long, you were starting to like it."

"I told you, I love the picture. It just lost its value when you glued it down," she said, her impatience causing her to focus more intently on her work. "You know, with that couch over there now, we don't need this lamp anymore. Here, could you take it out to the garage?"

Jack, in reflection, realized he should have been tipped off about Bobbi's rearranging mood the minute he drove up the driveway and saw the picture. These moods always came complete with a swift ax to any undesirable object, such as a plant or a picture or a vase that Bobbi hadn't picked out herself but had tolerated for a suitable amount of time. Anything marginal was history. The only exceptions to the rule were paintings or art projects created by the children. Little molded clay hand prints from kindergarten, construction-paper pictures taped to the refrigerator, and primitive third-grade pottery were treasured like gold. This same rule did not apply to Jack's efforts, however. The fact that he had personally framed the U.S. Navy World War II poster was not sufficient reason to qualify it for a similar enshrinement—a little piece of inequity that Jack chose to take personally and hold inside. It came out in the pathetic look that Bobbi saw and chose to ignore.

The conflict over the picture was, at its root, a conflict of values. Jack had never considered the value of the poster itself. He only saw its meaning as it related to Bobbi's character. That's why he chose to frame it as he did; he valued the overall appearance. He had tried setting the poster loosely in the frame, but the glass pressed down on it, accentuating the ripples in the paper and the creases from being folded for so many years. When the man in the frame shop suggested that gluing it to a stiff Styrofoam backing would completely smooth it out and make it look like new, Jack had immediately liked the idea. The man had warned him that it would ruin the value of the piece as a collector's item, but it would display itself better. "*It just depends on what's important to you,*" he had said, and in that statement was foreshadowed the essence of the conflict that began on Christmas morning.

The value of the poster itself was what was important to Bobbi. To her, the poster was a fifty-year-old treasure from World War II. It was tangible evidence of the importance of the female contribution in a time of world conflict and national pride. There might only be a handful of these actual posters still in existence. This was a museum piece, a relic of history that carried with it a mind-set of a bygone era worth remembering. To display it with all its creases and ripples was to attest to its authenticity. She wanted it in a frame more to protect it than to show it off. In her mind, Jack might as well have taken an original Van Gogh and stuck it to their bathroom wall with wallpaper paste.

In Jack's mind, the picture was a symbol of Bobbi's character. It did not carry any value in and of itself, but only in what it represented. He had chosen to glue it because it would best portray that significance. It made perfect sense to him to display this poster in its frame as proudly as he would want to display his wife. Bobbi's character was where the worth lay for him. He saw no value in the poster itself. That is also why it was so hard for him to understand her rejection of it, since in his mind, it gave glory to her.

"This is a good example of how little you know me," Bobbi had said, and it wasn't the first time Jack had heard that comment.

It could have been made anywhere, anytime, during their nineteen years of marriage. "You think I'm only interested in the appearance of things. It's the value of things that is important to me."

Jack carried the lamp out to the garage for storage and noticed the picture again, standing crooked against the wall, a monument to his misjudgment of his wife. Substance, not perfection—that's what she wanted. Value, not appearance. She was right; he had her figured wrong. He thought she would choose how things looked over what they were really worth. When she suggested, in an earlier discussion, that he was the one who was more concerned with appearances, that had troubled him. He had always seen the two of them the other way around. Perhaps he didn't understand his wife very well after all.

In the garage, he had to climb on top of the washing machine in order to find a place to put the lamp. He marveled at how it was possible to acquire so much stuff in seven years—the length of time that the Acres family had occupied this house. *Probably time for a garage sale*, he thought. On the shelf where he set the lamp, he found a cheap pair of earrings that he surmised were costume pieces Bobbi had bequeathed to Brook for dress-up play when she was younger. How they had gotten on a top shelf in the garage he didn't know, but he decided to put them in his pocket and check with Bobbi before he did anything with them. In his present frame of mind, he was not going to take any chances on the significance of objects. The earrings made him think of the ring that Bobbi was so eager to reclaim along with her mother's ashes, and a discrepancy came to his mind. With the picture, it was the value of the poster that had won out over what it represented. But with something like her mother's ring, probably worth little more than the forgotten earrings he'd just put in his pocket, it was what the ring represented that made it so priceless to her. That seemed inconsistent to him, and he determined to ask Bobbi about it at his next opportunity.

Returning to the family room, he noticed a good feeling about the room as he walked into it.

"You know, I like the couch over there," he said.

"I do too," said Bobbi. "So you'll help me finish?"

Jack answered that question by rolling up his sleeves and smiling.

Jack could accept the fact that Bobbi was tied to this earth in ways in which he was not, or at least in ways he would never understand. And that is why he would end up rearranging his day as he and Bobbi rearranged the furniture; and once over his resistance, he would actually enjoy this little episode. They'd laugh, bang heads a couple times; he'd watch Bobbi rave about not having enough space for things or not enough things for space, and she'd watch him move one thing over and another thing back, and another thing where the first thing was—both of their minds running like a sped-up silent movie.

And Jack would finally admit, though it might have taken some coercing, that he did enjoy living in the environment Bobbi created. After all, when he married this person, there was something he had liked, though so different from him. In his best moments, he admired and even cherished that difference; in his worst, he sought to destroy it.

"Brook's home," Bobbi said even before she heard the door slam.

"Hi! I'm home!" Brook's voice echoed, and she quickly bounded up the stairs, then froze in the hallway in front of her father's desk when she saw the state of the room. Quick on her feet, she announced, "You wouldn't believe how much homework I have today! I'm so dead!" and turned back toward the stairs.

"Not so fast, young lady," said Bobbi. "Where's my kiss?"

Brook turned around cautiously, ran up and gave each of her parents a quick peck on the cheek, and started for the stairs a second time.

"Don't worry," said Bobbi, "we're not moving the piano."

Five minutes later Brook called to them from the other end of the house, "Get on the phone, you guys. It's Grandpa!"

"Sam?" said Bobbi. "I never heard it ring."

Jack headed toward the stairs. "She probably picked it up on call waiting. I'll get to the other phone."

Bobbi went to the phone at Jack's desk and Jack picked up downstairs just in time to hear, "Pop! Is that you?"

"Well, last time I checked . . ." came the familiar gruff voice.

"You rascal! Where are you? We've been worried sick about you."

"Why?"

"Sam! You left home and didn't tell us where you were going! We *do* love you, you know. Where are you, anyway?"

"I'm in a very nice hotel in Naples."

"I *knew* you'd end up in Naples. You're there to find J.W. Dean, I bet."

"Well, I won't be seeing him tonight."

"Why? Is something wrong?"

"That's what I wanted to ask you."

"Ask *me*?" said Bobbi. "I'm fine. It's *you* I'm worried about."

"The last time I saw you, you were falling over backwards."

This was followed by a long pause in which Jack could hear a crowd of loud voices. "You were there?" Bobbi asked. "At J.W.'s crusade? You saw me?"

"You went down like a rock. I tried to get to you, but they ran me out of the place."

"Who ran you out? Would you please tell me what's going on?"

"Uh-oh, gotta run. Someone else needs the phone. By the way, I have your mother. She's doing just fine. Talk to you later."

"Pop. . . !" Bobbi cried, but there was only a click followed by a dial tone.

"Well, what do you make of that?" asked Jack, returning upstairs. Bobbi was leaning on his desk, staring into his dark, silent computer screen.

"I *hate* that man sometimes," she said, pressing her fingertips into the desk top. "Most of the time, actually. Did you hear all of that?"

"Pretty much."

"He was there—in Naples! He saw me! Can you believe that? Why does he wait until now to call?"

"He's a strange bird. That's all I can say."

"I mean, given the fact that he missed me at the crusade— though that's hard to believe—why wouldn't he have called you to find out where I was staying? He knew I was going to be there on business. He could have found me if he wanted to."

Jack could only shrug his shoulders and return Bobbi's bewildered look. "It seems pretty obvious," he finally said, "that he doesn't want to be found just now."

"I can't believe I was actually that close to him," she said, easing herself down into his chair and swiveling toward the revamped family room that was nearing completion. They both stared at the results of their afternoon project as they talked, eying the new relation of things from a different perspective. "What do you suppose all that noise was in the background?"

"Sounded like a busy restaurant to me," said Jack, glancing again at the nude wall opposite his desk. "Or the lobby of a hotel maybe?"

"That was awfully loud for a lobby; people were shouting. I've had some strange conversations with that man, but that was the strangest ever. And what was that he said about Mom? Do you think he has her ashes?"

"That's what it sounded like to me," said Jack.

The phone rang. "I'll get it!" Brook's distant voice yelled.

"I bet I know what all the noise was on the phone," said Jack. "It could have been a whole bunch of people checking into a hotel at the same time, like a convention or something."

"Most likely a low-budget tour bus," said Bobbi. "I doubt Sam would stay in a hotel nice enough for a convention."

"It's for you guys again!" shouted Brook from the bottom of the stairs. "It's Uncle Will this time!"

Jack looked at Bobbi. "Boy, it's the Florida connection!" he said, then raced downstairs again.

"Hi, Will," said Bobbi. "Guess who we just talked to?"

"Surprise me."

"Pop."

"No kidding? Where is he?"

"In some hotel in Naples. He wouldn't tell us."

"Boy, this thing is getting more bizarre by the minute," said Will. "*I'm* in Naples."

"You are?" Bobbi asked. "What are *you* doing there?"

"You told me to come here, remember? I'm looking for Sam."

"Well, you should be able to find him tonight," said Jack. "He's bound to be at the J.W. Dean meeting."

"Not likely," said Will.

"What do you mean?"

"I guess you haven't heard. They arrested J.W. Dean last night for the murder of his wife."

"No!" Jack exclaimed. "Sheriff Buford finally got his man."

"On what grounds, I wonder?" asked Bobbi.

"Apparently someone in Cocoa Beach came forward with some new information that might implicate J.W. That's all they're saying in the news down here."

"How are you going to find Pop now?" Bobbi questioned.

"Beats me," answered Will. "You know how many hotels there are in Naples? And knowing Sam, he's probably in some run-down motel that isn't even listed."

"This is so frustrating! What are you going to do?" Bobbi said.

"What *can* I do? I've got some business here tomorrow—that's partially how I justified this trip. I'll just have to take care of it and head back home. Unless you can think of something."

"Are they still holding J.W. there?" said Jack. "Hey, wait a minute . . . maybe that's it!"

"What?" said Bobbi.

"Maybe Sam was calling us from the jail and that's why it was so noisy. He was keeping an eye on J.W."

"Nice try, but J.W. went back to Cocoa Beach this morning," Will commented. "He's in police custody."

"So much for that idea."

"It was noisy from where Sam called you?" asked Will, backing up again to Jack's comment.

"Yeah," said Jack, "noisier than any lobby I've ever been in."

Bobbi chimed in, "You know, he did say he was in a very nice hotel in Naples. Maybe he actually was. Jack thought the noise could have been a lot of people checking in for a convention or something like that. Could you at least call some of the larger hotels and see if any are hosting a special event today? It's a shame to have you that close and not even try."

"Sure, sis. I'll do my best."

Bobbi took down his Naples numbers and said good-bye. When Jack returned upstairs, they could only shake their heads at each other in disbelief.

"First I find out Sam and I were in the same tent and I didn't know it; now I find out Sam and Will are in the same town and Sam doesn't know it."

"If we only knew where Sam was," said Jack.

"Yeah. I thought you had something there with your jail idea. That could have easily been the inside of a noisy precinct."

"Like the background noise on *Hill Street Blues*," Jack said, referring to what used to be their favorite TV program before they had kids and there was actually time to watch TV.

"Exactly."

Jack and Bobbi were still staring out at their remodeled family room and didn't notice Alex creeping up on them from behind.

"Boo!" he screamed, and Bobbi jumped right out of Jack's chair.

"Alex, you must stop that," said Jack. "We're not going to live through you scaring us like that."

"What are you guys looking at?" said Alex, and then he saw the room. "Uh-oh, Hurricane Bobbi strikes again. Too bad I missed it."

"There's still some picking up to do," said Bobbi, "since you're so eager. . . ."

"No, thanks."

Bobbi grabbed her son's flannel shirt as he turned to walk away and pulled him down and kissed him all over his face until he squealed.

"I get to do that whenever I want because you're just so cute."

"Hey, what happened to the picture that was here?" Alex said, straightening up and trying to change the subject.

Jack and Bobbi rolled their eyes at each other. "Never mind," they said in unison.

⌒

Later that night when Jack was emptying out his pockets, he came upon the earrings he had found in the garage. Bobbi was putting Brook to bed when he walked in on them.

"Either of you seen these before?"

"Where did you find those?" Brook asked, taking the earrings out of his hand.

"On a shelf in the garage that I had to stand on the washing machine to get to."

"Alex did that. He was hiding them from me."

Bobbi watched Brook set the earrings on the table and snuggle back into bed. She pulled the covers up to her daughter's chin and stroked her hair.

"Do you think you'll ever get Grandma's ring back?" Brook asked.

"I hope so, because it's going to belong to you now."

Brook smiled, warmed by fresh stories of the farm at Parker Corners that Bobbi had been telling her. "Tell me another story about Great-Grandma Martin," she said.

So Bobbi launched into memories of her favorite grandmother—the good smells of country cooking, the hungry workers around the table, the light in Grandma Martin's eyes, and most of all, that big, soft lap that used to pillow Bobbi while she listened to her grandmother's strong, sweet voice reading from the Bible.

Meanwhile Jack went and made sure Alex was tucked in bed and nighttime prayers were prayed.

"Whatever we do, we've got to get Mom's ring back," Bobbi said to Jack later as they got ready for bed. "I've promised it to Brook, and she asks about it every night now."

Jack didn't say anything. He wanted to encourage his wife, but he doubted, knowing what they were finding out about Reverend Dean, that they would ever recover the jewelry.

"Explain something to me." Jack was sitting on the edge of the bed running his fingers between his toes. "The picture I framed that now resides in a corner of our garage no longer has meaning because it has lost its value, and yet this ring you keep talking about, which you have said is almost worthless, has great value to you. I don't get it."

"It's what it represents."

"I was hoping you'd say that, because as far as I'm concerned, that is the value of the picture, even if it is glued down. It represents you."

"Not anymore," said Bobbi from the bathroom sink as her makeup was being transferred to a washcloth. "Once it was glued down, it lost its value. It's more than just the picture that represents me. It's the poster itself. It's original and classic, and there are probably no more like it anywhere. Just like Grandma Martin's ring. It's the ring itself that has value to me. Not to anyone else. I would never shine up that ring and put a new diamond in it—even if it might look better and be worth something—because then it would cease to be what it is to me: something of value that represents a history and a tradition I can pass on. You understand that, don't you? Brook does."

"But I didn't want to frame the picture with wrinkles and creases in it."

Bobbi glared at him through the mirror over the top of her washcloth, the makeup now completely off her face. *Not a good time to bring up wrinkles and creases* was what her eyes said.

"I know what I'll do." Jack was thinking fast. "I'll reframe the picture and put it in my office. Do you mind?"

"Not at all," she said, looking at Jack as if he had just narrowly escaped a near-death experience.

TEN

Escapee

Sam woke up to a vague sensation rooted somewhere in his memory of upstate New York. He concluded a jail cell must be cold anywhere, if it was this cold even in Florida. This one was underground, which explained its dampness in April, though the weather outside was heating up. The smell in Sam's cell was that of mildew mixed with human sweat, like a high school locker room of a disintegrating old gymnasium after a game. Sam was dying for a smoke, but they had taken his cigarettes away from him.

After a tasteless breakfast and the worst coffee in memory, a guard came and escorted him to a small room where he was left alone with a table, two chairs, and four bare walls. On the way there he endured the taunts of some of the prisoners, most having to do with his age. Sam was surprised to discover himself more curious than humiliated by all of this. He was already logging it in his mind as merely one more experience in this new adventurous life that

Betty had introduced him to by getting mixed up in all of this mess after she died. *If only she could have been around for this*, he thought. *She just might have liked it.*

Sam paced the room for only a minute or two until a man came in, set a small box on the table, and introduced himself as Lieutenant Brand. He was short but stocky with a large square head and a grinding voice that did not seem to be coming out of his mouth but from somewhere in the vicinity of his left front shirt pocket after getting tangled up in five colored pens and a mechanical pencil. The man offered Sam a cigarette, which he took gladly while noticing his own fingers shake as he reached for it. Finally, something to cover up the taste of that awful coffee.

"Have a seat," the lieutenant said as he lit Sam's cigarette, then one for himself. He began pacing on the other side of the table as blue smoke curled around the green shade covering an otherwise naked light bulb that hung by a bare wire from the middle of the ceiling. Sam noticed his hand steady almost immediately as the nicotine took effect, and the visibility in the room rapidly diminished. The box on the table looked like the one he had tried to take from J.W.'s car.

"Mr. Dunn, I'll tell you right up front, we're not sure you belong here, but we're holdin' you due to a number of unanswered questions. You may or may not know it, but you walked right into the middle of a serious homicide investigation, so I must ask for your cooperation. Sir, do you recognize this here box?"

Sam didn't speak.

"You've seen this box before, haven't you, Mr. Dunn?"

Sam let a few more seconds go by, flicked his ashes, then spoke. "Aren't I entitled to a lawyer?"

"I beg your pardon; I thought you knew. We aren't pressing any charges as long as you can help us with a few simple questions."

"And if I don't answer your questions?"

"Well, let's see. . . . We could book you on burglary, breaking and entering, and unauthorized crossin' of a police line, for starters. It just seems hardly worth it for two jelly donuts and half a cheese croissant now, don't it?" The detective leaned in so close with that last statement that the lampshade swayed slightly with the pulse of his breathing.

Sam blinked and tried to figure out the part about the donuts. His characteristic blank stare conveniently masked an inner confusion and surprise. Glancing at the box a second time, he noticed a small grease stain on the side of it. A donut box? Slowly he reached out and opened the box. He had not had a chance to look in it before; the officer had taken it from him immediately upon arresting him. There it was, just as the detective had said. Sam was in jail for stealing a box of leftover donuts.

"I still have a right to a lawyer," Sam said.

Lieutenant Brand grew impatient. "Mr. Dunn, you're right. You do have a right to a lawyer, but so do a dozen other people in our jail right now who have committed or are being accused of committin' far more serious crimes than stealing a box of donuts. You and I can solve this in a few minutes and I can send you on your way. You are not a criminal, Mr. Dunn, and to treat you like one would tax an already overburdened system. Now, let's try this again: Have you ever seen this box before?"

"Yes."

"This is the box you had in your possession when you were arrested two days ago at the Vagabond Inn, ain't it, Mr. Dunn?"

"This one, or one like it."

"Mr. Dunn, are you aware of a certain snake-handlin' preacher named J.W. Dean?"

"Yes, I am."

"And did you know that it was J.W. Dean's car that you stole from?"

"No."

The officer let out a big sigh. He knew that answer was a lie, and it meant it was going to take that much longer to get to the truth. "Let me guess . . ." He began pacing again. He had a line of questions already predetermined in the event he needed them. Lieutenant Brand could carry on these investigations in his sleep. "The pancakes you ordered that morning at the motel coffee shop weren't to your liking, so when you happened to spot a box of donuts in the backseat of a car, you just decided to help yourself in spite of the police tape on the vehicle. Is that it, Mr. Dunn?"

Sam was quiet. This guy had sure done his homework.

"Perhaps this note will refresh your memory, Mr. Dunn." Lieutenant Brand then reached into his coat pocket and brought out an envelope.

Sam recognized it immediately as the one he had given to J.W. right before his arrest. He had forgotten about giving it to him and realized that it would inevitably land in the hands of the police. That meant they knew everything about the ashes. No more need to hide anything. The detective unfolded the letter and smoothed it out on the table in front of him.

"Is that your handwriting, Mr. Dunn?"

"Yes."

"And are you a guest at the Vagabond Inn as it says here, room"—he twisted his head to read it upside down—"one twenty-seven?"

"Yes."

"Actually, Mr. Dunn, you've been trailin' J.W. Dean for some time, haven't you?" When Sam didn't respond, he went on. "You've been lookin' for the ashes of your wife ever since you found out the funeral home switched them by mistake. Right?"

"I want to get my Betty back."

"You know, Mr. Dunn, I understand completely, and that's why you have to realize we're on your side. You've got to leave it in our hands now. J.W. Dean is in police custody; he will soon be tried for the murder of his wife. The whereabouts of them ashes will not exactly be top priority around here for the next few months. You will just have to be patient."

That last word, *patient*, was not even present in Sam Dunn's personal vocabulary. Already he was figuring out how he might be able to get to J.W. Dean in jail. Lieutenant Brand, in the meantime, was ready to wrap up this little investigation and move on. He reached into his crowded shirt pocket and pulled out a business card.

"If you have any questions, call me. We ain't gonna book you, but we are gonna keep a keen eye out for you. Any more snoopin' around J.W. Dean's affairs, and we'll throw you in the slammer just to keep you out of our way. You understand?"

Sam stared forward, looked down at the card and back up. Lieutenant Brand took it for a nod and picked up the box to leave.

"Okay. Follow me and I'll introduce you to Deputy Long. He will get your things and take you back to your truck at the Vagabond Inn."

"One thing . . ." Sam said.

"What is it?"

"My wife had jewelry. It went with her ashes . . . to J.W. Dean. I'd like it back if you find it."

"Here." He handed Sam a piece of paper and one of his pens. "Write me a detailed description of the items. If you can accurately identify them, I'll contact you. I believe there was some jewelry found in the glove compartment of his car. Just give the report to Deputy Long; I'll send him right in. Good luck, Mr. Dunn . . . and in the future, give the right answer the first time."

Sam turned out onto the highway less than two hours later, a free man. Though he endured only a very short stint in jail, it was still long enough for him to gain a new appreciation for being able to get in his truck and go where he wanted. For that reason the road looked wider, the asphalt blacker, and the white lines whiter as they flashed against a wall of black clouds that stretched from overhead down to the horizon, absorbing the afternoon rays of the sun from behind him and deepening the tones of every color and hue.

Sam allowed himself a rare smile as he sped his truck eastward along Alligator Alley on the way back to Cocoa Beach. He rolled along as the clouds closed in behind him and finally shut out the sun, heavy drops of an afternoon shower pelting his windshield.

The man at the front desk of the Vagabond Inn had tried to get him to pay for the extra night since he failed to check out after being arrested. Sam had been belligerent with him, refusing to pay for a night he never used. When the manager threatened to call the police, Sam said "fine" and showed him Lieutenant Brand's card, insisting he give him a call. "He's the one who took me out of here before I could check out. Deal with him."

Sam discovered that Lieutenant Brand's parting word about giving the right answer the first time still irritated him. He hated sermons, especially from someone in a position of authority. Still, things couldn't have gone much better. His twenty-four hours in jail had gotten him some important information. He knew that J.W. still had the ashes somewhere, if he hadn't disposed of them along the way, and Sam now had an "in" with the police. Even if they were not awarding his case the importance he wanted, they at least weren't against him. Of course, he was not going to wait for Betty's ashes to become a priority with the Cocoa Beach Police Department. He didn't need their cooperation anyway; he could get to J.W. himself. On the drive back to Cocoa Beach he worked on a plan in his mind.

Back in Naples, Will Brewster had just about exhausted the phone book on convention-sized hotels looking for Sam. He had worked his way down through the alphabet, calling the Hilton, the Holiday Inn, the Ritz Carlton, the Sheraton, and a few of the non-chain hotels that he knew were large enough to house a small convention, like the Surf and Sand Hotel or the Sea Horse Inn. After working down to the Vanderbilt Inn on the Beach, his eye for some reason caught the Vagabond Inn listed right before it. Even though it seemed too small for a convention, he decided to try it anyway, since it was on the east side of town, where J.W.'s crusade was held, and he had time for one more call.

"Did you say Sam Dunn?" the desk clerk repeated to Will's astonishment when he called. "Yes, we have a Sam Dunn checked in here, but he's not actually here anymore."

"What do you mean?" asked Will. "Has he checked out?"

"Well, not exactly. He was arrested yesterday morning. As far as we know, he's in jail."

"In jail? Must be the wrong Sam Dunn. This guy drives a blue Chevy truck."

"I'm lookin' at his blue truck as we speak," said the man.

"Old guy with white hair and a dent in his forehead?"

"That's him."

"This is impossible," Will said. "What's his address?"

"Just a minute, I'll check . . . 513 Paradise Cove, Cocoa Beach."

Will hung up the phone in shock. What he didn't know was he had called literally minutes before Sam and Deputy Long arrived at the Vagabond. By the time Will gained his composure enough to locate the number for the sheriff's department and call, Sam was already on his way down the road, enjoying his newfound freedom. Will got a police officer at the station, but all he could do was confirm that Sam Dunn was indeed a prisoner. If he wanted any further information, he would have to visit in person.

Will's arrival at the county jail began a comedy of errors that would take another twenty-four hours to unravel. The first error was that Deputy Long was new to his post and unfamiliar with the proper procedure for signing out a prisoner. Since he was personally responsible for seeing Sam on his way, he decided he would complete his report when he returned. He knew it would take him some time to fill it out and he did not want to appear to his prisoner as the incompetent rookie that he was. He also knew that Sam Dunn was a very low-priority prisoner—an old man who was in jail more as a fluke than anything else. Coupled with this was the fact that Lieutenant Brand had left the building shortly after questioning Sam and he was out on location the rest of the day. So when Will got there and started asking questions about Sam Dunn, everyone had seen the old guy, but no one could find him or any record of his release. It took only fifteen minutes for them to decide to put out an all-points bulletin for an escaped prisoner matching Sam's description.

Will called Bobbi and Jack from the station. "Recognize the background noise?" he asked after saying hello and getting them both on the other end of the line.

"No . . . wait a minute," said Bobbi. "It sounds like the place

Sam called us from yesterday. How did you find it? Where are you?"

"The county jail," said Will.

"I was right," Jack said excitedly. "Have you found Sam?"

"Well, not exactly. Seems like our stepfather is an escaped prisoner."

ELEVEN

Late Show With David Letterman

Florida dangles. It hangs freely and unpredictably off the bottom of the United States like a snake off of Bonnie Dean's hand. Like the alligators that still lurk in its swamps, Florida's history is crawling with smugglers, fugitives, poachers, conquistadors, and veterans of Indian wars. Its current society is a melting pot of drug traffickers, vice cops, golfers, gamblers, baseball trainers, Cuban refugees, sports fishermen, Jewish retirees, European tourists, Mafia warlords, military personnel, and young families dragging their kids with mouse ears and Goofy hats to and from Walt Disney World, oddly juxtaposed in the middle of everything.

And Sam Dunn loved it all. He loved it the first time his family brought him down to the Miami shore in 1936, and he loved it even more the first time Crocky took him and his brother and cousins out sailing into a silky indigo bay in his thirty-foot sloop three summers later. Those rediscovered memories were so fresh in his mind that Sam almost turned south again when he hit Fort Lauderdale, but J.W. Dean was north in Cocoa Beach, and Sam was not going to rest until this mission was accomplished. He would be back, though, and sooner than he thought.

He checked into the Starlite Motel on the Old Highway 1 business route just in time to catch David Letterman's opening monologue warning all wives of snake-handling preachers to keep their hands out of boxes with crawling things inside. "You never know what you're going to pull out of one of them there boxes," he said, leaning into the camera until his face distorted. Then he pulled a rubber coral snake out of his pocket and acted like he was struggling with it before he threw it into a screaming audience. It landed right on top of a shrieking woman who jumped out of her seat and climbed over four people to get away from it. The camera kept following her horrified face as the crowd went wild.

"What's your name, miss? Somebody get her name! What is it? Cheryl? Cheryl, you'll be excited to know, I'm sure, that tonight on the show we're going to have an expert on snakes show us the difference between the snake that killed the preacher's wife and the ones that J.W. Dean usually handles. So, Cheryl, and wives of snake handlers everywhere, don't go away! We'll be right back." And just before the cameras broke for the commercials, he threw four more rubber snakes into the crowd and shouted, "One of those is real!"

Obviously, the news about J.W. Dean's arrest had gained national attention, though Sam's brief imprisonment had kept him from finding out about it in his daily *USA Today*. Sam was surprised to find David Letterman's joking somewhat distasteful to him. Could it be that he was getting soft on J.W.? He shuddered to think he was, but he had to admit, now that he had met the preacher and heard him speak, something was different. Few people, in person, completely embody the stereotypes that society—and in this case, the media—force on them. Sam now realized he would have to acknowledge that there was something very real about J.W.'s faith or be dishonest with himself. Perhaps even more real to him was the simple faith of those who believed J.W. and J.W.'s God. Even if they were wrong, there was something pure and childlike about their belief that made it seem right. And if they were right, then Sam had a lot to think about.

He picked up the phone and called Bobbi. "Hi, little girl," he said when she answered.

"Pop?" she said dreamily, awakened from a sound sleep. "Sam?" she repeated more loudly. "Sam!" she said with quiet intensity. "Where are you?"

"In a motel room."

"Did you escape from jail?" she asked in a hushed voice.

"Well, I got out, if that's what you mean."

"Aren't they after you?"

"No, not as long as I stay away from J.W. Dean," Sam stated.

"Well, stay away from J.W. Dean, then."

"Nope. I'm not done yet."

"Pop, what on earth are you doing? Where are you? What were you in jail for?"

"Stealing a box of donuts."

"What? You got put in jail for stealing donuts?"

"I'll tell you all about it sometime."

"Tell me now," Bobbie said, exasperated. "You woke me up."

"I know I did. Turn on your TV. David Letterman is talking about the snake that killed Bonnie Dean. Quick. He's coming back on."

"Sam! Don't you dare hang up on me again!" And then there was a long pause.

"He hung up on you, didn't he?" Jack asked, rubbing his eyes.

"I can't believe that man," Bobbi said, turning on the light and sitting up in bed. "That's downright rude!"

"Well, where is he? Did he tell you?"

"He's in a motel room. Isn't that great? A motel room somewhere in Florida. That narrows it down considerably."

"Did he sound like an escaped prisoner?"

"No. He didn't seem worried about anything."

"Well, what did he call for?"

"He wants us to watch David Letterman."

"Now?"

"Apparently he's talking about the snake that killed Bonnie Dean. Come on, bring your pillow."

"It's moments like these that I wish we were an average American family with a TV in the master bedroom," Jack stated as they made their way into Alex's room and turned on the small TV on top of his dresser. Bobbi got into bed with Alex, who groaned as she moved him over but did not wake up. Jack sat on the floor next to the bottom bunk. They were just in time for the Top Ten.

"Ladies and gentlemen," said David Letterman, "as most of you probably know, snake handler and faith healer J.W. Dean was arrested earlier this week in Florida for the murder of his wife by a coral snake. Now, we've all heard the tragic story of how the Reverend Dean claims he didn't know the snake his wife handled was poisonous. For a guy who handled poisonous snakes for a living, we find that a little hard to believe. But in case there are any other preachers out there with this problem, we have a solution. That's right, folks, direct from the home office in Tallahassee, Florida, we have, for preachers-only tonight, the top ten ways of telling whether or not the snake your wife handled was poisonous."

The music played, the countdown graphics twisted and turned, and the crowd went wild.

"Oh no," said Bobbi.

"Oh yes!" said Jack.

"All right, ladies and gentlemen, here we go! The snake your wife handled was probably poisonous if, number ten: She doesn't object to you watching *Monday Night Football* in bed. Number nine: You offer to take her shopping, and she has no comment. Number eight: You start getting a lot of comments on what a great person your wife *was*. Number seven: She has no objections to you hiring Mallory Blaine as your personal secretary. Number six: Your next revival service is attended by numerous law enforcement officers. Yes, all you snake-handlin' preachers out there, the snake your wife handled was probably poisonous if, number five: You get a Christmas card this year from the county coroner. Number four:

That guy that called about donating organs was not talking about a new one for your church."

"I can't take any more!" Bobbi cut in. "Poor J.W."

"Quiet," Jack motioned to her, "we're missing the top three!"

"Who cares?"

"I do! Wait. There's number one: 'No more charges on your phone bill to your mother-in-law's phone number.' That's not very funny. I liked the one about donating organs best."

"I don't like any of this. I think these jokes are cruel."

"Well, he had it coming," Jack replied.

"And why do you say that?"

"He tricked the people," Jack said. "They weren't poisonous snakes. If he's going to trick people like that, he's got to expect ridicule once they find out. You live by the sword; you die by the sword."

"That still doesn't mean that he might not have a legitimate ministry in spite of that," Bobbi said. "Remember, Paul said he would rejoice even if Christ was preached for the wrong reasons. I heard J.W., and he preached Christ."

"Okay, I'll grant you that," Jack admitted. "Oh no, look. Now they've got real snakes on the show."

They turned their attention back to the TV in time to hear David Letterman ask, "And what do we have here?"

"This here is a scarlet king snake, David," said his guest. "Perfectly harmless. Here, I'll let him bite me."

"Yikes!" David exclaimed as the man held up a snake clamped on to his hand with its tiny jaw. "Doesn't that hurt?"

"Hardly. Not as much as it would hurt if you bit me."

"Don't worry," David stated, looking suspiciously at his audience and snapping his teeth. "So this is the snake J.W. Dean used in his services?"

"Yes, David. This is a harmless king snake—no more dangerous than the garter snake many people find in their garden at home. Now, over here, on the other hand, we have the coral snake."

"Joe, get the camera up close here," David directed, "and let's look at how similar these snakes really are. They're hard to tell apart.''

"Yes, they are, David. You can see that it's only the order of the bands that keeps—whoops! One got loose there. . . .''

"Hey, he's slithering across my desk! Wait a minute! Which one is this?''

"I'm not sure,'' the man said, smiling. David Letterman jumped back from his desk just as the snake man grabbed the runaway reptile by the neck.

"Yikes!'' said David. "Don't go away, folks. We'll be back with the Red Hot Chili Peppers after this.''

"You can turn it off now,'' said Bobbi. "I've seen enough. People sure love to jump all over preachers when they mess up, don't they?''

"Sure. It makes us all feel better about our own screw-ups.''

Jack and Bobbi then shuffled back to their own room, jumped into bed, and curled up together. A full moon made the whites of their eyes shine like pearls.

"I wonder when we'll hear from Sam next,'' Jack said, drawing Bobbi close. "Do you think we should call Will?''

"No. Wait until tomorrow. It's too late now. If Sam's not worried, I don't know why we should be.''

"Bobbi, when you talked to Sam, do you know that you whispered?''

"Did I? I guess I did.''

"Was that because you didn't want to wake me?''

"No. I knew you were awake. I didn't want anybody to know I was talking to Sam. He's a fugitive, you know.''

"I thought so. I love the way you think.''

"I'm glad you do,'' Bobbi said, tucking herself into the cocoon Jack made with his body.

TWELVE

The Interview

J.W. Dean was a phony in more ways than one, but J.W. Dean was not a murderer. He did not kill his wife with a snake, nor was he capable of such a thing. J.W. didn't even have it in himself to deal with real poisonous snakes in the first place. How a real coral snake got into his collection of harmless scarlet snakes, the ones he fooled his audiences with every night, was as much a mystery to J.W. as to anyone. When he checked the snake box the morning after Bonnie died, he found not five snakes, as there should have been, but six. How long that coral snake had been cohabiting with the scarlets was a mystery of equal perplexity. How long had J.W. and Bonnie been playing at snake roulette—putting a hand in the chamber with five harmless reptiles and one poison round? One could only speculate. It made J.W. shudder just to think of it. It could have been his hand in that box just as easily as hers.

Had J.W. ever encountered a real snake-handling service in his travels, he would have been scared right out of his ever-lovin' imitation rattlesnake-skin boots. As it was, the closest he ever got to the real thing was his television set. It was a video of a snake-handling in Alabama that had given J.W. the idea for his scheme of using scarlet snakes to stage a snake-handling demonstration in his meetings. The first time he did it as a lure to advertise the crusade, the audience went from twenty-five to sixty and the number of converts from two to nineteen. For J.W., there had been no looking back.

Of course, J.W. knew he was deceiving the people, though he would never have used that word. He was *attracting* them to hear the gospel. For him, a nonpoisonous snake-handling isn't much different than telling stories from the pulpit that grip people's hearts and bring them to the Lord, even if they were made up or greatly embellished. And J.W. could easily point out the phrase "evangelistically speaking" as a euphemism for a common pastoral tendency toward exaggeration, which would never have arisen were it not something that everybody already did—at least everybody *he* knew in the ministry. J.W. was of a belief, not uncommon among revivalist preachers, that the end justifies the means, especially in something as important as the eternal destiny of a person's soul.

Besides, the snakes were not the main thing anyway. Like a sideshow in a circus, J.W. used the snakes only to draw a crowd. To draw them and keep them coming back, because they'd want to return the next day to see if he and Bonnie lived through the bites from the night before. That was no different to J.W. than the stories he'd heard about pastors going up in the steeples of their churches and refusing to come down until attendance at Sunday services reached a certain goal. According to J.W., marketing gimmicks like this were on the same par as his handling of harmless snakes, and J.W. outlived being "snake-bit" with the same amount of evangelical fervor as any pastor up his steeple.

It's amazing that he got away with this charade as long as he did, however, in an area of the country where people should have been more knowledgeable about the similarities and differences between coral snakes and scarlet snakes. But such is the power of the pulpit. Both varieties of snakes are about the same size, roughly two to three feet in length, with a slim, graceful head and body that flow together without a visible neck. Colors ring their slender bodies in alternating black, yellow, and red bands that follow a consistent pattern, and herein lies their only recognizable difference. Though the colors of the two snakes are the same, the order in which they appear is not. "Red against yellar kills a fellar." So goes the saying in parts of the southeastern United States where both snakes are prevalent, to help people remember the difference.

Anyone could have noticed, had they been looking, that J.W.'s snakes had their deadly red and yellow bands separated by harmless black bands, but people are gullible—especially in the hands of a powerful spell such as one J.W. could weave. And even if someone did suspect something, they probably wouldn't speak up. They would go along with the story for the sake of the gospel for the same reason J.W. did. They would have to be a doubter or a skeptic to care enough to say something, and skeptics rarely bothered to attend a J.W. Dean service. Like supermarket tabloids, everybody knows "them stories ain't true"—everybody, that is, but the millions of people who keep buying them and believing them anyway. So the snakes did their job, and the people who wanted to believe kept coming.

J.W.'s services primarily drew an audience tied to the local church that was hosting him. Though there were a few exceptions, he usually landed a small independent congregation. J.W. was not legitimate enough to be endorsed by a denomination, even one that might feature signs and wonders. His appeal remained among the little struggling churches on the outskirts of town that needed a special shot in the arm. And as promised, J.W.'s services jumpstarted many a church. Though much was usually made of inviting the public to his crusades, more often than not, guests were former members who had left the fold for another, or they were "backslidden" relatives and friends of the more faithful who had been prevailed upon to come see J.W. and Bonnie handle snakes.

J.W. Dean's own variety of snake handling would come at the

end of a meeting, right before he invited people to come down front for prayer. The local musicians he had organized for the services (hopefully a guitar, bass, keyboard, and drums, plus three or four vocalists, though he learned to work with any combination of these) would start into the song J.W. always used for this part of the service. It was a song he wrote himself:

> Take them up, take them up,
> There is nothing that can harm you;
> Take them up, take them up,
> See them dangle in the air;
> Take them up, take them up,
> The devil cannot charm you
> When you throw your spirit into prayer (into prayer),
> When you throw your spirit into prayer.

And while the music worked its own magic on the crowd, Bonnie would come out with the box of snakes and open the lid, and she and J.W. would put their hands in until they each produced a snake attached to the fleshy part of their palm by its powerful little jaw. If it was an especially good night and the crowd was getting into the spirit, they would get one or two on each hand. Then, while everyone was still singing and swaying, they would swagger around the platform and up and down the aisles, waving the dangling reptiles like priests brandishing the sleeves of their robes. J.W. liked to call it his snake dance. After the snakes were put away, J.W. would accomplish his greatest work.

"There's poison in my system, but the Holy Ghost is fightin' it right now. I can feel the battle ragin'. Can I get an 'Amen'?"

Amen.

" 'They shall take up serpents and it shall not hurt them,' saith the Lord. Can I get a witness?"

Yes! Thank you, Lord!

"It's God's Word!" he would shout, holding his large blue Bible up. Often he would feign a slight weakness in his body—a sagging of his heavy Bible or a little tremble in his legs reminiscent of an Elvis twitch—to remind the people that he was struggling with the venom, fighting it off before their very eyes through the power of the Holy Ghost.

"There's sin in your life, but the blood of Jesus can CLEAN IT OUT! He can take it away! He can give you POW-er over your sin! Do you believe that?"

Yes, Lord! We believe.

"There's sickness in your body, but the Holy Spirit can Ha-EEL you! Do you believe that?"

Amen! We believe!

"Then I'm going to ask you to come down here and get healed. Come down front here and get your sins forgiven. Come and RE-CEIVE-ah the POWER." At which point the singers would start singing:

> *Throw them down, throw them down,*
> *All those sins and tribulations,*
> *Throw them down, throw them down,*
> *See them trampled on the ground;*
> *Throw them down, throw them down,*
> *Give your heart in consecration,*
> *So the filling of the Spirit will abound (will abound),*
> *So the filling of the Spirit will abound.*

J.W. was fairly safe with his pseudo-snake-handling service as long as he stayed in Florida. Real snake handlers rarely come that far south anymore. Most of them stay in the hill country that touches portions of Georgia, Alabama, Tennessee, Kentucky, the Carolinas, and the Virginias. These are the regions where authentic snake handlers have been practicing their deadly art for over eighty years in the back hills of the southern Appalachians. They handle real snakes and many of them die real deaths.

Though these gritty mountain folk might occasionally take up a coral snake now and then, they are far more interested in the challenge of the wild rattlesnakes, cottonmouths, and copperheads they collect from the surrounding hills. And unlike J.W., though part of their spiritual ritual might include surviving numerous bites (for they always refuse treatment when bitten), the whole point of their handling services is to not get bitten at all. For them, handling the snake safely is the spiritual experience itself. It is the ecstasy of the moment—the immediate faith-tester—to be so anointed by the Holy Ghost that you can hold death coiled in your hands, draped over your shoulder, trapped under your bare feet, or even catch it when thrown to you, and survive . . . that you can have it staring you in the face and not be struck by its venom. It's all about the power of faith over fangs. To be bitten means that the protective fabric of faith has broken down in some way, be it sin, a compromise of values, or lack of concentration on the Lord. But even to die is to die staring at the enemy and triumph over him in the promised resurrection. And these practices don't stop with rattlesnakes. They cast out demons, drink strychnine and Drano, and put their hands in flames to test the power of the Holy Ghost. For these believers, faith is a life-and-death struggle every time. Way beyond J.W. Dean. Some of them have even served time in jail because of local laws forbidding the handling of snakes in public meetings.

And yet here was J.W. Dean, in a life-and-death situation in prison for reasons other than staring down snakes. The death penalty was a possibility for him, although remote. The end of his ministry, however, was in doubt and his future uncertain as well. But J.W. Dean had not lost heart. It would take more than this to break his spirit. He saw his time in the maximum-security holding facility outside of Orlando as not unlike Paul's experiences in prison, and like Paul, he spent much time singing hymns and praying. In fact, J.W. Dean had never been closer to God than he was during his days in prison.

J.W. had no trouble getting legal representation for his case. His publicity had already attracted nothing short of a feeding frenzy among the gray suits that patrol the shallow waters of Florida's courts in search of high-profile media cases. But J.W. chose to pass by the sharks and settle for a relatively unknown Orlando attorney named Harvey Finklestein, who, instead of a suit, wore cheesy short-sleeved flowery shirts, the kind tourists buy in hotel gift shops. J.W. liked Harvey because he was a born-again Jew, and

J.W. was convinced he was getting a perfect combination of shrewdness and sympathy.

"I followed up with that guy who wants to interview you for *Current Christianity*," said Harvey during a visit with J.W. a few days into the second week of his confinement. "I think you should take it."

"Why?" said J.W. "I don't want to talk to anyone yet."

"You need all the publicity you can get, baby."

"How do we know this story will help? That magazine has never been kind to charismatics."

"Look, J.W., you know and I know that news is news, and the more controversial it is, the better chance it has of being noticed. Besides, I've guaranteed our right to okay the story before going to print. We're not happy? We call it off. Fair enough?"

"So you set up an interview already?"

"Tomorrow."

"Harvey! I can't be ready to talk tomorrow!"

"Sure you can. You can talk right now. Just tell the truth like you told me. Don't worry. I'll be here with you to make sure you don't get in trouble. It's a Christian magazine, J.W. They'll be sympathetic."

"Fellow Christians can be meaner than the world. You don't realize that yet. You haven't been a Christian long enough."

"I know human nature. I'm a lawyer, remember? Trust me. This is the right exposure for you."

Both J.W. and Harvey were surprised the next day when the reporter from *Current Christianity* showed up at the prison. As uneasy as J.W. was about this interview, the reporter seemed even more so.

For half an hour the man questioned J.W. about his background, his ministry, handling snakes, Bonnie's death, and his future goals and dreams. He took painfully laborious notes on a yellow legal pad, often asking J.W. to repeat himself or stopping him while he wrote down something important. All this time, J.W. continued to study the man curiously. Something seemed familiar to him—his white hair . . . the dent on his forehead. . . . And then ten minutes short of their allotted time, something clicked inside his head.

"Wait a minute," J.W. exclaimed, suddenly pointing a finger at the reporter. "I know you."

At that, Sam Dunn came out from behind his legal pad for the first time in the interview and said something that took J.W. and Harvey by surprise: "Yes, you do, Mr. Dean."

"I do?"

"I was standing in front of you the night you were arrested in Naples," said the reporter. "My name is Sam Dunn, and you have something that belongs to me." Sam had been using the name S. Dunn with J.W. and his attorney, but now that J.W. was starting to figure things out, Sam decided it was time to drop the pretext and simply go for the information he wanted. He was actually surprised to have gotten as far as he had playing the role of a writer for a Christian magazine, of all things. Sam was not good at being anything other than Sam, and he knew it. Nor had he gone into this meeting with any clear plan other than to get himself once more in J.W.'s face.

"That's it!" exclaimed J.W. "You're the guy with the ashes!"

"No, *you're* the guy with the ashes," said Sam. "My wife's ashes, to be exact."

"Will someone please tell me what's going on here?" said Harvey.

"So you're not a reporter for *Current Christianity*?" said J.W., somewhat relieved and slightly amused.

"No, I'm not."

Harvey was not amused at all. "What? You're an impostor? You came in here under false pretenses to obtain information from my client? Do you know that I can have you arrested for insubordination of justice?" The lawyer started to motion for a guard through the window, but J.W. caught his hand and pushed it back down on the table.

"Settle down, Harvey. The man only wants an exchange."

"Can you tell me where the ashes are?" said Sam.

"Yes, but you'll never find them. I'm sorry to have to tell you this, but I threw them off a bridge in the Florida Keys."

Sam's countenance fell.

"And what did you do with Bonnie's ashes?" J.W. asked.

"In the bay off Cocoa Beach," Sam stated, shaking his head. He saw no reason for the fake ashes now that it was clear he had nothing for which to trade them. He also didn't want to further complicate matters with the police should they come looking for his barbecue version of Bonnie.

"But your note said you could trade." J.W. was puzzled.

"I was bluffing," said Sam. "I was just trying to get you to talk to me."

"Anyone want to clue me in here?" Harvey Finklestein was losing his patience.

"Our wives were both cremated on the same day," said J.W., "and the mortuary got the ashes mixed up. This man has been following me for weeks trying to recover his wife's remains."

"Were you surprised at how heavy they were?" Sam asked, suddenly feeling an unexpected camaraderie with the preacher. "The ashes, I mean."

"Yes," J.W. said. "More like sand than ashes."

"That pouring sound"—Sam recounted, his eyes drawing back into his head as he remembered it—"I can still hear it."

J.W. broke in on Sam's memory. "I wouldn't know."

"One of the high bridges?"

"No. I just chucked the box out the window. It was an impulse. I was running away from everything at the time and I wanted it all behind me."

Just then the guard on the other side of the double glass signaled them five more minutes.

"Mr. Finklestein," Sam leaned in, "I promised you a story and you will have a story. By the end of this week. It will be yours to do with as you please."

"But can you write?" asked Harvey.

"What I have promised, I will deliver."

"Harvey, let's go along with the man's story." J.W. was warming to the idea. "What do we have to lose?"

Harvey was not convinced, but Sam did not seem to care. He had another question for J.W. "You wouldn't happen to remember which bridge that was you threw the box off of, would you?"

"It was somewhere along the Seven Mile Bridge," J.W. said.

"I'd like to know so I can remember her there," Sam said.

"Of course," J.W. agreed. "You must have loved her a lot."

Sam needed to press a little further. The Seven Mile Bridge was just that—seven miles long. "You wouldn't remember *where* on the bridge you threw the box out, would you? Something to mark the spot for her daughter and me?"

"I was on my way to Key West," J.W. said, "and I think it was right around that little island they call Pigeon Key."

The guard came and escorted Sam away while the lawyer stayed for a private conference with his client. Sam walked out of the prison that day wondering about two things: one, how long can plastic and cardboard hold up in salt water? And two, maybe he had himself a real story after all.

THIRTEEN

S. Dunn on Snake Handling

"It's for you, honey," Jack said, turning on the light and looking at the clock. "It's from Shaughnessy—Sam's brother. It's two o'clock in the morning, for heaven's sake."

Bobbi sat up in bed squinting and took the phone. "Albert?" she said. "What's wrong?"

"Lose the light," she whispered to Jack, but he had already flopped back on his pillow, so Bobbi leaned over him and turned it out herself, smothering his face as she did.

"Uh-huh," she kept saying. Then, "No kidding. Well, where do you think he is now? . . . And you're going to go down there? . . . What do you make of all this? . . . Yes, I think he's up to something, too, but maybe now we'll all find out. When are you leaving? . . . Will you please keep me posted? . . . Okay. You take care of yourself. . . . No, that's all right. I'm glad you called. We've been worried sick about him. . . . Yes, we'll be praying too. Uncle Albert, you sure you're not too old for this? . . . I knew you'd say something like that. All the same, you be careful, you hear? . . . You too. Good night." She then hung up the phone, leaning over Jack once more to do so, and pressed his face farther into his pillow.

He let out a muffled groan. "Couldn't this have waited until morning?"

"The Dunns don't wait for anything. He heard from Sam."

"I figured that. Where is he?"

"Albert doesn't know. Sam wants Albert to meet him in the Florida Keys right away. Something about scuba diving."

"Scuba diving in the Keys? That's what he woke us up for—to tell us his vacation plans?"

"Jack, something's up. Sam never calls Albert unless there's a death in the family. Why would he suddenly want him to fly down to Florida and go diving with him?"

"Beats me." Jack rolled over on his side and propped his head up, reluctantly becoming more awake. "Except that it's obvious that since Betty died, Sam has gotten a second lease on life. He bought the truck; he turned detective overnight; he traipsed all over southern Florida keeping his whereabouts a secret; and now he wants to vacation with his estranged brother? Seems like a perfectly natural progression to me."

"I don't think it's a vacation." Bobbi was silent a moment, her gaze locked on the intertwining pattern of leaves the moon was shadowing on the bedspread. "He *is* crazy, isn't he?"

"Nothing ever surprises me about Sam. But why do you think Albert had to call us at two in the morning to tell us this?"

"He's leaving first thing in the morning; Sam wants him there that quick. I think he wanted to know if we knew anything about what Sam was up to before he left."

"Sam never lets anyone know what he's up to."

"Can you believe this? Scuba diving at their age? And Albert's doing it. He's so sweet to pick up and leave at the drop of a hat just because his brother finally reached out to him."

"I agree with you; there's got to be more to it than a sudden urge to go diving." Jack locked his hands behind his head and stared up at Bobbi's flattened hair in the silver moonlight. There was something bouncy and beautiful that he liked in her hair's imperfection after a few hours on a pillow. He never tired of being the only person in the whole world who ever got to see this magical wayward hairdo. Of course, he never told Bobbi this. To her it would be far from a compliment.

"Remember all those bizarre stories about Sam and Albert and their mystery grandfather in the Florida Keys?" Bobbi asked.

To Jack's dismay, Bobbi seemed to be waking up.

"I overheard them at the funeral talking about going back there someday."

"You did?"

"Yeah. It was real strange. Whenever they talk about the Keys, they drop all their animosity and suddenly become friends."

They were quiet for a while, and Jack contemplated waking himself up too.

"Jack, hand me the phone," Bobbi commanded.

"It's two in the morning. Who are you going to call at two in the morning?"

"Sam. I have a feeling he's home right now."

Jack handed her the phone, but all she got was his answering machine. "Sam, I just talked to Uncle Albert. Diving in the Florida Keys? You be careful, now, and *please* call us sometime. Bye for now."

She handed Jack the phone, and without looking, he fumbled with it until it clicked into the receiver. His arm went immediately limp as if the act had exhausted him.

Bobbi, however, sat up staring at the shadows. "Now I'm wide awake," she said flatly after a long sigh. Once more she pressed Jack into his pillow, this time to turn the light back on.

But before she could reach the lamp, he suddenly sprang to life, grabbed her arm, and rolled her over on her back until they were nose-to-nose in the moonlight, a sliver of which caught Bobbi's eyes, wide with surprise.

"So am I," he said. "And I'm not alone. It seems a whole bunch of surfers just showed up on the beach."

"What a coincidence," Bobbi said with delight, "because I just checked the marine forecast for tonight, and guess what?"

"I bet I know," said Jack, and the next part they said together: "Surf's up!"

⌒

Sam didn't even flinch when the phone rang. The top quarter of a clean sheet of white paper had been staring back at him for hours from under the roller bar of his old black Royal. The stale air in the room was being pushed around slowly by an off-center ceiling fan that rocked rhythmically against its base. There was no movement outside his open window and no sound except the creaking of the fan and the automatic sprinklers turning on and off in the yard. Ever since Betty had died, Sam kept his air conditioner off. He preferred to feel the air and smell his own sweat. On his desk were three recent issues of *Current Christianity* he had stolen from the library, and an ashtray, crammed with crushed Marlboros, overflowed onto one of the magazines. Finally he hunted through the round enamel typewriter keys and began pecking out letters slowly, deliberately.

John Wesley (J.W.) Dean has a dream, he started.

He wants to be on television someday like his hero, Jim Bakker. In the meantime, however, he hasn't wasted any time following in his hero's footsteps. Not even bothering with the prerequisite television show, J.W. just went straight to jail. And the way publicity works in this country, he may get his show after all. Nothing like tabloid coverage to get your career up and running.

"All I ever wanted to do was get people saved," J.W. said during an interview from a maximum-security holding facility outside of Orlando. To get people saved, J.W. and his late wife handled snakes as an attraction. Until now, everyone thought they were dealing with deadly coral snakes, but J.W., though he claims to have nothing to do with his wife's death, does admit to trickery in that he and Bonnie handled harmless scarlet snakes instead. The two types of snakes are easy to confuse. Especially on that one fateful night in March, when a real coral snake clung to Bonnie's

wrist in a service in Rockledge, Florida. That snake now resides in custody in the Cocoa Beach Police Department as evidence in a murder. Where did it come from? Who put it in the snake box? And why? These are the questions no one has any answers for yet.

A sly smile crept across Sam's face as he leaned back and surveyed the words on the page. Suddenly he stared uninterestedly at the Christian magazines and started looking around the room for something else. He found his current copy of *USA Today*, which he unfolded and spread out next to him on the other side of the typewriter. After studying a few articles, he went back to his own writing with increased vigor.

"How could I have done it?" J.W. revealed from prison. "I had my hand in the same box!" And if that is true, it's hard to believe he could have been the culprit. It's hard to believe anyway, once you meet J.W. Dean. A murder is the last thing anyone would think J.W. could commit.

John Wesley Dean grew up the son of a coal miner in Dryfork, West Virginia. His sickly mother succumbed to a long bout with cancer when he was nine, and his father was buried alive three years later in a mining cave-in. J.W. got his first visions of the ministry from his grandmother, a devout Christian woman who raised him and took care of his dying mother at the same time. She was the one who persuaded him to pursue the ministry and attend a holiness college in Missouri on the insurance money his father left them.

Sam was transfixed by the flow of words that poured from his brain. For years he had read the paper, never knowing *he* could write an article. His ability to write something he actually liked to read took him by complete surprise. He was so intent on his discovery that he didn't notice the light creeping into the early morning sky outside his window.

⌣

It was only a week later that Bobbi and Jack encountered the very same words that originated from Sam's black Royal typewriter, reprinted in the *Boston Globe* by way of the *Cocoa Beach Bee*. Jack didn't notice anything about the origin of the article at first, except that it was a more extensive and entertaining editorial than the bits and pieces the national news had been printing on the story so far. Harvey Finklestein had been pleasantly surprised to receive the story from Sam and immediately had it placed in the Cocoa Beach paper. He knew the story was a good one and would go further than just the local news. This was better than *Current Christianity* could ever have been, and quicker too.

Jack was reading the article to Bobbi as she got ready for work. It didn't matter that she would be working out of the house that day; Bobbi always dressed for work as if she were in visual contact with everyone she talked to on the phone, prompting Jack to peg her as someone who, unlike everyone else, won't have to change any habits when the videophone becomes commonplace.

Jack often read to Bobbi during her morning ritual over hair and face. He had gotten as far as the part about J.W.'s college experience and was reading on in the bathroom while Bobbi's makeup was applied and curlers flew in and out of her hair, his voice rising and falling to the sporadic hum of the hair dryer.

" 'J.W.'s road to the traveling circuit occurred after two failed prostates'—I mean 'pastorates . . .' "

"Was that Freudian?" Bobbi asked, laughing.

"I think so." Jack continued. " 'It was his own brand of pseudo-snake-handling that finally put him in business. Snakes turned J.W. into a mild success, at least among the Coalition of Independent Holiness Churches of Florida and southern Georgia. So J.W. took to the road with his reptilian traveling salvation show and his wife of six years, the former Bonnie Brumfield, a college sweetheart from Holiston, Missouri.' "

"Poor Bonnie," Bobbi interjected.

" 'But you live by the snake, you die by the snake, or so it went for poor Bonnie.' "

Jack looked at Bobbi and they both smiled as the newspaper echoed her sentiment.

" 'And for J.W., it was the snake that eventually put him out of the preaching business and into jail. The particular snake that killed his wife has since enjoyed the status of mascot around the Cocoa Beach Police Department, where it now even boasts the name "Serpico." They call it that for the serpent that tempted Eve, as well as for the famous police officer who rid the New York City Police Department of corruption and graft. Sheriff Buck Buford of the Cocoa Beach Police is convinced that J.W. is the one who put Serpico in the snake box that fateful night. Buford, in turn, credits Serpico with cleaning up J.W.'s act when his plan backfired and got him arrested.' "

"I don't think Buck likes J.W. very much," said Bobbi.

"I don't think so either," Jack repeated.

" ' "Gonna put J.W. right out of business with this here snake," said the sheriff. "We've not only got the murder weapon, we've got motive and we've got proof," though he's not divulging any information before the trial.

" 'J.W., on the other hand, has pleaded "not guilty" to murder by coral snake and steadfastly holds to his innocence. "It could have been me just as easily as her," he claims, and most of the Rockledge congregation tends to agree with him, though no one has come forward who can recall Bonnie's husband handling any snakes on the night she died.

" 'All of which is greatly disturbing to Elvis Brown, pastor of the Mark 16:18 Gospel Church of Blackwater with Accompanying Signs, a tiny mobile-home church in Blackwater, Georgia, in the shadow of the southern Appalachians, where the handling of poisonous snakes is commonplace.' "

"What's the name of that church?" Bobbi asked without taking her eyes off the mirror.

"The Mark 16:18 Gospel Church of Blackwater with Accompanying Signs."

"What's Mark 16:18?"

"It's a controversial passage that has to do with snakes and poison and stuff like that."

"What's controversial about it?"

"It's not in all the original manuscripts," Jack stated.

"So? It's in *their* Bible."

"Well, it means a significant number of biblical scholars question the reliability of a whole paragraph at the end of Mark. The New International Version even has it separated from the text with a note about it."

"But these people don't know that." Bobbi finally looked straight at Jack.

"Of course they don't," Jack replied. "They've never seen anything but the King James Bible."

"Go on with the article. This is fascinating."

" 'Elvis Brown, who claims to have been bitten fifty-one times by rattlesnakes, is not happy about the shadow of publicity this incident has cast over his church and its two generations of worshiping by handling snakes and drinking strychnine.' "

"Drinking strychnine?" said Bobbi. "Why would they do that?"

"It's in the verse."

Bobbi kept fooling with her hair, deep in thought. Jack went back to reading when she had no further reply.

" ' "We risk our lives every time we worship. It's the power of God or death. Mr. Dean's wife dyin'—that was God's judgment. He put a real snake in that box and showed everybody that J.W. was backin' up on the Lord. Play with God and you're gonna get snakebit every time." ' "

"Almost done." Jack noticed that Bobbi was about to wrap up her morning date with the mirror.

"Finish it; this is great." Bobbi threw her makeup in the shoe box she kept it in while her eyes remained connected to her reflection in the mirror, checking every possible angle.

"Here you go," said Jack, reading a little ahead. " 'Elvis's church gets its name from a passage in the Gospel of Mark where it states that "these signs shall follow them that believe: In my name shall they cast out devils; they shall speak with new tongues; they shall take up serpants; and if they drink any deadly thing, it shall not hurt them." All of these signs, and then some, occur at the Mark 16:18 Gospel Church of Blackwater with Accompanying

Signs where faith is tested on a regular basis, and a snakebite or a sickness—even death—is interpreted as evidence of unconfessed sin or a momentary chink in the armor of faith.

" 'On the occasion of Bonnie Dean's death in Rockledge, Florida, however, there was not even the honor of a lapse in faith. There was only the uncovering of a spiritual hoax. Bonnie Dean put her hand in a box, pulled out a deadly snake, and died. Elvis Brown thinks God put the snake there. Sheriff Buford is convinced that it was J.W. who planted it. Since snakes don't talk, at least since the Garden of Eden, how Serpico got in that box may be something no one will ever know for sure.' "

"That's it?" asked Bobbi.

"That's it."

"Great article."

"Yeah, it is pretty good," Jack agreed with a little more reservation, being a writer himself and threatened by anyone else's good writing.

"Whoever wrote it seems to give that Mark 16 church some credibility. Did you get that impression?"

"Well, compared to J.W., anyone would look pretty credible. Says here: 'This story by S. Dunn first appeared in the *Cocoa Beach Bee*.' "

"S. Dunn?" Bobbi's face was incredulous. "You don't think. . . ?"

They both stared at each other while the name slowly set in.

"Have you ever known Sam to write anything like this?" Jack asked. "This is pretty good writing."

"Well, he reads the newspaper religiously," Bobbi offered.

"Reading is one thing. Writing is another."

"I don't know. Maybe after all those years some of it rubbed off."

"It would explain what he's been doing with all of his time lately," said Jack, now lathering his beard over the double sink. "You don't suppose he went to Georgia himself and interviewed this Elvis guy, do you?"

"We stopped being surprised by Sam some time ago, remember?" Bobbi picked up the paper and checked the by-line for her-self. "I suppose there could be another S. Dunn in Cocoa Beach."

"That would be a remarkable coincidence." Jack shook out his razor. "It's him. I bet it's him."

"Well, if it is, then we should praise God because I think that snake handler from Georgia might be getting through to him. He seems to be pretty impressed with the genuine faith of these weird people."

"It would take someone as ornery as a snake handler to make Sam believe."

"Jack, what do you make of all this? Are these people for real? Do you think God is in this snake-handling stuff? I mean, it's in the Bible."

"Yeah, in a passage with questionable validity. You've got to remember that."

"Oh, come on, Jack. Do you really buy that? Why would God have allowed something to be in our Bibles for almost twenty cen-turies and then suddenly take it away because some guys on some committee somewhere decided they weren't sure about it any-more?"

"Well, look in your Bible."

Bobbi's Bible was sitting on the back of the toilet, so she picked it up and found the Gospel of Mark and read out loud the small print between verses eight and nine of chapter sixteen: " 'The most reliable early manuscripts and other ancient witnesses do not have Mark 16:9–20.' "

Bobbi watched Jack wipe off his face with a towel and then commented, "Has anyone tried telling that to these people? How would you like to have a rattlesnake in your hand, then have some-one come up and tell you that the verse you are risking your life over was not in the early manuscripts? I bet these people haven't even heard of the New International Version. They've built their whole church around a verse that was in *their* Bible."

Jack brought the towel down off his face and looked on while Bobbi messed with her hair some more in the mirror. If she wasn't done with her hair, she wasn't done with her thoughts either.

"You know what I think?" she said, turning to him.

"What do you think?"

"I think that God honors what you believe, even if it isn't in the early manuscripts."

Jack looked at her in amazement, leaving her with the last word.

FOURTEEN

Map of Florida

The Everglades of southern Florida hold a rare and hidden beauty that few ever witness up close. Driving along the Tamiami Trail across southern Florida at sixty-five miles per hour, one sees only tall brown grass with patches of green trees in the distance. The only break in the monotony are the periodic hand-scrawled signs advertising airboat rides through the marshes, a major source of revenue for the remnant Miccosukee and Seminole Indian tribes forced to live here on reservations. Take one of those airboat rides, however, and a delicate and sometimes violent world comes into view.

Most of Florida south of Lake Okeechobee is actually slow-moving water running off from the lake's overflow during the heavy thunderstorm season that occurs annually from May to October. The gradual but steady slope of the land west, east, and southward—a drop of no more than two inches a mile—creates a wide swamp spotted by islands of hardwood and cypress trees called hammocks. Some water is visible in channels and sloughs, but the majority is hidden by a hearty sawgrass that can root in the sandy peat bottom of a few feet of water and flourish on the surface so that, from a distance, one sees what appears to be dry, tall grassland broken by clumps of trees. That is why the Everglades is often called "a river of grass."

These hammocks that have formed on the slightly elevated ground of old ridges, beaches, or even Indian burial mounds teem with tropical plant and animal life. Dry hammocks support yucca and several kinds of cacti. Moist hammocks hang with Spanish moss and rare air plants from the pineapple and orchid families thriving in the shelter of the tall trees. Here a garfish might flash silver-gold in a slough of amber water as ghost-orchid flowers spray overhead like cascading fireworks. As the water seeps slowly to the sea, it mixes with the salt water of coastal estuaries where pink shrimp, snook, and snapper have supported the local fishermen for generations.

Out on Florida Bay, the groping roots of the mangroves crowd the shoreline with their exposed tarantula legs that appear and disappear with the tide, making amphibious passage possible only for the great wide-winged heron, stork, and ibis. Endless secrets lie below sea level as well. These are found in the coral reefs that dot the Florida Keys. Indeed, much of the Keys are the remains of an old coral reef, the Key Largo Limestone. And somewhere on top of this ancient underwater limy ooze rested the most important secret of all for Sam Dunn: the plastic-wrapped, donut-boxed ashen remains of the body of Betty Dunn.

Sam was concerned about getting to those ashes as quickly as possible. The decomposition of plastic in salt water was an unknown, given they could even find the box. That's why he picked up his brother Albert from the Miami International Airport and immediately headed south. During their first dinner together, Sam decided to let Albert in on the real reason for their expedition.

"How long has it been since you went diving?" he asked, lighting a cigarette before the food arrived.

"Oh, fifteen years . . . maybe twenty. How long has it been since you went back to smoking?"

Sam looked at his cigarette as if it held the answer. "Since Betty died."

"I thought so."

Albert was devoid of sharp edges. Everything was rounded off, including his head, on which his hair was cropped short, leaving salt-and-pepper stubble. He had an extra layer of pale, almost translucent skin that folded around his neck and turned various shades of white, pink, and red when he turned his head or became overly emotional. The crows'-feet around his eyes made him look as though he was always smiling.

"You'll have to renew your certificate, you know," Sam reminded him, getting back to the subject.

"Renew it? I was lucky to even find it. How about you? You all current?"

"Ha! I can barely swim," Sam said.

"You're kidding, aren't you? You have your certificate, of course."

"Nope. Never been underwater before in my life . . . unless you count submarines in the war."

"And here I thought I was the one who was going to have to brush up on his dive tables," Albert replied. He hesitated a moment, then turned to his brother. "Sam, why does this sound more like a project than a vacation?"

"Because it *is* a project," Sam announced. "Didn't I tell you? I want you to help me find Betty's ashes."

Albert's face turned grave. So far there hadn't been any indication that Sam was losing his grip on reality. He seemed to be his usual ornery self. But scuba diving in the Florida Keys for ashes that had been poured in the water two months prior from a boat off Merritt Island was indicative of a very serious problem. Albert's mind started spinning. He had already committed to this trip. But how far was he willing to go with a bizarre mission like this? Suddenly he saw himself in scuba gear with Sam, diving for invisible bits of his cremated sister-in-law in a vast green sea. Albert decided to see how far this insanity had progressed.

"Where do you suppose the ashes are now?"

"Under the Seven Mile Bridge near Pigeon Key."

"I see. You've certainly narrowed it down, haven't you?"

"Yep. Shouldn't be too hard to find."

Shouldn't be too hard? Albert repeated in his mind. *The hard part is going to be figuring out how to get Sam professional help without him suspecting it.*

"What about the currents under those bridges?" Albert said, testing him further.

"They reverse with the tides, with a half-hour window of calm in between. That's when we dive."

Albert had never been able to figure out how his brother could make so much sense on one hand and so little sense on another. Albert couldn't take any more.

"Sam, come on, now. How can you possibly know that Betty's ashes have somehow settled under one particular bridge in the Florida Keys?"

"Because that's where Reverend Dean chucked them."

"Reverend Dean? Who's Reverend Dean?"

"J.W. Dean. He's a snake-handling preacher."

"I know who J.W. Dean is, but what does that have to do with the price of beans?" The skin color on Albert's neck was turning.

"Nothing," Sam said, putting out his cigarette and picking a carrot out of the condiment tray, "but it has a lot to do with Betty's ashes."

Albert fell back in his chair in frustration. Right then he could barely look at Sam. Every time he did, he saw the dent on Sam's forehead as a blow he wished he could deliver to try and knock something loose from his brain. Maybe someone else had already tried it and that's where the dent came from in the first place. Albert would certainly understand if that were the case. Especially when Sam didn't show any concern at all with how much he frustrated people. Albert watched him munch on his carrot while staring right at him with the indifference of a cow chewing on its cud.

It took Albert some time, but he finally managed to knock out enough answers from Sam while they waited for the food to arrive to figure out why he was suddenly having dinner with his brother in Florida, "I know you've never been much for explaining things, but this is one time a simple explanation would have been helpful," he said, exhausted with his questioning.

"Well, you're here, aren't you? We start diving lessons in Key Largo this weekend. I found a place that will certify us in two days."

"Are you sure we're not too old for this?" Albert gazed at the grilled snapper on a bed of rice that was placed before him. Sam had ordered his standard steak and potatoes.

"How's your heart?" asked Sam.

"As good as ever, but that cough of yours . . ." and Sam obliged by rattling his damaged lungs.

⌒

Jack was up early grinding beans to make a fresh pot of coffee. The house was quiet with sleep as he brought in the *Boston Globe* and smelled the oily brew. It was a perfect spring day and a holiday at that. At least it was a holiday for the kids—one of those administrative days that come once or twice a year for students—resulting in the promise of a private holiday for the whole family. Jack and Bobbi controlled their own schedules enough to turn one of these unexpected free days into a family outing when it seemed no one else in the world had the opportunity. This translated into uncrowded excursions, empty restaurants, and short lines at the movie theater.

Jack made it through half of the front section of the paper, then checked the clock and started fixing breakfast for two. Cereal, juice, wheat toast, and some marmalade. The marmalade he put in a small dish with a miniature spoon and suddenly the tray was starting to take on the look of a room-service order. "One more thing . . . ah yes . . ." He plucked a single white daisy from the flower arrangement on the breakfast table and popped it in a little ceramic vase that had accidentally found its way to the Acres' house from a real room-service tray out in a world of big hotels and fast planes. His two hands full with the tray, thermal coffeepot, and newspaper, he kicked the door to his bedroom open and went to where his wife lay fast asleep.

"Mrs. Acres, your breakfast is ready." He unburdened his hands on the table next to the bed when Mrs. Acres didn't move and opened the curtains to the small, twelve-paned eighteenth-century window facing east, letting in a beam of golden sunlight. Two late commuters whizzed by on the road outside heading for the Interstate and Boston, thirty miles away. Then he tried again.

"Mrs. Acres . . . your breakfast."

Bobbi's eyes flickered and opened. A smile of delight slowly spread across her face like the sunlight in the room as Jack and breakfast came into focus. "Oh, how nice."

"The weather report for today couldn't be better," he said in his best room-service voice as Bobbi sat up and made room on the bed for the tray. Jack crisply snapped a small towel he had brought in over his arm and spread it out on the bed and then set the tray on top of it and poured the coffee. He kept talking as he did this: "High sixties . . . scattered clouds . . . It should be a perfect day for whatever you have planned, Mrs. A.: boating, hiking, wind-surfing, bungee jumping, ballooning, roller coaster riding, or just plain sightseeing. Here's your paper. And if I can be of any more assistance, please don't hesitate to call."

"How about shopping?" she said with a sly grin.

Jack winced and recovered. "Perfect day for shopping."

Bobbi was now awake and blushing over this surprise role play. As Jack headed for the door, she said, "Don't I need to sign for this?"

"Actually, it's complimentary this morning—compliments of the management."

"How nice. Listen . . . if you have a free moment, why don't you come back and join me?"

"Well, it's not exactly hotel policy. . . ."

"Perhaps it would make a difference if you knew I owned stock in this hotel, and I'm changing the policy right now."

"Well, in that case . . ." Jack said, leaping squarely onto the bed. Bobbi saw it coming and lifted the coffee safely into the air.

"I like the other guy better, Jack." She checked the tray for spills. "Do you think he'll be back anytime soon?"

"Maybe next weekend." Jack fluffed up a pillow and settled in with the paper.

"Why don't you wake me up like that every morning?"

"Really? You wouldn't get tired of it?"

"Try me," she said, and he knew she wouldn't. "So what shall we do today? Bungee jumping is definitely out."

"How about that amusement park up in New Hampshire? What's it called?"

"Cranberry Lake. We should save that for Alex's birthday. It's only a month away now. It won't be as special if we go today."

Just then Brook barged into the room. "Did I hear somebody say Cranberry Lake?"

"Shhh," Bobbi said, "not today. Good morning, baby. Come give me a kiss."

"I'm sure Alex wouldn't mind going again," Brook said after kissing her parents halfheartedly. "Oh please, Mom. A bunch of kids from school are going up there today. That would be so cool!"

Jack was suddenly ready to change his mind on the amusement park idea. "For you and them, maybe. Not for us," he stated. "You would have to lose us as soon as we got inside the park if your friends are going to be there. Kind of defeats the purpose of a family day, don't you think?"

"Very smart, Jack," Bobbi agreed. "You're catching on to this teenage thing."

"Well, I'm dropping her off three blocks from school now. Doesn't take a rocket scientist to figure this out."

"Dad, it was only a couple weeks ago that you walked me onto the school bus for the away game. I thought I was going to die!"

"I wanted to be sure it was the right bus," Jack said, looking for the sports section.

Brook rolled her eyes at her mother.

"Your father's right, Brook. We'd never have a family day at

Cranberry Lake with your friends there and you know that."

"Pleeeeease?" begged Brook, fighting a losing battle. "Trevor's even going."

"Oh, well, that settles it for sure," said Jack.

"Cranberry Lake?" chimed Alex, running in and jumping on the bed, prompting Bobbi to lift the coffee once again. "Today?"

"No Alex, not today," said Bobbi, and Alex got a sandwich kiss from his parents.

"Yuk!" he complained, wiping his face.

"I have an idea," said Jack. "What about Rockport? We haven't been there in a long time."

"Dad," said Alex, "isn't that where they have that awesome kite store? Could we get a kite and fly it on the beach like we did that one time?"

"Sure, and your mother can still shop. Are you game, honey?"

"It's not quite the shopping I had in mind, but . . . Brook?" she said, deferring to her daughter.

"Sure," Brook agreed flatly.

"Well," Jack concluded, "this is probably as close as we're going to get to a consensus. I suggest we get ready and out of here before anybody changes their mind."

～

Rockport is a quaint New England seacoast town barely twenty-five minutes by car southeast of the Acres home in Ipswich. It sits on the easternmost tip of Cape Ann, a sort of fatter, smaller Cape Cod north of Boston. To reach it you must pass through the larger, less attractive port of Gloucester until the village of Rockport comes into view, literally nestled into the rocks that form the jagged coastline of this charming eastern seaboard village. The small harbor is mostly populated with weathered fishing boats, lobster being the main attraction in the icy, deep purple Atlantic water. A string of small shops follows the peninsula north to Pigeon Point. Many of the shops share with upstairs renters the tiny narrow street that passes by their windows, and their Dutch doors are always open to traffic on the weekends.

Never in a hurry on days like this, the Acres family arrived in Rockport in time for a late lunch of clam chowder, followed by a stroll through the boutiques and the obligatory ice-cream cone along the way. Jack and Bobbi then left the children to explore on their own among the rocks off Pigeon Point after agreeing to a time and place to meet up again.

Most of the shops—with the exception of the tourist T-shirt and souvenir traps—were specialty art galleries, and the one that interested Jack the most was a new shop with detailed and exquisite maps of various topographies. The best sellers seemed to be the large, colorful maps of individual states of the Union, suitable for framing. Not a map person, Bobbi objected at first to bothering with this shop, and yet once inside, she spent a long time in front of a two-by-four-foot map of Florida.

"Trying to find Sam?" Jack asked as he walked up behind her.

"Sam and Uncle Albert, both. What is it about those islands that is so fascinating?" she said, staring at the Florida Keys.

"The fact that they string out there in the middle of nowhere? The fact that they are so small? The fact that they can all be connected by one two-lane road—that you can drive out there literally on the ocean? That's what fascinates me."

"No, I wasn't thinking of any of that. I was thinking of how surprised I was to find so many tacky places right there in the middle of paradise. Remember when we took a day trip down there two years ago on our vacation? Honestly, I don't think there was a motel on any of those islands that I would want to stay in."

"That's what I liked about it. It's not spoiled by tourism."

"Give me tourism any day."

"You folks vacation in Florida often?" the voice of the shop owner cut in as he strode over to join them.

"We have relatives there," Bobbi replied. "Hi. I'm Bobbi and this is my husband, Jack, and I think we'd like to buy this map."

"We would?" Jack raised his voice and eyebrows in surprise.

"It's only twenty-five dollars," Bobbi reasoned, "and I think it would look great in that spot across from your desk. It's got all the right colors for the living room."

Jack could only think of the picture that used to be there and how perfect he thought it was. He figured, however, that twenty-five dollars was a fairly painless replacement. "Sounds like a good idea to me," he agreed.

"Good," Bobbi said. "What frame would you recommend?"

"This is our standard black frame over here" said the owner. "That's a hundred and fifty dollars. We also have it in red mahogany for two hundred. All our frames include museum mounting good for the lifetime of the print."

"The black one would be best," Bobbi said, ignoring Jack's convulsive faces. "Can you have it ready by the end of the day?"

"I believe so. It's slow today. If it were the weekend, I'd say forget it. Come back at four-thirty and we should have it all ready for you."

"A hundred and fifty dollars to frame a twenty-five dollar map?" Jack asked once they were just outside the door. "We could frame a Rand McNally atlas and make a fortune."

"Those pieces are works of art," Bobbi said. "I like it because not everyone has a map on their wall."

"Gas stations do."

"Look, Jack, just trust me. The map will look great in that spot."

"But why couldn't we just buy the print and frame it ourselves?"

"Are you sure you want to try that again?"

Suddenly Jack remembered that even when he'd made the frame for the World War II poster at a do-it-yourself shop, it had cost almost a hundred dollars, and this print was even larger.

"As long as we won't have to rearrange the whole room again."

Bobbi turned to look into Jack's eyes. "It will be perfect."

When they reached Pigeon Point, they found the children playing near the water down an embankment of large, angular rocks. They waved to get their attention and sat down on a gull-stained wooden bench. It was an unusually mild day, and Alex was skimming pebbles on the calm water between breakers while Brook looked on.

"Ten to one I know what Brook is thinking," Bobbi said after a little silence.

"What's she thinking?" asked Jack.

"She's wondering what happens to all those rocks when they stop skipping."

Jack seemed confused by the obvious but didn't speak.

"That's the difference between you and me . . . even Alex and Brook, for that matter," she said, turning to face him so that the afternoon sun set the edges of her auburn hair on fire. "You and Alex will always be skimming along the surface of the water. Brook and I will always sink to the bottom."

They both turned their focus back to the children, and Jack asked, "Is that supposed to mean we're shallow and you're deep?"

"No, not at all. I didn't say 'deep'—I said 'bottom.' There's a big difference. You live in one reality, we live in another. You and Alex move freely along the surface of many things. We sink down wherever you stop."

Jack said nothing. He knew there would be more coming.

"Think about it, Jack. What's the first thing I've wanted to do every time we've moved to a new place?"

Jack thought of each of the three houses they had occupied during their marriage, and the one activity common to them all popped into his mind. "Change it."

"Exactly. I have to put my signature on it somehow. Where I am is very important to me. You don't really care where you are as long as you can perform certain tasks. Am I right?"

"I think so."

"Can you maybe understand why a place for Mom is important to me? And don't spiritualize it with heaven and all that. I know she's got a place there. I'm talking about me right now. I'm the one stuck in the here and now. Mom needs a place here for *my* sake—a place at least to be remembered by those of us who knew her. Besides, if you can't ever be rooted in life, you should at least get to be planted in the ground when you die instead of being scattered on the wind. Don't the Scriptures even talk somewhere about our bodies being seeds that are planted in the ground?"

"First Corinthians fifteen," Jack cited. "Death is like the planting of a seed that God later resurrects to a new body."

"See? That's just what I mean. If this body—when it dies—is like a seed, then . . . what do you do with seeds? You plant them. So we should have planted Mom in the ground, not burned her up and thrown her on the water. You wouldn't do that to a seed, would you?"

"I think it's just a metaphor, Bobbi."

"I'm not so sure."

Alex and Brook were starting up the embankment toward them. Jack and Bobbi let their conversation die and watched their children step and teeter along the jagged rocks. As the afternoon sun played on their faces, Jack and Bobbi both captured some snapshots.

"Dad, we want to fly the kite now," Alex said when he got within earshot. "Is it still in the trunk?"

"I think so." Jack dug in his pocket for the keys to the car. He started to throw them and then thought better of it. One drop and they'd be gone forever in the deep, rocky crevices.

"Will you come help us?" Alex said when close enough to take the keys.

"In a minute. Your mother and I are talking right now."

"You two are beautiful children," Bobbi stated with strength and simplicity. The children's faces glowed against the backdrop of the deep blue water and flushed with pride at their mother's compliment.

"Go fly a kite," Jack called to them as they ran off toward the car.

After a few minutes of taking in the beauty of the coastline, Bobbi spoke again. "Jack, I want to go down there."

"Down where? Florida? Why?"

"To find Sam and get Mom's ashes back before he does something stupid with them."

"Bobbi, we don't even know where he is, and it doesn't seem like he plans on telling us anytime soon. If you went down there right now, where would you even start?"

"I'd probably start at his house and see if I could find any evidence of where he was going. If that didn't turn up anything, Albert said they were going diving in the Keys."

"Oh, that narrows it down considerably."

"Well, they aren't divers. They've probably got to rent stuff—get some kind of license. You can't just strap on a tank and jump into open water. That much I know."

Jack shook his head in disbelief. "I think I remember reading somewhere that there are over three hundred dive shops in the Florida Keys."

"Got to start somewhere."

Alex and Brook came back into view down by the water. They had taken a path to the beach from the parking lot that avoided the rocks. Alex was holding the rolled-up kite and motioning to Jack to come help.

"Just a minute!" Jack shouted, and the children started unwrapping the kite on their own.

"Bobbi, you can't be serious. When are you going to find time for this?"

"I'm still working on that project in Naples. I can justify another business trip just about any time. I was even thinking of going down as early as tomorrow. The week after next is spring break. You could all join me next weekend."

Jack stared out at Brook and Alex, who were now having some kind of disagreement over the kite. "I've gotta go help them," he said. "Give me a chance to think about this. Want to come fly a kite?"

"Not that way. I'll go around through the hotel and meet you on the beach."

Jack kissed his wife and started down over the rocks. He was glad he had worn his hiking boots that day because the rocks were quite slippery. From the shoreline where he jumped down to the sand, he looked back up to see Bobbi still sitting on the bench, separated by jagged rocks that were impassable to her in her fine shoes. He waved and she waved back, smiling.

FIFTEEN

Big Mo

"You boys fixin' to go divin'?" a crusty gray-haired man inquired, looking Sam and Albert over as if they were not old enough to swim. "Got yer certificates?"

"I called you about the weekend course," Sam said.

"How old are you boys, anyway?"

The brothers looked at each other and then back at the old man behind the counter. The dive shop was nothing more than a shack across the street from the entrance to John Pennekamp Coral Reef State Park on Key Largo, the only underwater state park in the country. Scuba gear hung on the walls in a disorderly fashion, and pictures of underwater scenes peeked through the stacks of carbon-paper forms and goggles that crowded the glass-covered counter.

"We're younger than you, old man," said Sam.

"You over sixty?"

Sam and Albert did not reply.

"Gonna need a physical if you're over sixty."

"Who's the instructor here?" Sam questioned.

"You're lookin' at him. Name's Sarge."

"How old are *you*, Sarge?" asked Sam.

"Seventy-two, and I've got almost as many hours underwater as you boys been breathin' on land." It was a line he must have used on everybody, and it might have been pretty much true for most of his customers, who were probably half the age of the two men now standing in front of him.

"What about *your* physical?" Albert said jokingly.

"Every six months." Sarge sported a better physique under his faded red tank top than most men twenty or even thirty years his junior. He made Albert and Sam think they were ready for a rest home. "Sorry, boys. Insurance requires it. Here's the name of a clinic in town that will take care of you without an appointment. Have them fill out this form, and I can get you into a class this weekend."

"Guess we don't have much choice," Albert said.

"You can try somewhere else, but I guarantee you, it will be the same story. I have the only two-day course on the Keys. If you're in a hurry, better stick with me."

"We can rent everything we need, right?" asked Albert.

"Yep. Tanks, vests, fins, goggles, weights . . ." Sarge stared at Albert's round girth.

"Why didn't you tell me about this physical when I called?" Sam questioned.

"Didn't tell me you was old guys."

Sam and Albert stared speechlessly at the "old guy" behind the counter, and neither of them ventured a comment on the obvious. They decided to sign up for the course and left with the forms for their physicals, plus a training booklet they were supposed to read before their first lesson.

"Well, if he can scuba dive at seventy-two, I feel better about our chances," Albert stated on the way to the car. By the time they found a motel, it was too late to check on the clinic. It was only Wednesday, so they planned on getting their physicals the next morning, leaving them a day and a half to explore some of their old haunts on the Keys and scope out the bridge under which Sam was convinced they would find the ashen remains of his former wife.

"You didn't tell me there was going to be homework required for this trip," Albert said as the two of them sat outside their motel room in the twilight. Sam had agreed to refrain from smoking in the room.

"Aaaah," Sam waved him off, "I'm not doing mine. Never did; not about to start now."

The motel they found was a small one-story rustic with a thatched-roof patio area behind it next to a patch of tall palm trees. The patio might have been charming with its wrought-iron furniture and canvas umbrellas, except that it sat on a slab of unattractive concrete that afforded an exceptional view of the cluttered backside of a strip mall next to the motel. Nothing even close to the famous glamor of Key Largo that adorned the lyrics of so many popular songs. But Sam and Albert didn't care. They were not on vacation; they were on a mission, though not the same one. Albert didn't share Sam's intent on finding the box of ashes, but he did have his own objective—to take this rare opportunity to be with his estranged brother as far as it would go. Though he knew well how his brother could beat down his spirit, he was determined to not let Sam get to him this time.

"What do you think of our chances?" Albert asked.

"What chances?"

"Of finding the box."

"I have no idea," Sam said.

Albert let that typical Sam Dunn response dangle as his brother took a drag on a cigarette.

"How long do you expect to look for it?"

Sam chuckled through the smoke. "I have no idea."

"Are there any concerns . . . besides our age?"

"Are you concerned, Albert?" Sam looked his brother right in the face. "Do you want to go home?"

"I didn't say that. I'm just wondering what we're up against."

Sam leaned back in his chair, checked his cigarette ashes, and answered, "Shifting currents . . . maybe a hammerhead or two."

"Sharks? They don't come into these shallow waters, do they?"

Sam laughed again. "Well, sure they do."

Albert thought of his life back in Shaughnessy as an elder in his church. He thought of his relatively secure finances, his gratifying volunteer work helping minorities establish small businesses downtown. And though he still continued to tell himself he could never marry again, there had been, of late, a formidable challenge to that sentiment by the name of Irene that had been making some headway in his mind.

"Do you think you'll ever marry again, Sam?"

Sam looked at him as if he had just asked him to jump in the water and swim to Cuba.

"I'm sorry," Albert apologized. "It's much too soon for that question. I should know better."

"No, it's too *late* for that question. I shouldn't have married Betty in the first place," he said, grinding his cigarette butt into the concrete with his shoe, "but I won at the races."

"Come on, Sam. That wasn't the only reason you married Betty." But Sam was staring the doubt right out of Albert. "You were good to her," Albert kept trying. "There was more to it than that."

"I made good on my bet, that's all. And I can tell you that when it comes to women, all bets are off."

"Are you saying you regret marrying Betty?"

"You're darn right I do."

Albert stared at the pink sky filling in the gaps around dark palmetto branches. The conversation had taken the type of turn he dreaded, but he could not leave it alone. "You regret having someone love you? You regret having a reason to live? You regret waking up in the morning and having someone warm and breathing next to you?"

"If they're gonna up and die on me . . . you bet I do."

Sam's voice was now like a chain saw ready to level the entire stand of palm trees within view. Albert was trying hard not to get pulled down into his brother's pessimism, but it was difficult. It had always been. Albert collected his voice and tried to monitor it in controlled tones: "Then why are you so bent on finding Betty's ashes if you wish you'd never married her in the first place?"

Sam reached into his shirt pocket. "Something to do," he said, knocking a fresh smoke out of his pack and clicking his lighter.

Albert weighed the foolishness of diving in shark-infested waters for the sake of "something to do," and a major inequity filled his mind. Sam was asking Albert to risk his life for something that didn't seem to mean that much to him—neither the ashes nor his own life. *Something to do?* Albert thought better of it. He surmised there were other things at work in Sam that Sam wasn't even aware of. He seemed to be following some course of destiny that he could not admit to himself. He was contradicting himself mightily by going after his wife's remains against such formidable odds, but Albert chose not to point that out. He hoped that time would tell.

"You're going to kill yourself with those cigarettes, you know."

Sam watched the smoke float up to the palm fronds and disappear in the darkening sky. "So. . . ?"

"Is there something you haven't told me?"

"You mean am I sick or something? I'm just dying, that's all, same as you. Life is hazardous to your health, Albert. It's not cigarettes. Life causes it. Life causes death. Pardon my language but it—"

"You're right," Albert stopped him short of whatever language he had coming, and Sam looked a little surprised. "You're right," Albert repeated, happy to have suddenly found a way out of Sam's pessimism. "Life causes death. That's why you need to have a plan for your death, brother. What's your plan, Samuel?"

"I'll figure that out when I get there."

"That will be too late."

"Are you preaching at me again?" said Sam.

"You bet I am," Albert smiled, gathering strength.

"Don't." Sam waved his arms, and the smoke zigzagged. "You always call me Samuel when you preach."

"But I care about you."

"If you care about me, you'll spare me the sermons."

"If I care about you, Sam—and I do—I'll do nothing of the kind. You'll hear sermons from me until my dying day."

Sam had been blowing his smoke away from the conversation in the still night air, but this time he let the blue spirals drift slowly across Albert's face. "Now I remember why I haven't missed you these last thirty years."

Albert felt the stinging pain of that comment for a few moments, breathed the smoke, and then slapped his knees. "I think I'll go inside and read up on that diving manual." He stood up and headed toward the motel.

"You do that," Sam said, aiming his chain saw at the middle of Albert's back. "And read up some for me. I'm not doing any old man's homework!"

The next morning found the brothers at the medical clinic, only to discover there were no physicals being given that day due to the number of doctors sick or out on surgery. Sam made some comment equating sick doctors with dead morticians, and they signed up for Friday and decided to drive down the Overseas Highway and check out the Seven Mile Bridge. The harsh words and feelings of the night before now hung over them like a thin cloud. At least Albert could feel it. He never knew what Sam was feeling.

The two men were quiet as they ticked off the mile markers one by one—those small rectangular green signs that number the miles from 126 just south of Florida City down to 0 at the corner of Fleming and Whitehead streets in Key West, the end of the line. The mile markers are a simple way of determining location in the Keys, since there is only one road that connects just about everything. For instance, at MM 100, you are across from the parking lot of the Holiday Inn Key Largo Resort. At MM 84.5, you are at a feeding station for abandoned cats on Windley Key. At MM 78 you will find the Lignumvitae Key State Botanical Site on the bay side of the road and the Indian Key State Historical Site on the other. At MM 63 is Conch Key, and at MM 61 is Duck Key, a downscale name that disguises one of the few upscale residential areas on the islands. For the most part, however, this road is nothing but a 126-mile traffic jam of garish billboards, hamburger stands, strip malls, and trailer courts.

The silence in the car was not all due to the conversation the night before. Albert had a lock on thoughts rich with sunrises, warm breezes, a hundred shades of blue, and the feel of a big game fish on the other end of a line. "Two lanes to the end of the world," he said at last.

Sam made no reply. They approached a jogger on the shoulder, and Sam noticed Albert instinctively brace himself by grabbing the door handle and the seat cushion. He didn't relax until he spotted the runner safely disappearing in the side mirror of Sam's truck. It was the third jogger they'd passed, and Albert had behaved the same way each time.

"Still makes you nervous, doesn't it?" observed Sam.

"I think it always will." Albert sighed. "I'm glad you're driving with so many of them out today."

It was a runner who wasn't paying attention to traffic that had caused Albert to swerve and crash into a tree sixteen years earlier, taking the life of his dear Doris while leaving himself relatively unscathed. It had been his bitterest pill and the severest test of his faith and optimism.

Albert's ability to trust God in the face of such a violent, senseless tragedy was something Sam chalked up to blind stupidity. The greatest discrepancy the two brothers shared, in fact, was the manner in which each dealt with the painful loss of their mate. The same loss that had ultimately deepened Albert's faith had only served to harden Sam, proving different things to each of them. To Sam, losing two wives only confirmed a belief that if there was a God, He was out to make his life miserable, while Albert continued to hold that faith is not created or destroyed by circumstances, only shaped by them.

"Sometimes I want to run them over," Sam said, passing another jogger coming the other way. "They think they're gonna live forever."

Albert wanted to say something about Sam's forever, but held back. Was Sam's statement a gesture of love—some form of blind retaliation for his own pain? A rare show of empathy? He decided to take encouragement from it, regardless.

At MM 53 they crossed the Vaca Cut Bridge onto Vaca Key and into the city of Marathon, commercial hub of the Middle Keys. At the lower end of Marathon is the beginning of the Seven Mile Bridge. As they passed a large, modern white building with big blue letters spelling "Fishermen's" over the entrance, Albert said, "Isn't that a hospital?" Sam slowed his truck down and made a U-turn. Inside they found they could both get physicals right away, from which they received a clean bill of health for diving, although the doctor did warn Sam about his diminishing lung capacity from burning tobacco and Albert his diminishing heart capacity keeping all his fat cells happy.

Sam blew off the doctor's comments later in a puff of unruly smoke. They were sitting at the Mile 7 Grill, MM 47.5, northeast of Seven Mile Bridge, waiting for their lunch order to arrive. Beer cans laminated the walls behind thrashing blue marlin and sailfish, shellacked and shining, frozen in their final resistance to captivity. Albert ordered conch chowder and a fresh fish sandwich, and Sam, always the meat-and-potatoes man, picked the foot-long chili dog without the chili.

Their lunch was soon interrupted by two crusty fishermen at the bar recounting their early morning's expedition in the Gulf waters. Albert recognized the inflection as being from upper New England, probably New Hampshire or Maine. "Darned if that big one didn't get my tarpon today," said one of them. "Pulled in nothin' but his head. Bit him clean off, he did."

"Eh, from the size of that mouth, I'd say you had a six-footer on the line, at least," said his companion.

"He was a beauty, all right. Biggest mouth I ever had a hook in. That thief!"

"Sounds like Big Mo," another fisherman commented from the other end of the bar. "Where were you fishin'?"

"Just off Pigeon Key in the channel."

"That's right where he likes to hang out," said the man, shoving some money across the counter and limping toward the door on a wooden cane. As he approached the two fishermen, he stopped and added, "Rascal's got the rest of my leg."

The man hobbled out the door and the blood drained from Albert's face. "Who do you suppose Big Mo is?" he said to Sam just as the waitress stopped by with coffee.

"He's a fourteen-foot hammerhead shark that's pretty famous around here," she said, pouring out of the side of the pot. "Took off Durwood's leg ten years ago when he was young and stupid, divin' off the Vaca Cut Bridge."

"How do they know one shark from another?"

"Everyone knows Big Mo. He's the only hammerhead around that big. He's even big enough to see from the air. They spot him in the channel all the time. If you get close enough, they say you can see the gash over his left eye where Sarge tried to beat him off his catch once with a crowbar. He's always robbing the big ones. Conchs don't even fish this channel anymore," she concluded in a flurry. "Your order will be right out."

Albert looked at Sam who, to his dismay, seemed to be slightly amused by all this. "You find this funny?" Albert's voice was rising. "That man lost half his leg right where we're going to dive. I don't see any humor in that!"

"Adds a little spice to our expedition, doesn't it?"

"Just because you don't care about your life—"

"Wanna go home, Albert?" Sam interrupted.

The food came and Albert stared silently at his unappetizing fish sandwich while Sam bit into his hot dog, chewing vigorously. Albert had never noticed before that the dent on Sam's forehead popped out each time he bit down. For some reason it reminded him of the tin alligators he used to play with as a boy, the ones with the metal tongue inside of the hollowed-out figure that clicked loudly when you pressed and released it.

"You used to always say that, remember?"

"Say what?" Sam asked, clicking away.

" 'Wanna go home?' " quoted Albert, imitating Sam's dry

monotone. "You said that when we used to come down here and vacation with Crocky. You said it when we went camping as Boy Scouts. Anytime you wanted to do something dangerous, you'd tell me I could always go home. You got me into more trouble that way. Well, I didn't go home then, Sam, and I'm not going home now." He picked up his fish sandwich and bit into it, having sufficiently talked himself out of his fear and back into his appetite.

"Suit yourself," Sam replied.

The next time the waitress came by, Albert asked her what she meant by "conchs" going fishing. He was sure a conch was a variety of shellfish.

"A conch is what they call you if you live on the Keys and fish all the time," she explained. "Conchs are the locals."

"Like they've been conked in the head," grunted Sam.

"Exactly," said the waitress. "Everybody on these islands is a little bit nuts. You've got to be to live down here."

Back on the highway, Sam and Albert came almost immediately to the Seven Mile Bridge, which they crossed over twice, checking out as much as they could from the car.

"It could be anywhere down there." Albert looked helplessly out at the expanse of blue surrounding the little five-acre Pigeon Key that looked to him like no more than a dropping from its namesake. In his mind he pictured the donut box Sam described to him resting on the ocean floor with schools of tropical fish nibbling at its folds and Big Mo cruising by. "That's if the currents haven't carried it out to sea."

From the new bridge they were on, Albert could see the old bridge that paralleled it by no more than 300 yards. The new bridge passed by Pigeon Key, but the old one connected to it. The little island was once a construction and maintenance camp for the Florida East Coast Railway, the brainchild of Henry Flagler, who first connected the Keys by rail in 1912. The old bridge was closed now, a section of it about a mile beyond Pigeon Key destroyed by the hurricane of '35 and never rebuilt again.

"Can you get out to the island by that old bridge?" Albert wondered out loud.

"I imagine so. We passed a sign for a visitor center back at mile marker forty-eight."

The old bridge was a romantic landmark, its concrete arches forming an endless chain of half-circles cutting the water. When the water was still and the sun low, the arches joined with their amber reflections to make full circles on the water. Humphrey Bogart and Lauren Bacall headed off into their dreams through one of those circles in the movie *Key Largo*, and Arnold Schwarzenegger pulled Jamie Lee Curtis out of a car plunging off the missing section of the old bridge in *True Lies*.

At the visitor center they found that the two-mile stretch of old bridge to Pigeon Key was passable hourly on an original Florida East Coast railroad car named "Henry" (in honor of Mr. Flagler, of course) or on foot. No cars were allowed on the Old Seven Mile Bridge.

"Let's walk," Sam pronounced.

"Don't want to take old 'Henry'?" Albert asked.

"No thanks. I'll trust my own two feet."

Out on the bridge, the two brothers began to appreciate anew the expanse, the beauty, and, in some ways, the terror of this maritime region. Most people who love the sea live near it on the mainland. They might see the sea every day, but they do not feel dominated by it or overwhelmed. It is out of their window—it makes a statement—but they can turn their back on it at any time and face a whole continent. Here the sea dominates. It is only occasionally punctured by small pieces of land. In the Keys, even on land where you cannot see water, you still always feel like you are "in" the ocean, and you wonder if without warning your little dot of terra firma could ever be swallowed up by a rising tide. Turn your back on the ocean here, and you merely see the blue pick up again on the other side of your little piece of land-lock. The Keys are no place for the weak-stomached or the claustrophobic.

Albert was surprised to find how even on a solid bridge—over what should have been a familiar sea—the assault of endless blue had the power to make the fresh cobia he had eaten in his sandwich seem to flap alive in his stomach.

Before starting out, Albert had grabbed a map of the Middle Keys from the visitor center. When they reached the island, he spread the map out on a picnic table while Sam paced the water's edge as if looking for something.

"Come look at this, Sam," Albert called after a few minutes. Sam came and peered over Albert's shoulder. "Look at the water depths around here."

"Can't see a thing without my glasses."

"Well, there's nothing deeper here than eight or nine feet, and that's only the two thin channels on either side of the island. Most of the area directly around us—all the way out there to the new bridge—is nothing but three to five feet of water."

"How far out to the channels?"

"Maybe half a mile."

"So what are you saying?" Sam looked intensely at his brother.

"If he tossed the box from this side of the bridge near Pigeon Key, then it's more than likely sitting in four feet of water."

They both stared out at the new bridge that rose high in the southern sky like the skeleton of a huge dinosaur looming over the water.

"Are you thinking what I'm thinking?" asked Albert.

Sam nodded. "No need to scuba. Let's rent a boat and get started."

SIXTEEN

Presumed I.D.

About the time Jack told Alex to start reeling in the kite, a woman regained consciousness in the emergency room of Saint Mary's and All Angels Hospital in Gloucester, Massachusetts. She stared at the ceiling, her eyes seeking the familiar. Finding nothing, she closed them and ran quickly through the rooms of her memory. In each one, she found only nondescript walls without pictures. Slowly she became aware of a fierce onrush of people and equipment in the room. Loud voices. Rolling metal. Lifting her head, she was immediately struck by a strong pain in her right temple. She felt for the spot and found a huge bump and a small bandage. *More bump than scrape*, she thought, thinking cosmetically of her face.

A nurse hesitated by the white cotton curtain that partitioned her bed from the rest of the room and hurried to her side when she saw her eyelids flutter. "You're awake. That's a good sign." She checked the woman's pulse. "How are you feeling?"

"My head hurts."

"I'm sure it does. The doctor will be by to see you, but I'll be quite honest with you—it may take a while. There are more injuries here than we can handle right now and others more serious than yours. For that you can be grateful."

"What happened?"

The nurse looked at her with concern. "A car went out of control and struck a group of pedestrians. You were one of them."

"Trisha!" someone shouted, and the nurse excused herself after admonishing the woman to try and stay awake.

With some difficulty the woman lifted herself up on one elbow, and another pain shot down along her right hip. She felt there and found a large bandaged area. It seemed to her to be a scrape, something she might get as a child slipping and falling on the playground at school. Scanning the area around her bed, she spotted a purse sitting in an empty chair. Gingerly, she brought herself up to a sitting position and slid off the bed. The pain in her head shot down through her whole body as her feet hit the floor, and she had to steady herself by grabbing a wad of bed sheet that fortunately held to its tucking. In the small mirror on the wall she noticed another patient with a head wound as she picked up the purse and started back to the bed. Suddenly she thought better of it and pulled the curtain aside and entered the bustling room, purse clutched to her chest.

"Oh, miss," said the nurse called Trisha, looking up from a patient. "You shouldn't be up. Please wait for the doctor."

"I need the restroom," she said, and the nurse motioned to a door and told her to go straight back to bed when she was through. The woman passed through the door and into a bathroom across the hall. Inside, she sat on the toilet without lifting her hospital robe. Her hands flew into the purse and nervously pulled out a brown leather wallet, which she unsnapped and opened. In the plastic window was the Massachusetts driver's license of a Barbara Ann Acres, 14 Deer Run Road, Ipswich. She stared at the picture on the license and then in the restroom mirror and saw the same unfamiliar face staring back at her from both places.

⌒

Jack was anxiously winding kite string on a wooden spool with repeated glances back at the hotel, through which Bobbi was supposed to have passed some time ago to join them on the beach. *Great! Now they're both lost,* he thought, wondering about the wisdom of sending Brook out after Bobbi. He regretted it the moment he'd let her go, and now his apprehension continued to mount. The kite seemed to take forever to bring in from its low and distant post in the sky. They had it out as far as two jumbo rolls of string could take it. Alex had lasted for all of five minutes winding and was down at the water skipping rocks again.

When he wasn't worrying, Jack found himself remembering his own childhood and wishing for a favorite kite reel his brother had made in wood shop that had a crank and a platform for the spool so you could set the whole contraption on the ground and reel in your kite like a big fish. The thought of that reel made him revel for a minute in his love for kites—the force of all that weight of string, the pull of the wind, the kite wanting to break free, not knowing that to have its own way would be its demise. It was the tension itself that kept it flying, the trying to pull free against the hands holding it that made it soar. Pulling against someone—even God—wasn't so bad as long as you stayed connected.

Glancing back again at the hotel, Jack saw nothing but empty sand between him and the white porch with its green awnings and tamarack chairs, so he resumed winding the spool, pulling back the line repeatedly with the sweep of his hand like rowing with an invisible oar. Pulling and winding. Pulling and winding. And with each pull the kite flew higher on a lighter string until it was high enough to catch a fading ray of sun from over Jack's shoulder, making it burn a fluorescent orange kite-shaped hole in the gathering clouds. It was late enough in the afternoon that everyone had left the beach, and a chill had moved in with the darkening sky. The blue ocean deepened to purple, and farther out it met a cold gray horizon. It made Jack shiver and wish for a jacket. "Come on,

Alex," he shouted. "Time to go."

"Go where, Dad?" Alex shouted back. "Mom and Brook aren't back yet."

"I know. I want to go find them."

"They'll come back. They know where we are."

Jack wondered if his son was right. Looking for Brook, who was looking for Bobbi, might get them all lost looking for one another, but the feeling of something wrong was gnawing at his insides. *Probably nothing*, he told himself. *Brook has probably found her and they are off shopping somewhere, oblivious to the time. It's happened plenty of times before. So why am I worried? Was it the sirens?*

"Come on, Alex," he finally said when the kite was almost directly overhead, twisting and ducking with animation—fighting the last shred of string. "I've almost got the kite in and I'm getting cold. We'll wait for them in the lobby."

Kite finally in tow, they plodded through the sand, filling their shoes so that they had to stop on the porch and empty them out. Jack was still cleaning out sand from between his toes when the porch door slammed behind him.

"I can't find her anywhere," Brook said, coming toward them.

"Have you been in all the shops?" Jack snapped his sock on the side of the deck and wiggled his toes. Alex mirrored his actions in miniature.

"Every one."

Jack looked at his watch and saw that it was almost five o'clock. "We were supposed to pick up something at that map shop. Let's go there before they close and see if she's already been there."

They got to the shop just as the man was turning the sign in the window. "Hello," he said, cracking the door open. "If you're looking for your picture, your wife already picked it up."

"How long ago?" asked Jack.

The man called to someone in the back of the store. "How long ago would you say that woman picked up the Florida print?"

"Couple hours ago, at least" was the reply from inside.

"I don't understand it," said Brook. "I've been everywhere."

The woman who had spoken appeared at the door, and the man

opened it a little wider. She had a spray bottle in one hand and a towel in the other. "You can't find her?" she said.

"No."

"When did you last see her?"

"It was probably around three o'clock," Jack said.

"I don't mean to alarm you," the woman warned, "but you did hear about the accident, didn't you?"

"I heard some sirens," Jack replied.

"Sirens?" Alex said.

Had the children heard them, they would have wanted to go check it out for sure. Jack had been glad at the time that they were playing nearer the water where the breakers were drowning out the whine, so he didn't have to face the dilemma of being stuck holding three hundred yards of kite string while his kids pleaded with him to attend the scene of some potential crime or accident, unsupervised.

"A car went out of control just up the street and ran into a crowd of pedestrians," said the woman at the door. "I heard they took a number of people to the hospital, but then again, I don't know for sure. Hard to say."

"But . . . cars aren't even allowed on this road," Jack said nervously.

"It came down from that hill up there and shot right across the road. They think the driver had a heart attack. Terrible thing. Look, I hope I'm wrong, but you might want to check the hospital just to be sure."

"Where is the nearest one?"

"Saint Mary's and All Angels in Gloucester. Would you like to use our phone?"

"Thank you. That's very kind of you."

At this point Jack was thinking that the woman was being a bit of an alarmist and that, most likely, nothing was wrong. But he figured it wouldn't hurt to take her up on her offer and eliminate all doubt.

"Is Mom okay?" Brook asked, making Jack marvel that the

childhood notion of parental omniscience still functioned at the age of thirteen.

"I don't know, babe. That's what I'm going to find out."

Brook and Alex fanned out in the shop looking at maps while the woman led Jack to the phone and the man looked up the number. After some time holding the phone, Jack was told that the hospital had indeed admitted a number of people from an accident in Rockport, but to Jack's relief, Barbara Ann Acres was not one of them. Jack thanked the shop owners for their help and returned to the street, expecting to run into Bobbi any minute.

Three doors up they came upon the aftermath of the mishap. There were beads of headlamp glass scattered on the sidewalk, water seeping from a broken fire hydrant into the cobblestones around it, ashes of spent flares in the street, and personal articles splayed out on the ground. And down an embankment of jagged rocks between two buildings of three-hundred-year-old brick and mortar, Jack could barely make out in the fading twilight the shattered black frame of a large map of Florida.

In a café in downtown Gloucester, a woman who presumed herself to be Barbara Ann Acres searched through the contents of a purse for anything recognizable. Everything was out on the table: a hairbrush, address book, lipstick, keys, sunglasses, shopping receipts, a couple pens, a few jewelry items, and two tampons. Except for the tampons, nothing was familiar.

"I do that myself from time to time," said a waitress, suddenly appearing at the table.

"Do what?" the woman asked, a little startled.

"Go through my purse."

"Oh yes . . ."

"You wouldn't believe what I collect in there. Say, are you all right? That's a nasty bump you've got there."

"I'm fine."

"You weren't hurt in that accident up in Rockport, were you?"

"No, I . . . uh . . . slammed into a cupboard at home."

"Terrible thing, that accident."

"So I've heard. How did it happen?"

"They're saying on the news that it was an old man who had a heart attack at the wheel. Rammed into a whole crowd of people. They sent six to the hospital. One of them is critical."

"How terrible."

"Everyone's in shock around here. Things like this aren't supposed to happen in our little town."

"You hate to see something like that happen anywhere."

"Yes, but people get used to it in someplace like Boston or Philly . . . but Rockport? What can I get you, honey?"

"Just a cup of coffee would be fine."

"Regular?"

The woman hesitated. How did she drink her coffee? What was "regular" coffee anyway? "Yes, regular would be fine."

The waitress left her, and she started looking at the receipts in more detail. One was from a cleaners in Ipswich. Another was a parking receipt for a garage in Boston. Then she found an unpaid parking ticket, also from Boston, and a receipt from a store called MapWorld in Rockport. It was dated April 7. Looking up, she spotted a newspaper on the counter and asked the waitress who was on her way with the coffee if she could bring her the paper as well. The waitress set the paper and the cup on the table, and the woman stared long enough at the light beige-colored beverage to make the waitress ask if there was anything wrong.

"What's this?" she asked.

"Regular coffee. You must be new to this part of the country. Up here cream and sugar is regular."

She took a sip and was convinced that Barbara Ann Acres did not drink coffee "regular," even if she had a Massachusetts driver's license. "I'm sorry, could you please bring me a cup without cream and sugar?"

"Certainly. No problem."

The newspaper matched the date on the Rockport receipt. *What was I buying?* She picked up the receipt and it read "16×20 map of Florida . . . $25.00, black frame . . . $150.00." *Now, what would I want with a map of Florida that big?*

Something about Florida immediately drew her. In the same way that she knew Barbara Ann Acres drank black coffee, she knew that Florida was very important. As soon as the coffee came back black, she got an idea. Scanning the address book she found two Florida addresses, a Sam and Betty Dunn and a Will and Jackie Brewster, both of Cocoa Beach. At the pay phone, she got no answer at the Dunns', but a female voice picked up the phone at the Brewsters' residence and she took a deep breath.

"Hi, Jackie, this is Barbara. How are you?"

"Barbara. . . ? Barbara who?"

"Barbara Acres."

". . . Bobbi?"

Bobbi, the woman repeated in her mind. She thought quickly. "Just wanted to see if you liked it."

"You'll never be anything but Bobbi. Barbara's too boring."

"Guess I just felt bored today. . . ."

"*That's* something I've never known you to be. You must be on the road. Are you back in Florida missing your family again?"

"You guessed it." She had to go along with the explanation, though she wasn't missing a family she didn't know she had. The Florida connection was taking on more significance every minute. On the back of the MapWorld receipt, the woman had found flight numbers and times to Cocoa Beach scribbled along with an Avis rental car confirmation number for the next day. "Bobbi" was planning a trip down there. Perhaps she could find out why.

"Well, I'm glad you called," said the voice on the line. "We tried to reach you at home a while ago but only got your machine. We've heard from Sam—well, not Sam, exactly, but Albert called yesterday."

"Really? What did he say?"

"Just a minute—here's your brother. I'll let him tell you."

So Will is my brother, the woman thought, *but who is Sam?*

"Bobbi?" A male voice came on the line. "Are you back in Naples again?"

"Yes," she said, relieved that he had offered her a place to be.

"Maybe we can see you this time around."

"Well, I'm not sure . . ."

"I know, you're busy. Actually, if you've got any time to spare at all, you might want to consider going down to the Keys. I think I know where you might be able to find Sam."

"Really? Where?"

"Uncle Albert called here yesterday—you *did* know that Albert was coming down to help Sam try and find Mom, didn't you?"

"Yes." *It's easier going along with everything*, she thought to herself. *But why doesn't he know where our mother is?*

"That's a story in itself, isn't it—those two together after all these years? At least now with Albert along we might get more information. Pop certainly won't be telling us anything."

Sam is my father? Bobbi's head was swirling. *This is all happening too fast.*

"What *is* going on?" Bobbi hoped he'd get back to her mother.

"Sam's now convinced that Mom is on the bottom of the ocean somewhere in the Florida Keys."

Oh great! "And how did she get there?"

"Apparently that J.W. Dean character chucked her off one of the bridges. Can you believe that?" Will asked in amazement.

What kind of family is this? Throwing bodies off of bridges? Am I in the Mafia? She rubbed her forehead in frustration.

"Bobbi—you still there?"

"Yes, I'm here. So you think I should go down there? What do you think *I* could do?"

"Well, you know Sam—he's gonna do what he's gonna do. I don't really care what happens to Mom's remains, but I know you do."

You bet I do! Somebody threw my mother over a bridge, and my brother doesn't care? Do I have to be related to these people? She took a breath. "Did he tell you where?" said the woman, trying hard to stay composed.

"Albert said something about the Seven Mile Bridge. It would be the longest one, of course. I think their chances of finding anything are pretty slim, but Sam is persistent."

"What do you suppose he's going to do if he finds her?"

"Beats me why he's so bent on it. He's got something up his sleeve. That's why you might want to get there first—just in case you might not like it."

The woman contemplated his words. *I must be in the Mafia; these people seem experienced at dealing with bodies.*

"Oh, I almost forgot," he went on. "Sam's been getting a lot of mail at the house for J.W. Dean Ministries. Can you believe that?"

"No, I can't." *Forget the Mafia. We have a ministry now.*

"You don't suppose Sam and J.W. have become some sort of friends, do you?"

"I'd believe anything right now."

"We've opened some of the mail and found checks. People still send money to that scoundrel! Do you suppose he's using Sam's address to keep the police from confiscating the money?"

"I wouldn't know," said the woman known as Bobbi. *Scratch the ministry; now the police are involved.*

"So are you thinking about going down there?"

"To the Keys? Well . . ." she hesitated, "what do you think?"

"I think Sam's become obsessed with this whole thing. I think it's time someone talked some sense into the man. I don't know if anybody can, but you've had the best success in the past. He seems to listen to you. I don't get what the big deal is anyway. If that Dean character threw Mom back in the ocean, then why not leave her be? It's all the same ocean, for heaven's sake."

You mean she's been thrown in once already? The woman heard some talking in the background and then Will continued: "Jackie just reminded me it wasn't Mom we threw in the first time, but you know what I meant."

"Sure . . ." *Now I know these people are crazy.*

"Sam and Albert are no spring chickens either. Diving at their age . . . Bobbi, are you okay? You're awfully quiet."

"I . . . I'm just a little thrown by all this, that's all."

"I know. Pretty wild, isn't it? How's Jack?"

"He's fine."

"And the kids? You must miss them."

"I always do."

"Well, I won't keep you. You sound pretty tired. Let me know what you decide."

"Thanks, Will."

"I'd go down there with you, but I just can't break away from the marina right now."

"I understand. Seven Mile Bridge, right?"

"Yes. It's all of seven miles, too, but finding two old guys out there shouldn't be that hard. I'll let you know if I hear anything more from Albert. Are you at the Ritz again?"

"Of course." *At least this Bobbi has class.*

The woman hung up the phone and made four more calls. One to her home in Ipswich—she got the number off her checks—followed by a string of calls to American Airlines, Avis rental car, and finally a call for a taxi to the airport. It was strictly impulsive on her part. She thought about reuniting with her husband and children, but a voice-mail message at her home was of a man's voice she did not recognize, and the thought frightened her. Though she had a longing for them, the idea of meeting her husband and children for the "first" time was greatly unsettling. Besides, she had all these questions about her family that she preferred to answer for herself, and there was already a reservation to Cocoa Beach in her name for the next day. For some reason she had been planning this trip alone before she got bumped on the head; she would go ahead and take it. Perhaps she would find out why in the process. The Sam Dunn in her address book was obviously her father, and the same Sam was looking for her mother, who had been thrown over a bridge at least twice into the Florida Keys. She would go to his house and see what she could learn about herself and this bizarre family. And she would go right away, on the evening flight, before anyone she knew found her.

SEVENTEEN

American in Gloucester

The emergency room of Saint Mary's and All Angels Hospital was still in a state of confusion when Jack walked up to the admitting desk at his wit's end. Two of the accident victims were still in emergency surgery. The driver of the runaway car had been airlifted to the Taft Clinic in Boston for a triple bypass operation and multiple head injuries. It was a miracle he was still alive. The nursing staff was overtaxed, and the usually pleasant young emergency room receptionist was ill-prepared for Jack's agitated nature.

"No, you *don't* understand. She *has* to be here."

"Sir, I don't know what to tell you. We have everyone accounted for, and there was no one by that name admitted today." Her voice was so tiny and childlike and on the verge of breaking that it was impossible for Jack to push her any farther. "What makes you so sure she's here?" the woman said timidly out of the tense silence.

Jack looked over at Brook and Alex where he'd left them in the waiting area already crowded with relatives and friends of accident victims. Brook was watching him with a worried look. Alex was watching TV. "We were in Rockport this afternoon." He was calmer now, trying hard to be reasonable by flattening his voice. "I haven't seen my wife since just before the accident. There was a framed picture that she picked up from a store three doors down from the scene of the accident smashed on the rocks on the other side of the street. I went back and checked with the store; it's the only one like it they've sold today. Now, if you found a picture you knew your wife had in her possession, smashed on the rocks at the scene of a place where numerous pedestrians were rammed by a runaway car, and she hasn't turned up anywhere in three hours, what would you think?"

Tears slowly began to form in the young receptionist's eyes as Jack systematically laid out his predicament. She had seen too much for her own sensibilities that day, and the calm yet intense desperation of the man in front of her pushed her emotions beyond the breaking point. It might have been easier had Jack yelled at her, but this was too real—too helpless—the way anyone feels at the hands of forces beyond their control. She bit her lip and spoke with her last ounce of composure before turning away quickly. "Just a minute, please."

Jack could only stand there and wait.

"What's happening, Daddy?" Brook was suddenly next to him, slipping her arm around his waist and trying to disappear underneath his arm. He wrapped her up in it tightly.

"They don't seem to know anything about Mom here," he said.

"God does." Brook said it into his shirt at one of those critical times when only children seem to be able to say the right thing and get away with it.

"You're absolutely right." Jack was suddenly steadied by her confidence. "God knows where she is," he said in a deliberate manner, as if each word was a leg that his hope could stand on. "I just wish He'd tell me."

The receptionist returned with red eyes and a nurse. She resumed her post behind the glass admittance window, and the nurse came through the doors from the emergency room and confronted Jack directly. As she reached out her hand, Jack noticed her name tag: *Trisha*. He let go of Brook to shake her hand.

"Mr. Acres, may I speak with you privately, please?"

Jack didn't like the sound of that. "If you mean without my children, no."

"Very well. You may all come with me."

Jack motioned to Alex, and the nurse led them down a short hallway where there was a vacant room. Jack's heart was pounding emphatically as they entered it, and Brook's fingernails dug into his arm.

"Mr. Acres," the nurse inquired as soon as they were settled in the room, "is your wife about my height with reddish brown hair?"

"Yes," Jack replied immediately, Brook's grip tightening.

"Can you remember what she was wearing today?"

"Yes. A long black dress, pleated at the bottom." He just described two-thirds of his wife's working wardrobe. She was always striking when she went out the door and always overdressed for New England.

"With crescent-moon buttons," added Brook.

"Then I think I know what happened to her."

"Is she all right?"

"Yes, I believe so. She just isn't here."

Brook's nails relaxed a bit, leaving four indentations on the inside of Jack's arm. Jack, numb to the pain, stared quizzically at the nurse.

"Your wife was unconscious when she came here. All her vital signs were good, but she had a severe bump on her right temple and a bruise on her right hip. I tended to her until I was sure she was not in any immediate danger. There were other patients demanding more attention, and as long as she was unconscious, there was nothing more to do until a doctor could look at her. The second time I checked in on her, she was awake. I told her to stay awake for a doctor, and a few minutes later she was up and walking, looking for a bathroom. I could not leave the patient I was with right then, so I directed her to the bathroom and told her to go right back to bed when she was through and lie down. Unfortunately, that was the last I saw of her. I'm so sorry we lost track of her, but it was like a war zone in here. We had three people in life-threatening situations, and clerical duties were simply not our first priority."

"You mean, she left the hospital?" Jack felt stunned and relieved at the same time.

"Way to go, Mom!" Alex exclaimed.

The nurse looked at him in surprise.

"She hates hospitals," Jack explained, looking for a place to sit down and think. Brook shadowed him and found a comfortable spot on his knee as he sat in a cold metal chair. Alex, satisfied that his mother was out of danger, started staring at the charts on the wall, paying close attention to the one on human reproductive organs.

"But where would she go?" Brook asked.

"And what would she do?" Jack wondered. "Take a cab back to Rockport? Hole up in a restaurant and call home? We should check our messages."

"You probably should be prepared for the fact that your wife may have temporary amnesia," the nurse said. "As soon as one of the doctors is out of surgery, I will have him brief you on the possibilities."

"You mean she could be wandering around out there and not know who she is?" Jack said.

"It's possible. She was somewhat disoriented when I spoke with her."

"She's always disoriented in hospitals."

"I bet I know where she is," Brook stated. "She's probably found a nice hotel somewhere."

"No, she's shopping," Alex said, still absorbed in the diagrams on the wall of the male and female anatomy.

Jack thought of money and credit cards—how she would get along. "Did she have her purse?"

"Her purse was near her bed," said the nurse, "and it's gone now."

While waiting for a doctor to brief him on his wife's probable condition, Jack was asked to give a complete description of Bobbi to the police, who were still in and out of the hospital finishing up their reports on the accident. Finally a doctor was available to answer whatever questions he could. Of course, all questions and answers were hypothetical, since no one was even sure of Bobbi's actual condition.

As they left the hospital and drove around aimlessly scanning the streets, Jack pictured Bobbi homeless somewhere, her greatest fear come true. He kept slowing down to take a second look at street people and bag ladies.

Brook contested him. "Dad, remember what the doctor said, she may have lost her memory but she hasn't lost her mind. Mom wandering the streets would be out of her mind. We're wasting our time. We should check out all the fine hotels and restaurants near the hospital."

"You're probably right," Jack conceded, and so they returned to the hospital and fanned out over a five-block circumference. There were two hotels and three restaurants, and no one fitting Bobbi's description had been seen in any of them that afternoon. There was one café they overlooked, based on the fact that they all three agreed that Bobbi would never go into such a tacky place. But with no more options, they decided it was their only unturned leaf. The first waitress they talked to identified her immediately.

"Yeah, she left here about an hour ago. Big bump on her head. Nice clothes too. We don't get people dressed like that very often in here."

"Did she say anything about where she might be going?" Jack asked excitedly.

"No. She spent some time on the phone and then left in a taxi."

"Can you remember anything else that might give us a clue as to where she was going?"

The waitress thought for a minute but only shook her head.

"Dad, she's got her purse," said Alex. "I bet she found our address and took a taxi home."

Jack was embarrassed by the reasonableness of this suggestion that had somehow escaped him. Before leaving the café he used the phone to call home again. It was only a twenty-minute drive; she should already be there. He found nothing except the same message on the answering machine from Will about hearing from Sam and Albert in Florida. He had already checked the messages once from the hospital. Sam and Albert's being in Florida was the last thing Jack was concerned about right then. Nevertheless, buoyed by the new information, they all decided the best thing was to go home.

All the way there, they encouraged each other with the good side of what they knew. Someone had actually identified her. She was alive and well enough to function. The doctor had said that if she was able to move about on her own, the chances were good that she would regain her full memory at some point, though it could come in pieces or all at once. Perhaps she was already at home and uneasy about answering the phone. But unfortunately, their mutual bolstering was met by an empty house.

"What should we do now?" Brook asked.

Jack had already been thinking on the way home that they should have gotten more information from the waitress about the taxi. If they knew what taxi company it was, they might be able to narrow it down to the actual driver. That threw them all into a search of all the taxi companies that could have possibly serviced Gloucester. No one could produce any reports of a pick-up at that particular café. Nor was the waitress that identified Bobbi still on duty. She had left five minutes before Jack called, and there was no answer at the home number the café manager was kind enough to give him.

Jack kept punishing himself with "Why didn't I think to ask her what cab company it was when we were right there in front of her?" and the children had no comfort for his remorse. He called the police and reported the waitress's testimony, and they said they would keep checking the taxi companies in town.

Finally at a loss, Jack rang up their closest neighbor, Sally McDermott, to see if she might have seen Bobbi come home and leave. She hadn't seen anything, and between her and her mother, Lyla, they didn't miss any comings or goings in the neighborhood. Sally invited herself over, and Jack didn't turn down the company. The idea of adult companionship right then was comforting, even if Sally was a bit of a busybody and prone to easy agitation. Sally's husband, Jake, was off playing hockey on available ice time, but he hardly ever spoke anyway. Lyla, a retired nurse, followed Sally over with a flask of scotch and two glasses, and for the better part of an hour, Jack was treated to colorful stories of her experiences with amnesia patients in her raspy, thick New England accent. The spry woman washed each major point down with a swallow of scotch, and each time she did, she offered the other glass to Jack.

"Do you good," she kept saying, prompting Jack to have to keep turning her down.

"No thanks, Lyla. I need a clear head right now."

Then the children started in on all the movies they could think of where people had forgotten who they were.

"Dad," said Brook, "you know Mom loves that movie *American in Paris*, where that lady gets hit on the head and wakes up believing she's a famous novelist in Paris researching a book and gets sucked into a real spy story."

"Yeah, and what about *While You Were Sleeping*," chimed Alex, "where that guy gets hit on the head and almost marries someone he doesn't even know."

"Yeah, but then she falls in love with his brother," Brook said dreamily. "I love that movie."

"*Overboard,*" said Sally. "That's the best one. Remember, with Goldie Hawn?"

"Oh yes," said Brook excitedly. "That's when she forgets she's high-class, and some unemployed construction worker tries to convince her she's his wife. He gets her cooking for him, doing the laundry and the dishes. I used to always think of Mom when I saw that movie. She'd be just like that."

"No, she wouldn't," said Alex. "She'd never do it. She'd tell the guy to get a job and a maid and walk out of the house."

"Yeah, but he had her trapped, remember?" argued Sally. "She couldn't get away."

"Mom would never allow herself to be trapped," Brook stated proudly.

Jack finally butted in. "Look, if you guys are trying to cheer me up, you're not succeeding. Now I've got Bobbi strapped to an unemployed taxi driver and on her way to Paris." Everyone would have laughed except he said it in a tone that made it anything but funny. Sally got up and started rinsing dishes that had already been rinsed.

"I'm sorry," Jack said. "I just wish I could *do* something."

Just then the phone rang and everyone jumped. Brook got to it first. "Hello? Just a minute. It's for you, Dad. It's the police."

"Mr. Acres," said the voice on the other end. "This is Sergeant Hamill at the Gloucester Police Department. We've just located a driver from Black and White Cab who says he took a woman matching your wife's description to the airport tonight around five o'clock."

"The airport? You sure it was her?"

"Right down to the crescent-moon buttons."

EIGHTEEN

Sam's Place

J.W. chalked it up to divine coincidence when he discovered that Barbara Walters was having a TV special on religion in America. He requested a trip to the television room, curious to find out if his own circumstances had landed him in the big league news. The promo had mentioned names such as Billy Graham, Jimmy Swaggart, Jerry Falwell, and J.W.'s personal hero, Jim Bakker.

J.W. felt rebuked, however, when an old clip of Jim's interview from prison came on the TV. He had forgotten how serving time had created such a personal catharsis for Bakker. Suddenly J.W. was sure, as he gazed intently at the TV, that he was the only man in America who was capable of mirroring the pain of Jim Bakker, for every word of remorse and contrition uttered by the defrocked evangelist was echoed in the heart and mind of J.W. Every tear found a salty counterpart down his face, for he, too, was a prisoner, watching from miles away in a faded blue convict shirt. The only difference between his shirt and the one Jim Bakker wore on television was the number stenciled over his pocket. It didn't matter whether or not Jim Bakker's tears were real; his tears were genuine. No glycerin here; no theater. No need, because no one was watching.

J.W. had also forgotten how gaunt Jim Bakker had looked. Gone was the boyish grin, the cocky turn of the lip, the raucous laughter, the full, bushy head of black hair he had sported during his PTL years. The man he was watching on television was old and gray and wrong. And that's just how he said it. "I Was Wrong." It was the title of Bakker's book, and J.W. couldn't help but feel those exact sentiments. He was wrong to fool the people. He was paying the price.

Watching Jim Bakker on Barbara Walters' special turned out to be J.W.'s penance. He saw himself on the screen. He watched Jimmy admit that he had misrepresented the Scriptures, and J.W. knew what that was all about. He watched Jimmy admit that he wasted millions of dollars on an extravagant lifestyle and that he twisted the truth to justify it, and J.W. knew that had he been as successful as Jim Bakker, he would have done the same thing. He watched Jimmy avoid trashing Tammy Faye, even though Barbara Walters kept setting him up for it, and he admired Bakker's refusal to fall into that trap. *Better than I would have done*, he thought. He watched Jimmy defend himself on a few accounts, pleading ignorance for things he should have known about, and J.W. saw himself doing the same. And when Barbara Walters asked the final biting question: "Jimmy, how do we know you're not conning us right now?" J.W. didn't hear Jimmy's answer because he was too busy forming his own answer in his head. "You don't, Barbara," he said out loud to the TV. "You don't."

J.W. Dean returned to his cell and to the three books that had been his company for the last three weeks. One was the Bible, and the other two were on snake handling—the real thing. J.W. Dean was done with quackery. He had even given his imitation rattle-snake-skin boots to his cousin in Port Mayaca, the only person besides Sam who had visited him in prison. J.W. had decided that if he ever handled a snake again, it would be a real one—a poisonous one with the power to bite quickly and painfully—like real snake handlers did. Life or death.

He also sat down that night and wrote his confessional:

> *I am sorry for all those I have led astray. The Bible says God is light and there is no darkness in Him at all. However hard you squeeze darkness, you just can't get any light out of it. I was wrong to think that I could make people believe in God by fooling them. It's because of me that He took Bonnie. It should have been me who got bit instead of her. God saw to it that a real snake put an end to my lie. I was wrong. I beg the forgiveness of any I have misled and count on nothing but the saving grace of Jesus on the cross for my own salvation.*

When J.W. presented it to Harvey Finklestein, wanting him to publish it, Harvey would have nothing of it. "Whose side are you on here?" Harvey asked when he read it during one of his regular jail visits. "I'm trying to defend you and you keep telling me you are prepared to pay for Bonnie's death. Will you please quit talking like that! What do you need me for, then? Go before the DA and take what they give you. Save us all the trouble."

"But I didn't kill her."

"Well, then stop talking like you did."

"But I did lie to the people, and God punished me with the snake. It should have been me."

"Oh, that's good. Shall I call God as a witness?"

That actually got J.W. thinking how he might call God as a witness in his life with real poisonous snakes, but he didn't say anything about that to his lawyer.

"Look, J.W.," Harvey said, "I'll stay with this thing for two more weeks. If I can't turn up anything new in your favor in that period of time, I'm off the case. You can get someone else to represent you or meet your beloved sentence alone for all I care." And with that he snapped his briefcase closed and called the guard.

The case against J.W. was mounting, and Sheriff Buford

couldn't have been happier. The DA had sworn testimony by three members of the congregation that J.W. did not handle any snakes on the night Bonnie died. In retaliation, J.W.'s lawyer had searched every congregation in Florida where the Deans had handled snakes, to find someone who would come forward and claim they had seen only Bonnie handle on other occasions as well. So far no one had, except for an overweight, emotionally unstable, middle-aged divorcee who found it impossible to conceal, at the mere mention of J.W.'s name, a mountainous crush on the handsome, silver-haired evangelist. "I wouldn't touch that witness with a ten-foot pole," said Harvey Finklestein. Then there was the hasty cremation to explain, the falsified death certificate, and J.W.'s quick exit from town. Not to mention his reputation for flashy women and his ambition to create his own television empire that was no secret to anyone who followed J.W.'s ministry.

The DA was prepared to show that Bonnie Dean would never have fit into the grandiose dreams of her husband. Where was the thick makeup, the false eyelashes, the bouffant hairdo that was standard equipment for this tacky charade they called "Christian television"? Bonnie didn't even have the personality for a makeover. Bonnie was plain Jane right down to her flat chest, flat hair, and flat personality. J.W. was going nowhere with this woman and anyone could see that. A perfect motive for death by coral snake that Brother Dean, of course, could get away with by attributing it to God's sovereignty. J.W. may have thought he could hide his act behind the wild circus of his reptilian sideshow, but this DA and police chief were on him like glue. The DA was also digging up the Mallory Blaine affair with some success in the news media, and what the news nibbled on, the tabloids gorged.

⌒

Little did any of them know that the key to J.W.'s release was at that moment thirty thousand feet in the air on her way to Cocoa Beach, Florida, in search of her memory and her mother. In her hand was a King James Version of the Bible she had commandeered from the magazine rack in the rear of the plane. Perhaps it was the

Bible, or perhaps it was the altitude—or some combination of the two—but the mind of Barbara Ann Acres was on the rebound. Bobbi was coming back, and the remarkable thing about this was *how* she came back. The mind of Bobbi returned in blocks, like giving character to the rooms of a house, one by one. Suddenly there would be pictures on the wall and furniture in one room, while the very next room, even the rest of the house, might still be bare. This provided Barbara with the rare opportunity of focusing on one thing at a time without any distraction. And for Bobbi, whose mind normally operated on a number of things at once, this was a rare opportunity indeed. To herself, however, she was not yet "Bobbi." That wouldn't come until she saw pictures of herself in Sam's house in Cocoa Beach. Right now, she was Barbara . . . Barbara Ann. . . .

Barbara Ann Brewster, a child slightly overweight, with a tendency toward boy friends—not boyfriends. Boys were buddies to her. They liked to hang out at her house. They liked her mother as much as they liked her (maybe more), and she remembered resenting that. They played football in her backyard, so to keep up with them—or perhaps to keep them at all—she played too. She skinned her knees, bloodied her nose, and stuck up for them while they dated softer, finer girls with smooth knees and mothers who worried about who their daughters went out with instead of inviting them over and making them part of the family. Somehow she made it through two years of college on intuition and speed (the drug), and then the obligatory social wedding from which a real marriage never materialized. That's when God had entered the picture—when she was divorced and disillusioned—and that's the room she was exploring now somewhere over North Carolina with the Bible open on her lap.

It all seemed to start just like the first book: "In the beginning . . ." He was there in the beginning, even though she did not know it, and He had been there all along. Now, with little else on her mind, He was all she could see. And she saw Him everywhere. She looked out the window at the clouds and saw His hand holding them up. She looked at the older woman next to her and saw His face etched in hers. She looked at the book lying on her lap and saw His love reaching out to her from every page. Suddenly she found herself surrounded by Him, overwhelmed by His Spirit like that first time He had come to her in the night of her confusion and loneliness. She wasn't even aware of the tears running down her cheeks until the woman in the next seat handed her a tissue.

"Are you all right, dear?"

"Oh yes, I'm more than all right."

"So they are good tears, then?"

"Yes."

"I like good tears the best," the woman said. "The older I get, the more I realize they're all good."

"Is that right?" asked Barbara, sniffling and wiping her nose.

"Tears keep the wounds clean so God can heal them quicker."

That only brought more water to Barbara's eyes. "I don't even know what my wounds are except for this bump on my head, and I'm still crying."

"What a lucky child," the woman softly commented. "What a fortunate child. You don't know what your wounds are, but you get to have them do their work on you anyway."

"Yes. I'm sure I do know—it's just that I lost my memory."

"I know what you mean. That's the problem with this world. No one knows how to suffer anymore. Suffering used to be a privilege. Now it's mostly an inconvenience."

Barbara looked at the woman more closely. She was probably in her eighties. Her eyes had clouds over them, but there was light coming from behind the clouds. In the margin of the open *Guideposts* magazine she was reading, the woman had scrawled several times, "I have read this page." Here they were, two women, previously unknown to each other and separated by decades, who had lost their memories, experiencing God and His ways with explicit clarity.

Barbara wasn't sure why she was flying into Cocoa Beach, except that's what Bobbi had already planned before the accident. Barbara's interest was in the Florida Keys, where two old men were scanning the ocean floor for her mother, for the purpose of doing who knew what with her body should they ever find her. Had she been going straight to the Keys, she would have flown into Miami. But Sam's house was in Cocoa Beach, and Barbara figured Bobbi was going there first for some reason—a reason that she hoped would become clear once she got there.

It was after midnight by the time she reached the gate of the Royal Golf Estates where Sam lived, and she had to grapple for answers to the guard's questions.

"Who are you visiting?"

"The Dunn residence."

The guard had a big grin on his face and ducked down to get a better look in the car window. "Wait a minute. . . . Aren't you Sam's daughter?"

"Uh . . . yes." And she must have looked surprised for a second. Then she thought quickly: "You have a good memory."

"Don't you remember me?" he said, appearing to be a little hurt. "Joe Paggliono—the former golf pro here."

"Oh, of course!" Barbara said, and for some odd reason, she remembered right then a tidbit of insignificant trivia to anyone but the man standing in the shack: "You're 'Pro Joe'!"

Pro Joe stood there basking in his recognition.

"So . . ." Barbara motioned to the gate. "Do I get in?"

"Sure thing. You know Mr. Dunn's not home."

"Yes. I'm picking up some things for him. I'll be seeing him soon in the Keys."

"How nice," he said, starting the gate up. He was still smiling proudly as she drove by.

The house was easy to find. It was a green house on a street of long, low-slung homes in shades of pink, yellow, and mauve, if not white. All the houses had ground-level lights set in their front-yard gardens, along paths to their driveways, even lights shining on the walls that put the whole house on nocturnal display. Sam's was a sensible house with lots of palmetto and high elephant-leaf plants hiding most of its unlit face. The front door was locked, but under the doormat in the back she found the proverbial "hidden key" she was hoping for. Immediately upon entering the house, she simultaneously entered another room in her memory. It hit her all at once with such force that she had to sit down and take it in.

Three feet from where she sat was the spot where her mother had died. Betty had been in a coma before Bobbi had arrived but showed renewed signs of life and recognition as soon as she heard her daughter's voice at the door and smelled her perfume. Her neighbor, who was right next to her at the time, said she saw a change in Betty the minute Bobbi came in the room. She perked up.

Now it was as if Barbara could smell the smell of death again, see the vacant face, hold the bony hand with the bruised, wrinkled skin. For three days she had talked to her mother—talked about anything and everything and sometimes nothing at all. It wasn't difficult because they had always talked easily when they were together. Barbara learned to "read" significance into her mother's placid face—a slightly raised eyebrow, the twitch of an eyelid, or the quiver of her lips. Then Jack, in a phone conversation, had asked if anyone had given Betty permission to die. The statement rang true with Bobbi, knowing how her mother's life, since her divorce, had been so full of denial. Everyone around her, right up to the end, had talked to her as if she would soon be over this illness and back on her feet. That's when Bobbi had asked if there was any scotch in the house, her mother's favorite drink. Sam brought her a glass, and Bobbi had touched some of the amber liquid to Betty's lips and told her it was okay to die. Immediately her mother smiled for the first time in three days, sat up, opened her eyes, and died.

"She was just waiting for permission," Barbara remembered the neighbor saying, to which she had replied, "No, she was waiting for the scotch."

That memory managed to bring a smile to her face, and with it, she became Bobbi again. She was, in fact, the Bobbi in the pictures on the mantel, having fun with all those people on the boat. None of the faces were familiar to her yet, except her own and her mother's. But there she was, laughing and carrying on—in such fine clothes too—while everyone else looked so casual. Why was she different? Was she trying to cover up something? Old football injuries? She lifted her skirt and found bruises on her legs.

Suddenly Bobbi felt lost. She felt the bitter absence of her mother close in on her like a cold iron gate. It was better on the plane, when she didn't know why she cried. Now with the memories came the realization that they were no more than that—only memories. With her mother's death she had closed the gate behind her and it mattered not whether the relationship was a good one or a bad one; it was simply over. She could never go back. Before, the gate had always been open. She could at least entertain the thought of going back and working things out if there was a problem, and like all mothers and daughters, they had their share of problems. But even the possibility, which had always been there, was gone now. The place she came from no longer existed. Bobbi felt like an emotional orphan.

How long she sat there she did not know. She felt this loss like a hand pressing on her chest, keeping her down. The worst part was not being able to pick up a phone and call her mother for any or no reason. She would never know the answers to questions she always meant to ask; she would never find out more about her grandmothers and how they played into her character. Then she thought of what the woman on the plane had said: *"Tears keep the wounds clean so God can heal them quicker."* And she cried.

Finally getting up from the chair, she had a distinct feeling that this was not her mother's place. Though the memory of her mother's death had come back vividly, her past was still inaccessible to Bobbi's fragmented mind. Looking around the house for signs of life before Florida, Bobbi found none. She vaguely recollected a former marriage—she knew then that Sam was not her father—but a former life was nowhere to be seen in this house.

This was Sam's place, and something about it didn't seem right. Bobbi was not remembering New York yet; she just knew Florida wasn't Betty's place. Bobbi searched the house for china, crystal, pictures with stories behind them, furniture from another time and place, but she found nothing. Nothing here to spark her memory. Only Florida chic, evidenced by so many of the mobile homes, condos, and pastel houses situated around endless rounds of golf. The house was pretty in its bright yellow decor and open-air ambiance, but it featured no past. She detested this aspect of Florida, where the aged golfed themselves to death in a pastel purgatory. Thoughts like this only made Bobbi long for her mother's terra firma—a place to root her own memories, should they ever return. Perhaps that was why she had planned this trip in the first place. She was rescuing her mother from this rootless place and taking her home.

Bobbi found the screened-in porch with all the beautiful orchids on the blooming table. Someone was taking good care of them.

In the study she found the first evidence of a connection to J.W. Dean, the guy who supposedly threw her mother over a bridge. There were stacks of mail addressed to J.W. Dean Ministries piled high on Sam's desk. *This must be the mail Will was talking about. Maybe I knew something about all this and came to take it to Sam. But who on earth is J.W. Dean, and what does his ministry have to do with Sam Dunn?* Bobbi wasn't remembering much about Sam, but what she could remember didn't seem to fit with his being in some kind of ministry.

One particular piece of mail caught her eye. It was the only piece of the few addressed to Sam Dunn that wasn't a bill. It was from a Lieutenant Brand of the Cocoa Beach Police Department. Bobbi opened it up and read:

> *Dear Mr. Dunn,*
>
> *The jewelry you correctly identified as belonging to your deceased wife has been found among Rev. Dean's things. It is presently impounded here at the police department as possible evidence in Mr. Dean's upcoming trial. This letter will serve as official proof that said items belong to you and may be recovered*

from the department sixty days following the conclusion of the trial. Said items are as listed below.

> *Sincerely,*
> *Lieutenant Adolpho Brand*
> *Chief Investigator*
> *Cocoa Beach Police*

#9864G 1 solid gold 24K twist bracelet
#9865G 1 diamond wedding ring

There it was, plain as day. J.W. Dean murdered Betty and threw the body in the ocean, and now he was on trial for it. Bobbi suddenly thought, *What am I thinking? No one murdered Mom. I was there when she died. So what is J.W. on trial for and what does Mom's body have to do with it? And, come to think of it, what are Sam and his brother doing messing around the scene of what must be a criminal investigation if the police are involved?* It was all too much for her head. The pain was throbbing inside it, and Bobbi was torn between wanting to try to figure it out and wanting to shut it all out. At least she was comforted to know she could get her hands on her mother's wedding ring. One thing tangible to remember her by.

Bobbi leafed through some of the letters to J.W. Dean just to see if she could get any help figuring out the situation. They were all addressed to J.W. Dean Ministries in Port Mayaca and had handwritten forwarding instructions to Sam's address. All of them were either encouraging J.W. to hang in there or raking him over the coals for being a fraud. There was no in-between for this guy. Some of the encouraging letters contained checks but none for more than ten dollars. From the letters, she was able to discern that J.W. was some kind of gospel preacher with snakes whose wife, Bonnie, had died from a snakebite that many were blaming on him, but the connection between him and Sam totally baffled her.

Bobbi decided she'd had enough of opening letters just when she came upon an unusual one marked PERSONAL & CONFIDENTIAL. It was unusual in that both the envelope's return address and its destination were J.W. Dean Ministries. The return address was printed, not typed, making it an envelope from J.W.'s own stationery, and under the address in the upper left-hand corner was written simply, *Bonnie.*

Now, why would Bonnie send her husband a letter through the mail? What did she have to put in print that she couldn't tell him in person? Bobbi could not resist. She had a slight pang of guilt opening someone else's PERSONAL & CONFIDENTIAL mail, but then again, this J.W. Dean guy had entrusted his mail to Sam for some reason, so Bobbi was simply appointing herself as Sam's personal secretary. She would be delivering it to him soon enough. What she opened was earth shattering, even with her own limited knowledge of the story.

> *My dear John Wesley,*
>
> *One of us might die tonight. I am sending this letter to you in case it is me and someone tries to put the blame on you. I cannot make a mockery of God anymore. I put a real coral snake in the box. I found it this morning while I was having my quiet time near the trailer court. I opened my eyes from prayer and there it was looking right at me. I knew it was from God and that I was to use it to test us like the serpent tested Eve. Yes, Eve may have eaten the fruit first, but this time she's going to be the first to put a stop to the lie. We cannot go on deceiving the people. It is not true to the gospel. Better to die being truthful than go on living a lie and discrediting the ministry. If we are bitten and live, then praise be to God for His miracle and the power of His word (Mark 16:17–18), and if we are bitten and die, then praise be to God for His judgment, which is always true and right and holy.*
>
> *If you are reading this, it is because His holy judgment has fallen on me and I have had the privilege of sharing in His suffering and death. Don't feel sorry for me. I am truly happy now and at peace with myself for the first time in a long time.*
>
> *"You shall know the truth and the truth shall make you free."*
>
> *I will love you forever,*
> *Bonnie*

N I N E T E E N

Cocoa Beach

The next morning Bobbi passed on the exit side of the guard shack of Royal Golf Estates just as Will was being detained by Pro Joe at the entrance. Joe was recounting to him how he was on a longer shift than usual, since the morning guy had overslept. Will couldn't care less about Joe's long night, except that it meant Joe had witnessed Bobbi's arrival the night before.

"Yep, she got in here about midnight," Joe said, shaking his head. "Can't believe I've been here that long."

Will squealed his tires as he pulled out, almost clipping the gate that was not rising fast enough for him. In Shaughnessy, he had served as a volunteer fireman, and the urgency of Jack's phone call had gotten the old emergency juices flowing again. Had Bobbi left even seconds later, they would have passed each other on Royal Golf Estates Road and Will would have noticed her because he checked every car he passed on the way in.

"Will, your home phone must be out of order," Jack had said when he finally reached Will at work at around nine-thirty. "I've been trying to call you since two in the morning."

"Two in the morning? Why? What's wrong?"

"Look, I can't explain right now, but I'm in the Atlanta airport waiting for a flight to Cocoa Beach. I need you to go right away to Sam's house and see if Bobbi is there. She's been in an accident. She may have amnesia. I've been able to determine she flew into Cocoa Beach late last night and rented a car; the only possible place she could be going is Sam's house."

"Hold it; slow down. *What* happened?"

"They're closing the door to my plane right now; I can't slow down. Just get to Sam's house as fast as you can and if Bobbi's there, don't let her out of your sight. I'll be about two hours behind you."

"Okay . . . I guess," Will had said sheepishly to the click on the line. He stared at the phone a few seconds before calling Jackie at home and telling her to come cover for him at the marina.

Airlines are not allowed to release passengers' names to anyone other than the police or the FBI, so with the Gloucester police aiding him, Jack had been able to determine Bobbi's flights, and once he had that, he found her car rental confirmation easily enough. Jack's hunch about Florida, coupled with the taxi driver remembering that he'd dropped her off at the American Airlines gate, had narrowed the chase considerably. Jack had barely enough sleepless hours to figure all this out, get his own reservations on the first flight out that morning, pack, tie up a few urgent items on his desk, since he had no idea how long he would be gone, and get the kids taken care of.

"Don't you worry about a thing," Sally McDermott had said when he called her at five A.M. "We'll take care of the kids and watch the house. You get down there and find our girl."

Knowing how long it usually took Bobbi to get ready in the morning, and factoring in how late she had gotten in the night before, Will was pretty confident that he would find her at Sam's house, but the house was empty.

"Couldn't have missed her by more than a few minutes," he told Jackie over the phone, trying to explain to her what was going on. "The shower was still dripping and the coffeepot was hot. By the way, did you notice anything wrong with our phone this morning?"

"It was off the hook," she said. "The dog must have knocked it off again sometime in the night."

"We've got to keep the boys from leaving it on the floor. Jack was trying to get us all night."

"Are you going to stay there and wait for him?" asked Jackie.

"How busy is it there?" he asked. They often tag-teamed their business.

"Busy."

"I'll leave a note for Jack. There's nothing more to do here. I'll see you in a few minutes."

"What if she just stepped out for a while—to get bagels or something? Maybe you should stay there."

"No. She would have left some things here if she was just going out. And she took all of Sam's mail, including the J.W. Dean Ministry stuff."

"She's taking it to Sam, I bet. Gosh, I wonder what she remembers."

　　　　　　　　　　　　⌒

Jack didn't arrive at Sam's house until about four hours later. His flight from Atlanta had been delayed by over an hour. Will came right over when Jack called him from the house, and it wasn't until then that they both started to piece together what had happened to Bobbi. It was also the first time Jack had heard of her phone call to Will the night of her accident.

"No wonder she didn't seem like herself," Will said. "She didn't want to talk at all. That's not like Bobbi. That also explains why she called herself Barbara at first."

"Barbara?"

"That's what Jackie said."

Sadness stabbed Jack's heart as he imagined his wife not even knowing her own name. "What did you talk about?"

"I told her we had heard from Sam and Albert," said Will.

"That's right . . . your message. Sorry, it's been a busy night. Where are they, anyway?"

"They're trying to find Betty where they think J.W. Dean chucked her—somewhere off the Seven Mile Bridge."

Jack thought for a minute. "Can you imagine what that would have sounded like to Bobbi without any idea of what you were talking about?"

"Yeah, like we throw people off bridges all the time."

"I bet that's where she's headed."

"The Seven Mile Bridge?" Will asked.

"Yep. Did you say who Betty was? How much do you think she's been able to figure out?"

"I can't remember many details of the conversation," said Will, "but she probably knows that Betty is her mother and I'm her brother. Don't know if she knows who Sam is."

They were sitting out on Sam's screened-in porch, staring out at the golf course through hanging orchids. Every few minutes a golf cart would whiz by. That, and the lazy whack of an iron shot were the only sounds besides their conversation. Sam's house was an eight-iron away from the seventeenth green of the Royal Golf and Country Club, a course Sam and Betty used to play, but they both had dropped their membership due to declining health. Sam could easily have taken it up again after recovering from brain surgery, but without Betty, he had no incentive. Sam had no real friends apart from her.

Feeling the warm Florida breeze on his tired face made Jack want to rest after his sleepless night, but he knew he had to keep going somehow.

"How long do you think it will take to get down there?" he asked Will.

"To the Keys? Oh . . . three and a half hours to Miami and then another two hours at least to the middle of the Keys. Could be more depending on traffic. Only one two-lane road down there."

Jack looked at his watch. "It's two-thirty right now. That means I couldn't get there before nightfall, could I?"

"You might get to see a nice sunset if you left right now and didn't stop along the way."

"But my only chance of locating Bobbi is to find those crazy guys diving for Betty's ashes, and they won't be out on the water that late."

"Not likely."

Just then a golf ball crashed high in the tree in the backyard, fell down through the branches, conked the bird feeder on the bottom branch—sending bird and seed flying—and landed on the ground two feet from the tree trunk.

"That's gonna be a difficult lie," Will commented. Of course, no one was allowed to hit a ball on private property. One had to throw it back onto the fairway. "Over here!" Will shouted at an old duffer in green shorts and hat and a bright yellow polo shirt who was headed in their direction. "Right next to that tree!" The guy waved him off, too embarrassed to come get the ball. He dropped a new one and shot, sending four inches of turf farther than the ball. Then he marched off after ball and turf and never looked back.

"With all the practice they get, you'd think these guys would get better."

"He probably has," Jack said, and they both laughed. "Do you think Sam's going to keep this place?"

"Naw. He's already talked about selling it."

"Where will he go? He doesn't have any family or friends."

"I wouldn't be surprised if he bought a camper for his truck and disappeared on the road," Will remarked.

Jack stared out at the serene scene and sighed. "Well, I'd better hit the road myself."

"You're welcome to crash at my place if you like. Get an early start in the morning and you'll be there by noon."

"Thanks for the offer, but I want to get there tonight so I can be out by the bridge first thing in the morning. I can't stand the fact that Bobbi's out there somewhere and I have no way of knowing where and no way of getting in touch with her. My only chance now is to be there when those crazy brothers show up in the morning."

"I understand," Will murmured. "Hopefully, they haven't found the ashes yet, or there will be little chance of any of you finding each other at all."

"You would have to say that," Jack replied. The thought had not yet occurred to him.

TWENTY

Trolling for Sharks

"Will you stop eating . . . and get your rear end . . . in the water. . . . It's your turn!"

Sam was hanging on to the side of the boat, waterlogged and out of breath. Even though it was barely the start of a new day, his impatience was already showing—impatience augmented by a week of unsuccessful searching.

Albert, who was leisurely enjoying his cream cheese on bagels, took Sam's outburst calmly. "Get in the boat, take off your gear, and I'll be ready." He said it in a slow, cheery manner, licking cream cheese off his chubby fingers. Albert was learning to let Sam roll off him like sea water off his sunburned back. He wasn't about to let anything upset this day's morsel of gourmet food from the 53rd Street Dock and Deli in Marathon.

The little white box had eluded them for a week, and the impossibility of the task was beginning to wear on Sam. With every day the sea looked more vast and the box seemed smaller in his mind. They were dealing with a potential seven miles of water under the bridge, with no knowledge of how far away the current could have carried the remains of Betty from where J.W. first threw her. They also lacked any sophisticated instruments for ocean-floor navigation that would ensure they covered every inch of the bottom, so there was always that haunting thought that perhaps they had missed a spot and should go over everything again . . . and again.

As ocean-floor navigators, however, they were becoming quite experienced. They were also becoming the talk of the town in all the dive shops and restaurants and bars in Marathon. That had started when Albert got the brilliant idea to hire a glass-bottom boat from Captain Hook's Marina and Dive Center for the first day out. "At worst, we can get an understanding of the whole area, and at best, we might even spot the thing from the boat."

The idea had proven to be a good one, not only because it helped them visually map the area they would be searching, but it also netted them a world of advice from the operator of the boat, a native conch who had been diving in these waters for over thirty years. Zeke (the only name he would give them) had plenty of suggestions for navigating the shallow ocean floor in these parts, and Sam and Albert ended up trying them all.

First there was the trolling method, where they rented a skiff with a small outboard motor and took turns towing each other back and forth slowly across the surface of the water. It was a little like the glass-bottom boat theory, only with the ability to scan a much wider area underwater aided by mask and snorkel. This method was initially quite useful because they felt they were able to see so much. But seeing so much also meant they were well aware of the presence of some pretty big tarpon cruising the same waters. The tarpon were no real problem to them; it was the bull sharks that were after the tarpon that made them a bit uneasy. Zeke had told them not to worry about bull sharks—they would be out feeding on tarpon and had never been known to attack humans— but Sam and Albert found out rather quickly that Zeke's comforting words lost their charm when they were being dragged behind a boat like a piece of meat in the presence of one of these six- to eight-foot beasts. Needless to say, they stopped the boat and got out of the water whenever they sighted one.

"No way I'm gonna be bull-shark bait!" said Sam when they decided for good to abandon the trolling method.

Albert, growing more feisty every day, had not been able to resist. "Wanna go home, Sam?" he asked, leaving Sam to eat his own words in the silence that followed.

Zeke did say that if they ever spotted a hammerhead, they should probably get in the boat pretty quick, and toward the middle of the first afternoon, Sam was convinced he'd seen Big Mo cruising by out of the corner of his eye. He scraped his stomach badly scrambling into the boat, and they both decided they'd had enough of the trolling method. It had not been a good first day in the water. Besides Sam's raspberry on his stomach, Albert had taken a big hit of sun on his back. That's how he found out that no amount of sun block was going to give his sensitive skin any protection in that constant exposure of sun and water.

The remaining days had been spent in a combination of two other methods Zeke suggested. The corkscrew method, as Albert named it, was to anchor the skiff, tie a rope to one of them at the waist, and swim in widening circles around the boat while the other let the line out four or five feet each time. This allowed the swimmer to dive for a deeper look if necessary and not worry about missing any coverage of the bottom. It was up to the one in the boat to control the line so that the circle gradually grew. The drawback with this procedure was that the farther away from the boat the swimmer got, the more anxious he became about sharks, so they had to keep the outer limits of the circle fairly tight for their own peace of mind. That meant moving often and repeatedly.

Finally there was the kick method: four kicks, then turn to the right; four kicks, turn to the right; four kicks, turn to the right; then eight kicks out and begin another four-kick square. This method allowed the swimmer to stay close to the boat, but it pre-

sented a problem when the current was moving swiftly in the channel, pulling both boat and swimmer off line. Twice a day there was
a thirty-minute window when the current shifted from bay side to
ocean side, and back again, and during that shift the water was relatively still. So they fell into a pattern of using the kick method
when the current was somewhat calm and the corkscrew when it
picked up speed in either direction.

Sam and Albert were becoming quite an item each night at
Crockogators Road-Kill Cafe, located a few miles north of Marathon on Grassy Key. Crockogators won out over the Seven Mile
Grill as their favorite dinner spot because Sam liked their Buffalo
Road-Kill Stew, and Albert was relatively happy to choose from the
wide range of nicely prepared fresh seafood items. Albert never did
get over the name of the place, however, and always wondered if
the meat they served had in fact been the fate of some wandering,
flea-infested critter's date with a hot Goodyear tire.

Each night the regulars at the bar asked for a report from the
visiting treasure hunters, as Sam and Albert had become known,
with Zeke spreading the word. The local conchs assumed it had to
be some kind of sunken treasure they were looking for, since Sam
refused to tell anyone about Betty. Sunken treasure was common
to the Keys, seeing as ships had been running aground on their
shallow reefs for centuries. This was obviously a different kind of
sunken treasure, though. No ship could have made it in this far.
Pretty much everyone had figured it was a "treasure" thrown from
the bridge that they were after, and Sam and Albert preferred to
let the speculation run wild. As the week progressed, the suspense
grew. Each day their tenacity at pursuing the search gave further
credibility to the hunting secret, prompting more outrageous
guesses.

"Come on out and join us if you want," Albert kept saying with
a twinkle.

"You cut us in on the booty and we'll be there," someone
would usually say.

Sam's unchanging response was simple. "What we're looking for is worth nothing to you."

"Hurry up with that bagel, Albert," Sam demanded as he climbed into the boat and took large gasps of air, happy to be free of his snorkel tube. "You're wasting valuable time."

They were out early this particular morning, trying to take advantage of the first tide shift. The sun was low enough to cast long shadows and yet still warm them, but not uncomfortably so. Color, temperature, and taste were all at their optimum for Albert, who was in no hurry to give up savoring the moment.

An uncharacteristic stillness added to Albert's enjoyment of his senses this particular morning. They were working close to the bridge again but without the usual clamor of cars and trucks. They had become accustomed to the snapping of tires on the concrete cracks and the reverberation of heavy trucks that seemed to drive down through the pilings and into the sea each time they clattered by. But this morning there was only silence, for this was the day of the annual Seven Mile Bridge Foot Race, and the bridge was closed to traffic from seven to nine A.M., meaning that Albert's distaste for runners was being severely challenged by the peace he was enjoying.

"It's so beautiful and quiet out this morning," Albert reflected. "I wish they'd shut down that bridge more often. You don't realize how annoying all that clatter is until it's gone."

"Albert, would you hurry up? Look at that still water." The raspberry on Sam's stomach had scabbed and now resembled the hard skin and shape of an alligator. Sam already had a good tan, and a week on the water had turned his skin to leather.

"You betcha." Albert stuffed one last bite into his mouth and grabbed his fins. No matter how much sun block Albert wore, he still looked like a big round beet. He simply couldn't tan. For that reason he had taken to wearing a T-shirt most of the time, even in the water. Once in a while Albert wished that they were working farther out off the east coast of the Keys where the beautiful coral reefs teemed with exotic fish and colorful undersea life, but he kept those thoughts to himself and chose to enjoy the array of beauty to be found above water. Here it seemed to him that God came up with a different shade of blue each day. Sometimes he could see the shades all at once out on the water as sun and cloud and shallow bottom mixed together in infinite combinations. His favorite time was in the early morning when they would creep out in their skiff through the mangroves on Vaca Key and disturb a rookery of snowy egrets or send a whirring pink cloud of roseate spoonbills beating upward.

Even below the surface of the water there was the occasional conch shell or yellow flash of jack crevalle darting by, but by and large they were combing a sandy, grassy area that contained a good deal of debris, especially near the new bridge. The construction crew appeared to have been pretty careless with their building materials. This area around the bridge was where Albert and Sam spent most of their time, theorizing that the box had sunk straight down and gotten wedged between some corroded pipes by the shifting tide.

Zeke was also of that opinion, though he warned them against reaching into any holes or crevasses. "There's a big moray eel that likes to hang out there close to the bridge. He could pop out of any one of those holes down there and have your finger for lunch."

The thought that there could be another fish lurking nearby that was capable of having more of him for lunch than a mere finger never crossed Albert's mind that morning. Perhaps it was the fine presentation of dawn and the rare silence that he was enjoying, or the fact that neither of them had had any further sightings of Big Mo since Sam's supposed one the first day out (which Albert had doubts about anyway). But Albert jumped into the water that morning with the casualness of someone jumping into their backyard swimming pool. After all, they had spent a week in these waters without major incident. Even the bull sharks had become commonplace.

Albert was still chewing on the last of his bagel and cream cheese when he felt something large and slippery slide against his leg. Looking down, his heart literally stopped in his chest at seeing a huge gray form pass under him, dwarfing their little boat and kicking up a bubbling wave that almost sucked him under as the big thing swam away. Albert was frozen with fear and unable to react for what seemed like an eternity but was really only a few seconds. Suddenly he noticed the gray image in the water turn and rapidly grow in size. A hump and a dorsal fin broke the surface of the water. Sam spied the wake approaching.

"Albert! Look out!"

A massive shot of adrenaline is the only way to explain how a man of Albert's age and girth was able to get himself so quickly back into the boat.

"Holy moley!" cried Sam, leaning over the edge and watching the huge gray beast disappear under their little skiff, rocking it like a teacup in a bathtub. "Look at the size of that fish!"

Albert couldn't look, nor could he speak. He was slumped against the back of the boat, gasping for air.

Sam was now on the other side trying to get a better look. On the next pass he was able to spot the telltale horizontal bar of the hammerhead's snout and—sure enough—there was the famous gash over the eye from Sarge's crowbar. "Albert, ol' buddy, you just had a brush with Big Mo and lived to tell about it!"

When Albert didn't reply, Sam turned around and saw his brother trying to speak, but only dry, guttural sounds were coming out of his mouth. His right hand was clutching his left arm up around the shoulder, and the force of the pain was prying him over on his side.

"Albert!" Sam screamed, rushing to him and rocking the little boat so that it threw his younger brother over onto his face.

TWENTY-ONE

Fishermen's Hospital

Ruth Farrington had to start as early as January going through the applications for the annual Seven Mile Bridge Foot Race. The race had been held every April for the past twenty years, and applications now poured into the Marathon Chamber of Commerce from all over the world: Puerto Rico, Japan, Africa, South America. Though Ruth received as many as three thousand, she could only accept the first fifteen hundred to cross her desk. The bridge simply could not hold any more runners than that in the amount of time the city could afford to shut down traffic.

The race always began at seven o'clock in the morning at the north end of the bridge leaving Vaca Key and finished seven miles later on Little Duck Key. For two hours, fifteen hundred runners would flow across the bridge like ants on a log. At nine o'clock sharp, buses would bring up the rear, sweeping up any who were unable to finish the race, and by nine-thirty, traffic on the bridge was flowing again.

One particular runner that morning—a Katie Lundgren from Wilmington, Delaware—was among the last to start, when she thought she heard a cry from below the bridge. She was running in this race for her tenth consecutive year, though this year she was running alone. She and her husband had made their reservations in advance, as they did every year, only this time, the reservations had been made in advance of their sudden divorce. Her husband had subsequently canceled his running date, but Katie had decided to run anyway.

She had just been focusing on the eerie quietness of the bridge and the runners' long shadows in the early-morning light, when over the soft padding of sneakered feet and the heavy breathing all around her she heard it again. It was a voice—someone calling out. It sounded painfully urgent. She was running right along the guardrail on the bay side, and the voice was coming from her right. It was so desperate that she had to stop and look over the rail. There, thirty feet below her, rocking on the blue water, was a small boat with a gray-haired man calling up to the bridge and waving his arms. In the boat she could see another man facedown in an awkward position. Katie looked over her shoulder and saw nothing but runners streaming toward her, many of whom were irritated at having to move to avoid crashing into her.

"Bad time for sight-seeing!" shouted one runner as he passed.

"Someone's hurt down there!" she called, but no one stopped. Slowly she inched her way back along the rail. The strong, steady flow of runners prevented her progress. Suddenly she hated their determination—a determination that seconds before she had shared, except that now there was something more important than the race. *Someone is in trouble down there.*

Working her way back was worse than swimming upstream. She could hear the man below yelling, "Hurry!" and she waved back to let him know she had heard him and was getting help. In a minute that seemed like an hour, she could see a break in the runners and some walkers in street clothes and a few vehicles some distance behind them starting their final sweep of the bridge. Charging, Katie broke through the last of the cursing runners and sprinted across the open space as fast as she could run. There was a man walking with a video camera on his shoulder. He had a cell phone.

～

Needless to say, Albert's opinion of runners was forever altered that day, for he had God and the Seven Mile Bridge Foot Race and one particular heads-up runner to thank for his life. Had it been any other day of the year, or any other time that day, no one on the bridge would have been able to hear Sam's cries over the roar of the traffic. He would not have even tried. Sam would have had to motor back to the harbor in Marathon to get help, and Albert would undoubtedly have died in that time.

As it was, the man who called for help turned out to be a reporter from the *Miami Herald* who was trying to find a human-interest story on one of the last runners in the race. He could never have imagined one this good. His call was immediately transferred to the Key Patrol, which had a boat two miles up the bridge at Moser Channel. They reached Sam and Albert's skiff in less than seven minutes from the time Sam first yelled for help.

Katie Lundgren never did finish the race, but that mattered little to her once she realized what had happened. "I wasn't even going to run this year," she told the reporter in a story that got national attention, "but the friends in my Bible study took up a collection and sent me. They thought it would do me good after my divorce and all. Little did we know, God would be using me to help save someone's life."

The race may have saved Albert's life, but it only made things worse for Jack Acres. He had reached Marathon the night before, dead tired, and after unsuccessfully checking hotels for Bobbi, he had decided to bed down for the night and get out to the bridge first thing in the morning. But the closest place he could find a room available was a roach-infested hole-in-the-wall without air conditioning twenty miles south of the Seven Mile Bridge on Ramrod Key. He took it, though he had trouble sleeping—even as tired as he was—in a sagging bed with the putrid sulfur smell of exposed mangrove roots at low tide wafting through his open windows. Then he got stuck in traffic the next morning and didn't make it any farther than Bahia Honda Key before they shut the bridge down for the race. It was after ten-thirty when he was finally able to cross over to the north side and pull off the road to view the area around Pigeon Key.

Bobbi had run into the same problem finding a motel room; she simply had refused to take no for an answer until the manager at the Holiday Inn Marathon and Marina serviced her with a room. (Jack had been with her before when she'd pulled this stunt, and he liked to joke that if she'd been the mother of Jesus, there would most definitely have been room for them at the inn.)

All that day, Bobbi and Jack somehow missed everyone—Sam . . . Albert . . . each other. It was actually hard to do, but they managed to do it. Had either one of them caught the local news on the cable station, they would have heard about Albert and Sam and the heroics of Katie Lundgren, but they were too busy in and around Pigeon Key looking for two old guys in a boat. Both of them visited the little island that day. Both of them checked out hotels and bars. When Jack stopped into Crockogator's Road-Kill Cafe, the man behind the bar said he was the second person that day to ask about these guys. Everybody at the bar knew who they were, but no one had seen them since the day before.

Bobbi had the same thing happen to her at the 53rd Street Dock and Deli in Marathon, where she stopped in for a sandwich at noon. One time they passed each other on the old bridge to Pigeon Key. Jack was on his way back from the island on the pedestrian walkway, while Bobbi was riding "Henry" on the 2:00 P.M. shuttle. Had she not been reading up on the island literature they gave her at the visitor's center, she would have seen Jack from the train.

Albert, meanwhile, was recovering nicely at Fishermen's Hospital. The doctors had contemplated sending him to Miami for surgery, but a resident cardiologist was confident he was out of immediate danger and could wait until he returned to his home in

Shaughnessy for more extensive testing and a likely bypass.

"Here, I brought you a T-shirt," Sam said when he went in to see him first thing the next morning.

"What's it say?" Albert asked, holding it up and smiling when he read, *I SURVIVED BIG MO.*

In truth, Albert was being charmed by it all—the attention in the newspaper, the television crew that did a story on him, the committee for the Seven Mile Bridge Foot Race that made him an honorary member. But most of all, he was charmed by Katie Lundgren, the cute little blonde from Delaware who had cut her race short to see how he was and had spent a good deal of the previous day checking up on him at the hospital.

"And who was that I passed on my way in here?" Sam inquired.

"Who, Katie?" Albert did a bad job of acting casual; it was only his sunburn that concealed his reddening face.

"Did she come early, or did she stay the night?"

"Come on, Sam, my heart's been through enough as it is. She just stopped by to see how I was before heading out to the airport. She's flying home this morning."

"I wouldn't be surprised if you're in love with her by now."

"Oh, I am!" Albert agreed. "I'm a gonner. She makes me wish I had a daughter."

"Pardon me, but will a niece do?" said a familiar voice in the doorway.

"Bobbi!" Albert exclaimed, a big smile washing across his beaming face. "Well, I'll be—how did you get here? When?"

Bobbi came over and kissed him on the forehead. "Careful now, you'll give me another heart attack," Albert said.

"Hi, Sam," Bobbi greeted her stepfather and kissed him, too, leaving a lipstick smudge right in the dip of his dent. Sam tried to conceal it, but his eyes were shining.

"I've been here since yesterday looking for both of you. It was your picture in the paper this morning that finally did it."

"Did it for me too?" said another voice from the doorway. They all turned to see Jack standing there.

"Jack!" Bobbi exclaimed.

"Thank God you know who I am." Jack walked over and hugged her. She held on and he held fast to his grasp on her.

"This is starting to feel a little like a scene from *This Is Your Life*," said Albert.

Sam looked at the two of them quizzically. "Jack, meet Bobbi. Bobbi, this is Jack. Will someone tell me what's going on here?"

"It's a long story," Bobbi said, still locked in Jack's embrace.

"Are you okay?" Jack finally released her and brushed the hair away from her face so he could inspect her bruise.

"I'm fine," she nodded. "The important thing is, how is Uncle Albert?"

"Uncle Albert couldn't be better," Albert stated. "Somebody ring up room service. Let's have a party!"

"Not so fast," said a nurse, entering the room. "There are entirely too many people in here. You're only allowed one visitor at a time, you know."

Bobbi grabbed Sam's arm and pulled him away. At the same time she laid a hand on Jack's chest and whispered to him to stay with Albert. "That's okay. We were just leaving," she said to the nurse. "See you in a few minutes, Albert."

Jack was reluctant to let Bobbi go just when he'd found her, but she left him little choice.

"Come with me. I want to show you something," Bobbi said to Sam as soon as they were in the hallway. Sam was still flushed by all the surprise. Things were happening too fast.

"What are you two doing here?" he said in the elevator, realizing it couldn't possibly have anything to do with Albert's brush with death. There was no way they could have found out that fast.

"Looking for you."

"Why?"

"I'm about to show you." Bobbi led him out the door of the hospital to her rental car, where she popped open the trunk lid. There, lying on the neat, clean gray carpet of the empty trunk, was a plastic bag with a rusted twist-tie, full of what looked like ashen-colored sand.

Sam stood there and stared, expressionless. "Where did you find it?"

"Washed up on the shore of Pigeon Key. It was in a foot of water. I didn't even have to get wet."

They both stared at the bag; Bobbi still had her hand on the trunk lid.

"Where's the box? How did you find it without the box?"

"It was in the box—that's how I recognized it—but it fell apart when I picked it up."

"What are you going to do with her?" Sam asked.

"Take her back to New York and bury her where she belongs."

"Oh no, you don't." Sam made a move toward the bag, at which time Bobbi slammed the trunk shut. Sam dropped his hands helplessly and stared off at the traffic on Overseas Highway and at the bobbing masts sticking up from the marina across the street. "Look, I've gone to a lot of trouble to find her. You just got lucky. I led you here."

"And I'm grateful—I truly am—but she's my mother and I know where she belongs."

"She's *my* wife," Sam said, looking directly at Bobbi for the first time, "and I know where she wants to be."

Bobbi bit her lip. That comment took something away from her. It had never occurred to her, in all this, that her mother may have had a say in the matter. "You mean . . . she told you?"

"Of course she told me. Did you think this was all my idea?"

Now Bobbi was the one looking off at the tilting masts as a warm breeze played with the hair around her injured forehead. Leaning against the trunk of the car for support, she turned to face Sam. "What did she say?"

"She wanted to be spread out on the sea. She wanted to play with the dolphins. That's why I had to find her. She can't play with dolphins on the floor of the ocean in a plastic bag!"

Tears filled Bobbi's eyes, and to keep them from spilling over, she tilted her head to the clouds. A lone pelican soared overhead and she blinked the tears away.

"Are you sure that isn't what *you* want?" she said, crossing her arms and dropping her gaze back at him.

"You don't think I know her, do you?" he responded. "Well the truth of the matter is: You don't know her as well as you think. You may have had her first, but I had her last, and I'm going to make sure her wishes are respected. Believe me, a hole in the ground in New York State is not where she wanted to end up."

Bobbi was staring down at the pavement now and her head was suddenly throbbing. At first she thought it was just the emotions, but then she knew it was something more. Her hands instinctively came up to cradle the heaviness.

"Can we talk about this later?" she asked. "This is just too hard for me right now."

"Are you all right?" Sam said, leaning in to get a closer look at her forehead.

"I'm okay. I just need to go inside and sit down."

They made their way back to the front door of the hospital, and Sam found it necessary to take Bobbi's arm to steady her. Barely inside the door, Bobbi reached for the arm of a vacant wheelchair just as her legs gave out.

"Help!" yelled Sam, enfolding Bobbi's limp body in his arms. "Will somebody please help me?"

TWENTY-TWO

Room 201

Bobbi woke up later that afternoon in a hospital and was sure someone had made a mistake.

"Where are my things?" she said, waking up Jack who was dozing in a chair next to her bed. Two nights on Ramrod Key had left him somewhat deficient in the sleep category.

"And where's Sam?" Bobbi questioned, remembering her conversation in the parking lot. "And what am I doing in here?"

"Whoa . . . one question at a time, please." Jack rubbed his eyes. "I'm still trying to figure out where *I* am."

"Is that my purse over there? Could you hand it to me?"

"That I can do." Jack reached for her purse, which was in the chair next to him. "Glad to see you're feeling better."

"I'm feeling perfectly fine," Bobbi retorted, rummaging through her purse and coming up with the keys to her rental car. "Which makes me wonder why I'm in here. Could you do me a favor and bring me the bag that's in the trunk of my car? It's a red Grand Am in the last row of the parking lot."

"Sure thing," Jack said, "but we have to talk. The doctor wants to try some tests on you."

"We'll talk as soon as you get back . . . but I can tell you my memory's fine."

Jack took the keys and noticed a familiar wrinkled spot on her forehead—right between her eyebrows—that furrowed when she was under stress. He pressed the spot with his thumb and made small circles, as if to rub it out. "You must be remembering enough to worry."

"I'll worry a lot less as soon as you bring me the bag."

When Jack returned he found Bobbi's hospital bed empty.

"Is that you, Jack?" she said from the washroom. "I'm in here."

He walked around an open door and found her in front of the mirror in her street clothes, making up her face.

"What are you doing?"

"Getting ready to leave."

"Bobbi, this isn't a hotel. You've only been here a few hours."

"Yes, I know. I've had a nice rest, too, but now I'm ready to go. Did you get the bag?"

"Well . . . no, actually. The trunk was empty. I forgot that Sam got all your bags out of your car already. I'm sorry; I wasn't quite awake yet. Everything's here in the closet. But, Bobbi . . . you can't leave the hospital."

Bobbi whirled and spoke. "Sam got my bags? How could you have let him do that?"

Jack stood there, confused. "I don't understand. He was just doing us a favor."

"Did you check the rest of the car?"

"There's nothing in the car. Everything that was in your car is here in this closet."

Bobbi slumped down on the hospital bed and looked as though she was about to cry. "No, not everything."

"What—what is it? What are you missing?"

"The ashes."

"What ashes?" Betty was the farthest thing from Jack's mind right then.

"Mom's ashes, of course. What do you think I'm down here for? Oh, I don't believe this is happening! What time is it? When did Sam leave? He's probably already done it."

"Done what? Bobbi, I wish you'd settle down and tell me what you're talking about. You know, we haven't talked since Rockport. There's so much to sort out, and now you're not making any sense at all."

"No, there's nothing to sort out, and I'm making perfect sense. I came down here looking for Mom even before I knew what I was doing. Then I remembered it wasn't Mom, but Mom's ashes I was after. Now that I know what I'm doing, I'm still looking for them. I had them—as a matter of fact, in my hand—except that now Sam has surely stolen them from me. For all I know he's thrown them back into the ocean by now. How long has he been gone?"

"I'm not sure he ever left. I haven't seen him since noon, but he could just be with Albert."

"Not when he had a chance to get a jump on me. I should never have shown him the bag." Bobbi heaved her chest in a sigh, then looked again at the clock. "We've got to try and find him. There might still be time. Come on." And as she stood up, Jack grabbed her by the shoulders and pushed her back down on the bed. Bobbi, unfamiliar with being physically restrained by her husband, blinked back a startled look.

"No, you don't. You're not going anywhere." He had her full attention now. "Bobbi, the doctor is very concerned. The blackout you had today should have been much more serious. This could happen at any time and probably will at least a few more times before your injury heals completely. There's even a danger of a stroke that could result in permanent brain damage—could even be fatal. That's why they have to keep you here for a couple of days to monitor the clotting level in your blood and keep you on the right drugs. The doctor said that, given the running around you've been doing since the accident, it's a miracle you're still alive."

Bobbi blinked as if to say, "So?" but what she really said was, "You go, then."

"Go where?"

"Go find Sam. It may not be too late. He's going to throw Mom's ashes in the ocean—I just know he is."

"Look, Bobbi, I don't care if Sam throws them in someone's barbecue, I'm not letting you out of my sight again. Every time I do, something bad happens."

Bobbi saw that Jack was determined and let her shoulders sag in disappointment. A look of almost childlike helplessness came over her. "Could you at least go see if Sam is with Albert?"

"We can call his room." And Jack rang up Albert and found out that he hadn't seen Sam all afternoon.

"I told you," she said when he hung up.

Jack backed away and pulled a chair up to the bedside. Bobbi was still in her clothes, sitting on the edge of the bed, with a small overnight bag next to her on the floor.

"Jack, do you know that I look in the mirror these days and see my mother? I hear myself talk and I hear her talking. I hear myself laugh and I hear her laughing. We are bound together, she and I. She is a part of me in ways I can never lose, but she left me nothing tangible to remember her by. It's as if she went out of her way to burn up everything. Do you realize that after her divorce, she got rid of everything that was ever important to her? I'm having a hard time forgiving her for that. It's as if she tried to start a new life down here with Sam—a life she wanted to burn up as soon as it was gone. I may never even get her jewelry back, thanks to J.W. Dean. And now Sam tells me it was her request to burn up the last bit of herself and throw it into the sea. Though I used to think it was Sam's idea, I'm starting to believe him. You know what that means, Jack?"

Jack simply looked at her. He was not grasping all of this. It was then that he noticed she had ripped off the tape holding her IV. The back of her hand was red and bleeding.

"It means she didn't want me to get even the last of her . . .

her remains. What was so awful about her life that she couldn't leave some of it to me? Maybe that's why I don't like cremations. Sure, everything's gonna burn someday, but that doesn't mean we light the fire. God's going to take care of that soon enough."

Jack got out of the chair and moved over next to his wife. He put an arm around her, and she rested her head on his shoulder. He had a feeling she wasn't done yet.

"I hate her," she said finally. "She was so selfish. She must not have been thinking about me. I just wanted something of hers—anything."

"And just where do we think we're going all dressed up?" said a nurse, walking in on their conversation. Then noticing the IV tubes dangling free, she asked, "Now what have you gone and done?"

TWENTY-THREE

An Unexplainable Absence

Sam unhooked the rope from the dock and let the little skiff drift slowly out into the bay before he started up the engine. It was hot—the kind of heat that dampened his shirt between his shoulder blades just walking from the car to the boat. By the time he pulled on the engine cord three times, perspiration was dripping off his nose. Sam checked the height of the sun and guessed it was about four o'clock. He was anxious to get started, if only to make the heavy air move around him.

He knew right where to go. There were two channels where he and Albert had spotted dolphins regularly during their diving expeditions. He was pretty confident he would find them in Knight Key Channel, since they had seen them there almost every afternoon about this time of day on their way back from searching for the box.

Sam made his way slowly south along the bay side of Vaca Key.

His favorite spots were around Stirrup Key and Rachel Key, north and south of the airstrip, respectively. These were uninhabited areas still thick with mangroves and roosting cormorants. On one spot opposite Rachel Key, they could almost always find a number of great white heron standing in the shallow water, their long white necks hooking into a feathery S and their stick legs reflecting parallel lines far across the water.

Sam reached Knight Key Channel and began cruising back and forth under the arches of the old bridge and the pylons of the new one. He could see Henry carrying tourists back from Pigeon Key and hear the traffic on the new bridge overhead. He marveled at the good fortune of Albert's heart attack coming at the only time all year that the busy bridge stands idle. Of course, Albert would never call it a coincidence. It was his date with destiny engineered by God. Sam had to admit, if it was a coincidence, it was a very mighty one. Was he getting soft on God? *Stranger things have happened to people who don't give God any credit*, he kept telling himself.

After about an hour of cruising the channel, he began to wonder where the dolphins were. He was so sure he would have seen a few schools by now. Finally he gave up on the Knight Key Channel and decided to motor farther south to Moser Channel. So certain was he of finding dolphins there that he got the bag of ashes out of the tackle box and set it down at his feet just in case. But Moser Channel produced only a school of tarpon and a great manatee that he mistook for Big Mo until he got a closer look at it feeding near the pylons.

Sam looked down at the little bag of ashes at his feet and marveled at how he had come this far and still couldn't manage to finish his task. He thought of dumping them anyway. The dolphins could be symbolic. Betty would be in the ocean, and somewhere, dolphins would dive in her honor. *No*, he thought. *Not good enough.*

The first time, when he had unknowingly dumped the remains of Bonnie Dean in the ocean, everyone thought the dolphins were a magical happenstance—a serendipity—but Sam had spotted them under the water. They were running with the boat as they often did, and that was why he had disposed of the ashes without warning. That, and the fact that he didn't want anyone turning sappy on him in the last few moments. Now that he had Betty for real, after all this, he wasn't going to just dump her randomly. He would wait for the presence of her sleek gray friends to christen the moment. He'd waited this long; he could wait a little longer.

The sun was an orange-red fireball low in the sky when Sam turned back from Moser Channel, leaving him with the thought that perhaps there were other forces at work in Betty's meeting with her final earthly destiny. Unless, of course, he met a few of her special graveside guests on the way in.

⌒

"Okay, I give up. How did you do it?" Sam bellowed as he barged into Bobbi's hospital room later that night, waking her up from a sound sleep.

"Shhhh!" Jack whispered. "Can't you see she's sleeping?"

"Not anymore," Bobbi said. "What did I do?"

"You kept the dolphins away."

"I know. I'm pretty good that way."

"Well, we'll see about that tomorrow."

"Tomorrow?" Bobbi asked, propping herself up and reading one step ahead of his every move. "So you're going to keep at it until the dolphins show up?"

"I promised."

"Why don't you wait until I'm out of here so I can at least attend? I know you're gonna do what you're gonna do. Might as well let me be there to remember the moment."

"I don't know that I can trust you."

"Fine one you are to talk about trust! Stealing her away from me at your first opportunity—and taking advantage of my helplessness at that."

"It was Providence. You were unconscious; I seized the moment."

"Hold it, Sam. Of all the things God does, creating an opportunity to break one of His own commandments is not one of them."

"And what one would that be?" Sam cast a bothered glance Bobbi's direction.

" 'Thou shalt not steal,' of course."

"I didn't steal; I merely took back what was rightfully mine. I'm on a mission here to complete Betty's wishes."

"So you can make up the rules as you go? I'm on a mission, too, you know."

"Maybe so, but I've got the Holy Grail."

"So you do. But I've got the dolphins on my side," Bobbi said with a twinkle.

"We'll see about that tomorrow."

"Wait for me, Sam. Please? Jack, make him wait."

Jack looked at Sam and shook his head, smiling. They both knew it was hopeless.

"Sam," Bobbi pleaded, "I just don't want my last memory of Mom to be the actual burial at sea of a snake handler's wife. Oh, and by the way, I have some important mail for you. Jack, could you get that mail out of the side pocket of my suitcase?"

Jack found the suitcase and handed Bobbi a wad of envelopes, which she started leafing through. "Did you know you were a clearinghouse for J.W. Dean Ministries mail?"

"What?"

"You're getting J.W. Dean's mail."

"Why?" Sam said with a blank look on his face.

"Probably to protect it from the police," said Jack. "Do you remember giving him your address?"

"His lawyer has my address."

"Well, you seem to be the newly appointed administrator of J.W. Dean Ministries," said Bobbi.

"Oh no, I'm not," Sam stated. "I'll just put all that into a box when I get home and ship it right back to them."

"Well, before you do, you might want to look at this one." Bobbi handed him Bonnie's letter.

Sam read in silence and then looked up. "She killed herself.

Incredible . . . J.W.'s off the hook.''

"Looks like it," Jack said. He and Bobbi had gone over the mail earlier in the evening. "Probably ought to get that to the police pretty soon."

"No. I'll get it to J.W.'s lawyer," Sam decided.

"You really think he won't throw the ashes in without dolphins?" Jack asked after Sam left.

"Sam's a man of his word, remember? And he gave Mom his word. The dolphins are my only chance now of at least being there when he does it."

"It sounds like you're giving up on the New York idea. Is that a resignation?"

"No . . . just a change of plans. I think I'm beginning to wonder if God just might be doing something with the dolphins around here. And if God is in this, perhaps that alone will be enough of a legacy."

TWENTY-FOUR

Waiting for the Dolphins

For the next three days, Bobbi healed and sent healthy brain waves rippling through the testing computers of Fishermen's Hospital, while nothing disturbed the calm surrounding the rented skiff of Sam Dunn in the endless blue around Vaca Key.

Sam couldn't believe it. He could never remember going four days without spotting a dolphin in Florida waters. He was so amazed, that by the third day he found himself secretly hoping he *wouldn't* see dolphins and then chided himself for having the thought. Such was the inner struggle Sam experienced. The growing question that plagued him was, if he found the dolphins, would he actually throw the ashes in? On the first day he undoubtedly would have. On the second day, he wasn't sure. By the third day, he was out on the ocean more to amaze himself with the silence of the unbroken waters than to actually do the deed. It was not like Sam to test the mysterious or the supernatural, but he was hard pressed not to notice something strange going on.

At the very same time, Bobbi was going through changes of her own. Bobbi saw the absence of dolphins as God secretly smiling on her. Sam had his chance—in fact, kept having his chance—to get a jump on her, but he was continually thwarted by something beyond anyone's control. That, in itself, was a new thing for Bobbi—making peace with something beyond her control. Being in control had always been Bobbi's forte. It was what had made her successful in business and sometimes problematic in marriage. Suddenly something very important to her was out of her control, and she found herself pleasantly surprised to be trusting God in it. Certainly God had more than her personal agenda in mind, but she liked to think it was their secret. She knew now that the dolphins would not come until the right time, and should they come while Sam was out there by himself, then far be it from her to stop him from doing whatever he was going to do. And yet somehow she knew the dolphins wouldn't come. That knowledge sustained her and gave her strength. She was so convinced of this that she found an unordinary peacefulness cohabiting with her, even in the confines of a dreaded hospital bed.

Something about the absence of dolphins changed everything for Bobbi. The more they stayed away, the more convinced she became that they were, in fact, inextricably bound up in the destiny surrounding her mother's final resting place. It made it easier to give up her insistence on a family burial plot in New York when something bigger than anyone's opinion was involved. For in truth, they were not waiting on dolphins as much as they were waiting on God. And if they were waiting on God, it would be a far better burial place than what anyone else wanted; it would be God's place, God's time.

"Just don't tell Sam that," Jack said when she shared this thought with him. "If Sam ever knew he was waiting on God, he would immediately stop waiting."

Each evening, as Sam visited her in the hospital, their conversation reflected the change that was being wrought in both of them by the sagacious dolphins.

First evening.

Bobbi: "Well, I suppose it's done."

Sam: "Nope. Flipper didn't show."

Second evening.

Bobbi studied Sam's face but it never showed anything anyway: "Well. . . ?"

Sam: "I've still got the ashes, if that's what you want to know."

Third evening.

Bobbi didn't even ask a question: "Sam, I think you'd better rent a bigger boat."

Sam: "Why?"

Bobbi: "Because I'm being released in the morning, and Brook and Alex will be here by noon. We might as well plan for a little cruise and do this thing right, the way we did it the first time."

Sam: "So you're going to let me throw her in after all?"

Bobbi: "You know, Pop, I don't think we have a choice. If we go out there tomorrow and find dolphins, we'd be defying God if we didn't throw her in. I think the dolphins are going to settle this."

Sam restrained himself from the obligatory negative comment that always popped into his mind whenever God or anything about the supernatural was implied, and in that restraint, Bobbi hoped.

"And if we don't find the dolphins?" Sam said as an afterthought.

Bobby was silent for a moment. "Then I get to take her back with me to New York."

To her surprise, Sam agreed, and Jack wondered later that night if Sam realized he had just wagered his bet on God.

⌒

The next morning, Jack went to pick up the children at the Marathon Airport. They had gotten a one-day jump on their spring vacation, but Alex wanted more.

"Why didn't you bring us down earlier, Dad?" he said, walking to the car after picking up their bags. "We could have missed more school."

"No way. Too many tests," Brook disagreed, always the conscientious one.

"Truth of the matter is, we weren't ready for you until now," Jack said.

"How's Mom?" they both asked in stereo from either side of the car as Jack unlocked the door.

"She's fine. In fact, never been better."

"I can't wait to see her," Brook said. "Will she know us?"

"Oh yes. She's got all her memory back except for the actual accident."

"What's the last thing she remembers, Dad?" Alex asked once they were settled in the car.

"Picking up the picture at that map store," Jack said.

"Whatever happened to that picture, anyway?" Brook wanted to know.

"They're framing us a new one."

"Well, that's nice of them," she commented, snapping her seat belt closed.

"Better get your seat belt on, Alex." Jack was checking on him in the rearview mirror. "I don't want anybody else I know taking up residence in this hospital. One more accident victim and we can probably take over a whole wing."

"That's right . . . Uncle Albert! How is he doing?" Brook had always had a special fondness for Albert.

"He's doing well. They're letting him out today, same as your mother."

"Dad, are we gonna bury Gramma again?" Alex asked.

"We're not burying her," Brook corrected him in a sassy tone. "We're throwing her ashes in the water."

"Same difference!" Alex shot back.

"No, it's not!"

"Yes, it is!"

"Hey, now . . . go easy. You guys been like this the whole time we were gone?"

"No, we're just tired of being nice for Mrs. McDermott," Brook said.

"She was pretty strict?"

" 'Strict' isn't the word!" Brook exclaimed. "She turns into the Wicked Witch of the West as soon as you guys leave."

"No kidding?" Jack was glad to hear of it.

"She makes me go to bed at nine every night," pouted Alex. "She must think I'm seven or something."

"And she won't let me talk to any of my friends on the phone for longer than five minutes at a time," echoed Brook.

"Say, those are pretty good ideas. What else does she do?"

Brook glared back at Alex to make sure he realized it was not in their best interest to answer that question.

Jack turned into the parking lot of Fishermen's Hospital a few minutes later, and Brook remarked, "Wow, that didn't take long."

"The whole island is only seven miles long. Nothing takes long around here."

"Mom!" shouted Alex, popping his seat belt before Jack even had the car in a parking place. He had spotted a nurse wheeling Bobbi out the front of the hospital.

As soon as Bobbi saw them, she jumped out of the chair and started toward the car, which Jack had to stop halfway into the parking spot to prevent the children from jumping out of a moving vehicle. There was a great reunion with plenty of hugs and kisses and squeals, especially on Bobbi's part.

"What's with the wheelchair, Mom?" said Alex, coming up for air.

"They have to wheel everyone out in one—it's hospital policy. Watch . . . in just a minute, Uncle Albert will be coming out too." They all looked up together. "There he is now."

Sure enough, out came Albert, pushed by his brother. They made quite a pair, the two of them. Albert, with his jolly, round self beaming with joy, pushed by a frowning, squinting Sam, whose dent made a shadow in the sunlight.

"Can I park the car now?" Jack was standing by the driver's side with the door open and the engine still running.

"Why bother?" Bobbi asked. "My stuff's already in Sam's

truck. Let's just go. Will and Jackie and the kids are meeting us at the marina in five minutes."

The children greeted Albert and Sam, and everyone piled into Jack's rental car for the short trip to the marina, where Sam had indeed rented a bigger boat, with none other than Zeke at the captain's wheel.

It was a boisterous group that set out to sea that day, so completely different from the solemn crowd only a couple months earlier that had set upon the bay in Cocoa Beach to bid what they thought was their final farewell to their mother, wife, and grandmother.

Zeke began by taking them straight out to the ocean. He didn't mess with the channels but headed for both bridges due east. He knew right where to go. Everyone snacked on a deli tray Jackie had brought and enjoyed the sun and the spray.

"Keep an eye out for dolphins," Bobbi told the children. "They're our honored guests today."

"Albert, I've never seen you look so good," Will said. "How do you explain that?"

"Heart attacks suit me, I guess."

"Hogwash!" said Sam.

"I really mean that I wouldn't trade any of this whole experience—heart attack included—for anything. In fact, I feel so good I'm going to go back to New York, get this operation out of the way, and get married."

"What?" several gasped at once.

Sam looked pained.

"Yep. Her name's Irene," Albert went on. "She's been my dear friend for a long time, but I haven't wanted to let go of Doris. Something about this trip—especially watching Sam be so persistent in making sure we finish well with Betty—has made me realize it's time to leave dear Doris behind and move on."

Jack threw a glance in Bobbi's direction. *Finish and move on.* She seemed to be sharing the same thoughts.

"Thank you, Sam, for showing me," Albert said, finishing his announcement and raising his glass in his brother's direction.

Sam, of course, made it look as though Albert had the wrong guy and walked over to talk to Zeke.

"Here's to Uncle Albert and Aunt-to-be Irene!" Jack raised his glass and they all saluted. "I hope she says yes."

"Don't worry," Albert reassured them. "I'm the one she's been waiting on."

"I don't understand it," Zeke said to Sam. "I've always found dolphins out here by now." They had been out in the open sea for almost half an hour, and everyone heard that comment because it was about dolphins.

"What do you suggest?" Bobbi said.

Zeke was at a loss.

"Maybe they're all at a dolphin convention," Kyle quipped, having just been at a weekend marina convention and boat show with his family.

"I have an idea," Jack said. "Remember when the disciples couldn't find any fish, and Jesus told them to throw their nets over the other side of the boat?"

No one responded to that comment because it was obvious that there were no dolphins on any side of their boat right then. They had four kids on constant watch.

"Why don't we try it?" Jack suggested. "We've got nothing to lose."

"Try what, Jack?" Will gestured all around him. "What side haven't we seen?"

"The other side of the Keys."

"The bay?" said Sam. "What do you think, Zeke?"

"They're easier to find out here, but there is one spot . . . I guess I could try. It's time to turn back anyway. There's more of a chance we'll see them on the way back in, though."

But they didn't. And crossing once again under the Seven Mile Bridge made everyone feel a growing sense of apprehension. What if the dolphins never came? What would they do then? Bobbi was surprised to realize, when presented with the real possibility that she could get her mother's ashes back, that she actually didn't want them anymore. She wanted the dolphins to come. Suddenly she had an idea.

"Hey, everybody," she said. "Why don't we all think of a characteristic of dolphins and call it out. Anything . . ."

"Intelligent," Brook said right away.

"Just a minute." Bobbi fussed with her purse and pulled out a paper and pen. " 'Intelligent.' Got it. What else?"

"Friendly to humans," said Jack.

"Sleek," Albert added.

"They communicate well," Jackie said.

"Hold it—slow down," Bobbi smiled. "I can't write that fast. 'They communicate well.' Okay, what else? This is great!"

"They like to play," Alex commented. "They do things just for the fun of it."

"And they're good swimmers." Brook was gazing out at the water.

"Anything else?" Bobbi asked after a short pause.

"They make good movie stars," Zeke said. "See that island right there?" He pointed as they passed by Pigeon Key one more time. "That's where they filmed *Flipper*."

"No kidding," Bobbi said. "I didn't know that."

"Squeaky," Kevin piped in. "They make squeaky sounds."

"That they do, Kevin. Anybody else? Well, this is good enough. What I've got here is just what I thought I'd have: a perfect description of Mom. What do you think?"

Suddenly they were all making connections in their minds. On each face was an impulse of surprise. Some memory of Betty that superimposed itself over a vision of a dolphin.

"Go back through them," Jackie said.

"All right," Bobbi agreed. " 'Intelligent.' I'll take this one. I bet some of you guys forgot Mom was a medical research assistant."

"Oh yeah," Will said. "Didn't she help some famous guy in the discovery of penicillin?"

"Amoxicillin," corrected Bobbi. "She helped discover it."

"Just think of all your earaches Gramma helped heal," Jackie said to both her kids.

"No kidding." Bobbi looked at her list. "How about 'friendly to humans'?"

"She was that, all right!" Jack cut in. "She was friendly to humans . . . animals . . . anything alive."

"Remember all that volunteer time she put in at the animal shelter?" Will recalled.

"No," Sam said. "I only remember all the animals she kept bringing home that I had to keep taking *back*!"

"What about 'sleek'?"

"She was sleek," agreed Albert. "Her silver hair . . . her petite figure . . . her golf swing."

"But did she hit the ball?" Sam asked.

"Oh, Sam," joked Bobbi. "Do you have to kid her about her golf game even after she's gone?"

There was a little laughter, followed by a gentle surprise that they were in fact laughing in such close reference to death.

"What's next?" Bobbi checked her list. " 'Communicates well.' "

Will jumped right on that one. "I swear I've caught Mom talking to trees."

"She did like to talk, didn't she?" Bobbi laughed in remembrance.

"Never send her to the market," said Jack, "unless you don't care when she comes back. Remember that? She'd talk to everybody in the process—people in the aisles, people behind the deli, the guy in the refrigerator. She once almost froze a guy because she had him trapped in the freezer, talking to him!"

"Don't forget the toll booth guy," Will added. "I remember cars honking behind us all the time while Mom was chatting away. She'd have their life history by the time she got her money out."

"How about 'playful'?" Bobbi went on. "Did she do things just for the fun of it?"

There was a brief pause. "She laughed and talked at the same time," Brook said.

"That she did," Bobbi nodded. "That she did."

"She squeaked." Kevin remembered his own offering. "When she sneezed, it was a squeak. Just like a dolphin squeak."

"You're right!" Bobbi exclaimed. "It was a little tiny thing."

"Just like your sneeze," said Jack.

"Well, that's about everything except 'good swimmer,' " Bobbi said.

"Sam, was she a good swimmer?" Bobbi was trying to bring him back in because it seemed Sam had drifted off somewhere else. At least, he was staring out the back of the boat. "Sam?" she repeated.

Sam couldn't talk because there was something in his eyes that made speech impossible. No one was expecting such a thing, since no one had ever seen anything like this in Sam's eyes before. Suddenly everyone who noticed had the same thing in their eyes, so that no one could speak for a while.

"Well . . ." He looked off the stern of the boat. "We're about to find out."

Suddenly everyone crowded to the back where Sam was standing.

"Oh, look!" cried Brook, who was next to him and pointing off into the foaming wake. "It's a dolphin!"

Sure enough, a playful gray bottlenose dolphin was actually surfing the wake of the boat. He'd slide down one side and then jump to the other and wash back toward the middle.

"He's a regular water-skier!" exclaimed Will. And it was almost like that—as if the animal were attached to the boat by an invisible cord.

"There's another one!" shouted Kevin from the starboard side, and this one was swimming right alongside the boat.

"No, there's two!" Jackie shouted as another came up from underneath and swam side by side with it.

"There's one over here!" Bobbi exclaimed, and everyone rushed over to join her on the leeward side.

"And another!" Alex was looking in the same area.

"We're surrounded!" Jack said. "Stop the boat!" And Zeke

slowly brought the speed down to a crawl as dolphins played in the water from every side. It was a great confluence of beasts.

"Have you ever seen so many dolphins?" Bobbi held her hands up to her face in surprise.

"Never," Will replied. "Kyle was right. It's a regular dolphin convention."

Everyone's face was bright with joy and wonder. Even Sam had a faint smile when he brought out the ashes and said, "I think it's time."

The next thing he did surprised everyone. He handed the plastic bag to Bobbi. Bobbi held it for a moment with her hand cupped underneath. She held it awkwardly, as if it didn't belong to her. With no more than the slightest hesitation, she turned and held the bag in front of Brook, who looked at it but did not receive it.

"To the next generation of Brewster women," Bobbi said, and Brook stuttered with her arms.

"Go ahead," Bobbi urged. "The dolphins are waiting."

TWENTY-FIVE

Postscript

Sam sent Bonnie's letter off to J.W.'s lawyer as soon as Bobbi gave it to him and figured that would be the end of it . . . and the beginning of J.W.'s freedom. But it turned out to be not so easy. In fact, the day Sam returned from the Keys to his home in Cocoa Beach, there was an urgent call from J.W.'s lawyer informing him that the court was still intending on pressing charges. They were now claiming coercion on J.W.'s part.

"So why are you calling me?" Sam asked.

"I want you to write another article for the *Bee*," said Harvey Finklestein.

"Why? What can I do?"

"Turn the tide of public opinion against the court. This thing has come down to nothing more than a personal vendetta for Sheriff Buford and the DA. It's no secret Buford has had it in for quack preachers for some time now, and he's simply not willing to admit he has to let this one go. All we need is a little pressure from the citizenry to get the whole case dismissed. Will you do it?"

And Sam truly outdid himself.

> In one of the most bizarre turn of events in legal history, the death of Bonnie Dean, wife of pseudo-snake-handling preacher, J.W. Dean, was found to have come at her own hand. J.W. Dean has been under investigation for the murder of his wife last March, ever since it was discovered that the snake box, usually filled with harmless scarlet king snakes for his services, contained a deadly coral snake the night Bonnie was bitten. But a letter, confirmed to be in Bonnie Dean's own handwriting and postmarked on the day of her death, reveals that she herself was the one who put the deadly coral snake in the box the night she died. The letter was found among a stack of other mail to J.W. Dean Ministries that had eluded investigation by being forwarded to an unknown mailbox in Cocoa Beach.

> The news came as no surprise to J.W. Dean, who for some time has held that it was God who put the snake in the box as judgment against the phony use of harmless scarlet king snakes in his services. "I knew God did it; I just never thought He would have used Bonnie. She was praying when she found the snake, and God told her what to do with it."

> The District Attorney is choosing to go ahead and try the case, but Harvey Finklestein, lawyer for J.W. Dean, insists they are wasting their time. "Their only chance is to try and prove that J.W. coerced his wife to write the letter, but such a thing is impossible to prove. Besides, even if she was coerced to write the letter, no one forced her to put her hand in that box. She did that of her own free will. She knew she was risking her life. The court is wasting its time and money on this case and should get on with more important matters."

> Indeed, that sentiment is sure to be shared by a number of citizens of Cocoa Beach who have already been heard on talk shows and in angry letters to the *Bee*. They think the jailing of J.W. Dean was a waste of taxpayers' money in the first place. Many believe that J.W. Dean is no threat to society and should be set free. Others feel this is something for the church to handle privately.

J.W. Dean, meanwhile, remains in maximum security patiently awaiting his fate. "It's all in God's hands," he says, claiming he has learned his lesson and will not return to the ministry. Some commentators find that highly unlikely, given the surge in publicity this case has given him. "If he's exonerated, he'll be the hottest thing on Christian cable stations since Jim and Tammy," said George Killian, professor of religion at Northwest Florida University, "and we'll have the TV empire of J.W. Dean to contend with." J.W. insists that he has no television aspirations for the future, and only time will tell if he's telling the truth this time.

So Sam stretched it a little bit. Maybe there weren't any letters to the *Cocoa Beach Bee*, but by the time this article had been out two days, there was a flood of them to the newspaper, the court, and the police department. In the end, the court succumbed to political pressure and dropped all charges, much to Sheriff Buford's dismay. "Just going to have to look for another chance to get the guy you want," Harvey Finklestein said as he left the courtroom with a free John Wesley Dean.

Sheriff Buford would never admit it, but Bonnie's letter and J.W.'s subsequent release saved him at least his conscience. Had he found the letter through his own investigation, it would have been hard for him to resist concealing it so he could have sent J.W. to jail—perhaps even to the chair. And then he'd have to live with that knowledge the rest of his life. He would have been severely tempted. As it was, the story went down as the most bizarre suicide on record.

~

As for J.W., he did two things upon his release. He had been planning this since the night he saw the rerun of the Jim Bakker interview, should he be fortunate enough to get out of prison. First, he went out and bought himself a pair of authentic rattlesnake-skin boots. Then, with those boots on, he went walking in the hills behind his boyhood home in West Virginia. He walked a long time, almost five hours, through pines and brush, waiting for an encounter he knew was inevitable. Around the backside of a large boulder it was waiting for him: a five-foot black timber rattler, old and mean as the hills it inhabited, curled up and shaking its noisy rattles like mad castanets. J.W. knew this was it.

For the longest time he was caught in the metaphysical power of this Edenic confrontation between man and snake. He knew the danger. A three-hour hike in was a three-hour hike out—plenty of time for the venom to do its deadly work. And should the snake bite him on his face, he would be unable to suck the venom out and save himself. That's why he knew it was going to have to be a face-to-face encounter. J.W. had asked God for this chance. He wanted to know.

He could feel the sweat forming under his arms. Soon it was running down his nose, but he did not wipe it away. He did not move an inch until the fear was gone, and with its leaving came an unexplainable urge to pick it up. It was an exuberant joy, an un-shakable confidence . . . not that he would be delivered from the snake, but that it didn't matter whether he was or wasn't. Whatever happened to him didn't matter because for the first time in his life, J.W. Dean didn't matter to J.W. Dean. God was all that mattered. Obediently he stepped forward and took up the serpent with one hand a few inches behind its head. The neck was free to roam and roam it did. With the other hand he supported the long, slender body that was both ugly and graceful at the same time. The body hung limp and the rattle that the reptile had been furiously shaking before he picked it up went silent.

For a while J.W. held the snake high above him and admired its evil head harmlessly weaving back and forth, its lightning tongue repeatedly striking the air and returning. J.W.'s sweating had stopped immediately upon picking up the snake, and a calm-ness and peace unlike anything he had ever known overtook him. Suddenly he started singing the song he had written and sung in his services, and the deadly snake seemed to dance in the trance of his voice.

Take them up, take them up,
There is nothing that can harm you;
Take them up, take them up,
See them dangle in the air;
Take them up, take them up,
The devil cannot charm you
When you throw your spirit into prayer (into prayer),
When you throw your spirit into prayer.

Then J.W. Dean brought the snake down until they were face-to-face, eye to eye. For a moment he thought of throwing the snake over his shoulder and walking back with it. He had done it. He had won. He could put the snake in a box and start a real snake-handling ministry. He could show the whole world this moment over and over again. Think of the faith it would inspire in people. He could go on television. Then they would all believe.

Suddenly it seemed to him that the snake's face had changed. Recognition came to its eye with a vengeance, as if the trance was somehow wearing off with the straying thoughts of J.W. Dean. The snake pulled its hoary head back and arched its neck with a terrible meanness in its eye, as if ready to strike. J.W. closed his eyes, banished the former thoughts, and began singing the second verse to his song.

Throw them down, throw them down,
All those sins and tribulations,
Throw them down, throw them down,
See them trampled on the ground;
Throw them down, throw them down,
Give your heart in consecration,
So the filling of the Spirit will abound (will abound),
So the filling of the Spirit will abound.

When he was done singing, he slowly opened his eyes and the snake was once again harmlessly weaving its head back and forth with glassy eyes. Reverently, he set the timber rattler back down behind the rock where he found it and turned and walked away.

Upon returning to the trail's head, J.W. got into a waiting blue pickup.

"Took you long enough," the driver commented.

"Let's go," J.W. said.

And from that day forward, John Wesley Dean never touched another snake again. Nor did he ever mention a word about this encounter to anyone.

ACKNOWLEDGMENTS

For a fascinating read on snake handling, try Dennis Covington's *Salvation of Sand Mountain* (New York: Addison-Wesley Publishing Company, 1995). I owe most of my understanding about snake handling and relative respect for these mysterious mountain people to Mr. Covington's fine book. I highly recommend it.

I also want to thank Bobby and Lee Michaels for showing me around the Keys—even trolling me through some parts of it the way Sam and Albert pulled each other around. Thanks to Beth Horveth, professor of marine biology at Westmont College for her expertise on marine behavior, and Jack Carlson at Captain Hook's in Marathon for informing me about diving and searching around Pigeon Key.

And finally, thanks to Bob Welch for an early reading and valuable critique.